ANYTHING

FOR BILLY

Larry McMurtry

SIMON AND SCHUSTER

NEW YORK   LONDON   TORONTO   SYDNEY   TOKYO

Simon and Schuster
Simon & Schuster Building
Rockefeller Center
1230 Avenue of the Americas
New York, New York 10020

SIMON AND SCHUSTER and colophon are registered trademarks
of Simon & Schuster Inc.

Designed by Mary Beth Kilkelly/Levavi & Levavi
Manufactured in the United States of America
1   3   5   7   9   10   8   6   4   2
Library of Congress Cataloging in Publication Data
McMurtry, Larry.
Anything for Billy/Larry McMurtry.
p.   cm.
1. Billy, the Kid—Fiction.   2. Southwest, New—History—1848—
Fiction.   I. Title.
PS3563.A319A84   1988
813'.54—dc19   88-22732
CIP
ISBN 0-671-64268-5

For Margaret Ellen Slack
and in memory of
Dorothea Oppenheimer

The flower of friendship never faded.

I

The Butler's Sorrow

1.

_____

The first time I saw Billy he came walking out of a cloud. He had a pistol in each hand and a scared look on his rough young face. The cloud drifted in from the plains earlier in the morning and stopped over the Hidden Mountains, in the country of the Messy Apaches—that was what buffalo hunters called the Mescalero.

It was a thick cloud, which made downhill travel a little chancy. I had found myself a seat on a rock and was waiting for the cloud to go somewhere else. Probably I looked as scared to Billy as he looked to me—my mule was winded, my gun was empty, my ears were popping, and I was nervous about the prospect of running into some Messy Apaches. One minute I wanted the cloud to leave; the next minute I was glad it was there.

Billy looked relieved when he saw me. I think his first notion was to steal my mule—it would only have been common sense.

"This mule won't make it far," I informed him, hoping

11

to scotch that notion—though if he had pointed one of the pistols at me I would have handed him the reins on the spot.

Billy gave me a chip-toothed grin. I would have guessed him to be no more than seventeen at the time, and short for his age at that. In fact, he was almost a runt, and ugly as Sunday. His dirty black coat was about three sizes too big for him.

He glanced at Rosy, the mule. She didn't like heights, or clouds either, and was in a foul mood.

"An Apache could take that mule and ride her fifty miles," he pointed out. "It's lucky for you I'm not an Apache."

"If you were I'd offer you the mule and hope for the best," I said.

He stuck one of the pistols into an old holster he wore and shoved the other one into the pocket of his black coat.

"Joe Lovelady's around here somewhere," he said. "It would be just like him to show up with my horse."

"I'm Ben Sippy," I said, thinking it was about time we got introduced. I stood up and offered a handshake.

Billy didn't shake my hand, but he gave me another grin. He had buck teeth, and both of them were chipped.

"Howdy, Mr. Sippy, are you from Mississippi?" he said, and burst out laughing. In those days Billy was always getting tickled at his own remarks. When he laughed at one of his own jokes you couldn't help liking him—he was just a winning kid.

Though now, when I think of Billy Bone giggling at one of his own little sallies, I soon grow blind with tears —sentimental, I guess. But there was a time when I would have done anything for Billy.

"No, I'm just from Philadelphia," I said. He was not the first person to make the Mississippi joke.

"Well, I'm Billy Bone," he said, with a flicker of threat in his eyes.

12

I guess I must have started or flinched or something, because the threat immediately went away and it seemed to be all he could do to keep from laughing again. I don't consider myself much of a comic, but for some reason Billy always had trouble keeping a straight face in my company.

"You act like you've heard of me, Mr. Sippy," he said.

Of course, he knew perfectly well I'd heard of him. Everyone in the West had heard of him, and plenty of people in other parts of the world as well. Since Wild Bill Hickok had let himself get killed in South Dakota two years before, I doubt there was a gunfighter alive with a reputation to match Billy's. But I just looked at him and tried to take a relaxed line.

"Oh, you've got a reputation," I said. "They say you're a cool killer."

"I am, but the cool killing don't start till around November," he said, giggling again. "This time of the year we mostly do hot killing, Mr. Sippy."

2.

Later on, I realized it was a good thing I had paid Billy's reputation that trite little compliment. If I hadn't, I doubt we'd ever have become friends. In fact, if I hadn't, he might just have shot me.

Billy expected people to take note of his reputation, though why he even had a reputation at that time was a mystery to me, once I knew the facts. From listening to gossip in barrooms I had formed the general impression that he had already killed ten or twelve white men, and scores of Indians and Mexicans as well.

But when I met him, Billy Bone had yet to shoot a man. A bully named Joe Loxton had abused him considerably when he was thirteen or fourteen and making his living cleaning tables in a saloon. Joe Loxton made the mistake of wrestling him to the ground one day when Billy had just been carving a beef and happened to have a butcher knife in his hand. When they hit the floor the butcher knife stuck in Joe Loxton's belly, and a day or two later he was dead.

"It was mostly an accident," Billy said, "though I *would* have stabbed that shit-ass if I'd had time to think."

That's not to say that Billy was a gentle boy. He was violent all right. In his case the reputation just arrived before the violence.

I felt a little peculiar for a moment. There we were, in a thick cloud in the Hidden Mountains, with only one mule between us and the most feared young gunman in the West making jokes about my name. Nothing unfriendly had occurred, but it's a short step, in some situations, from the unfriendly to the fatal—and a short step that often got taken in New Mexico in those days.

We had exhausted what few conversational supplies we seemed to have, and were just standing there. Billy had stopped giggling and looked depressed.

"I get a headache when I'm up this high," he said.

I was carrying one or two general nostrums, but before I could offer Billy one, Rosy, my mule, lifted her head and nickered.

I was horrified. Now all the Messy Apaches would have to do was ride in and make a mess of us, unless Billy Bone could shoot them all.

But Billy didn't even draw his pistol—he just looked irritated.

A minute later Joe Lovelady trotted out of the cloud, riding one horse and leading another.

"See! I told you it would be just like him!" Billy said.

Joe rode up beside him and handed him his bridle reins, but Billy didn't even look up. "It must get boresome being so danged competent," he said in a tone that was anything but grateful. "Did you scalp all the Indians, too, while you were rescuing these nags?" Billy asked, in the same annoyed tone.

"Nope," Joe Lovelady said. "I just snuck in and stole back our horses while they were taking a shit."

"I thought those dern Apaches were supposed to know their business!" Billy said in an ugly tone. He

15

seemed to be working himself into an angry fit just because his friend had recovered their horses.

Joe Lovelady, a calm man if I ever knew one, was unperturbed.

"It ain't getting any earlier," he said. "Why don't we lope on over to Greasy Corners?"

"In this fog?" Billy asked. "I couldn't find my hip pocket, much less Greasy Corners."

"I reckon I can find my way down a hill, fog or no fog," Joe Lovelady said.

Billy choked off his fit, sighed, and struggled onto his horse, a rangy black at least seventeen hands high.

"Gentlemen, could I ride along with you until we get out of these mountains?" I asked, seeing that they were about to ride off and leave me without further ado.

They both looked down at me. Joe Lovelady was a good-looking young man with a fine mustache. He could have been twenty-one or two, but no older, and he had more self-assurance than Billy Bone would ever have.

"I'm out of bullets and I'm lost and I'm not good at heights," I said, realizing it was a lame speech.

It had a good effect though—it put Billy Bone in a better humor.

"This old man's a total loss, but let's take him along anyway," he said. "Let's show him some fun."

Joe Lovelady seemed surprised at the suggestion.

"What's his name?" he asked, looking me over.

"His name's Mister Sippy but he ain't from Mississippi," Billy said, and laughed even harder at the joke than he had the first time.

He was still laughing when we started down the hill.

3.

_____

Joe Lovelady set a smart pace, cloud or no cloud. Rosy didn't appreciate it, but she was tired of living the lonely life with me and did her best to keep up for company's sake. Billy's horse was so tall it was like following a giraffe.

I don't think Billy much cared for horseback travel. His reputation was made in the Territory, but to me he had the look of a city boy—and in fact he had been born on the Bowery in New York and brought West as a baby. Something of the Bowery had stuck to him, even so.

Before we had been traveling an hour, he got bored enough to drop back and make a little conversation.

"We could all break our necks trying to follow Joe Lovelady in a fog like this," he remarked rather petulantly.

Finally we got down below the cloud and saw the great plain stretching away. By noon we had got pretty well out of the Sierra Oscura, but Joe Lovelady evidently had no intention of stopping for lunch. I began to

17

realize that he behaved with a certain relentlessness when it came to getting where he was going.

I suggested to Billy that we might stop and try to scare up a bite in Tularosa, but Billy immediately vetoed that.

"There are plenty of unkind sons of bitches in Tularosa," he informed me.

By midafternoon I had begun to feel a little desperate. Greasy Corners, our destination, I knew of only by hearsay. It was said to be a den of whores and cutthroats, but that part didn't worry me. Most of the local settlements were dens of whores and cutthroats.

My own hope was to find one a little closer. Greasy Corners was somewhere on the Rio Pecos—at least one hundred and fifty miles from where we hit the plain. I knew Rosy well enough to know she wasn't going to tolerate Joe Lovelady's pace for any one hundred and fifty miles. She was a mule with a lot of balk in her. I was not looking forward to being left on that vast empty plain with a stalled mule.

Besides, I was starving. By midafternoon I had begun to scrape little curls of leather off my saddle with my fingernails, just to have something in my mouth.

Billy Bone seemed a little gaunt too.

"You wouldn't have a biscuit, would you, Mr. Sippy?" he asked at one point.

I shook my head. "Do you think your friend will consider stopping for supper?" I asked.

"No, and if we did stop I don't see what there'd be to eat," he said.

"I've got a headache," he added in a sad tone. "If you don't have a biscuit you probably don't have a pill, either."

But I did have a pill—a bottle of them, in fact. I had bought them in Galveston a few months before and forgotten about them. They were just general pills, about the size of marbles and guaranteed to cure a wide range of diseases. I dug them out of my saddlebag and poured Billy Bone a handful.

"Let's just eat them," I said. "They're just general pills. It's better than starving."

Billy didn't say anything, but he gave me a kind of quizzical, grateful look. It may be that my sharing those Galveston pills sealed our friendship.

We rode out on the plain, munching the big pills. After he'd eaten about thirty, Billy got tickled.

"I may get so healthy I'll fall off this horse," he said, but before he could get any healthier we saw Joe Lovelady racing this way and that, whipping at something with his rope.

"Prairie chickens," Billy said. "He's good at catching prairie chickens. Joe just whacks them down with his rope."

That indicated to me that Mr. Lovelady was at last thinking of his stomach, which proved to be the case. That night we feasted on four fat hens, and our troubles seemed to be over. The big pills had left Billy and me with gaseous stomachs, and we did a lot of belching, which Joe Lovelady, an unfailingly polite man, did his best to ignore. Billy tended to linger over his belching, as kids will—some of his better productions gave the horses a start.

While we were polishing prairie chicken bones, Joe Lovelady suddenly looked at me and smiled—his first smile since we met.

"I know who you are," he said. "Sippy. You're that Yankee who don't know how to rob trains."

"Hey!" Billy said. "Are you *that* Sippy?"

I had to admit I was. My own little reputation had caught up with me again.

19

4.

When I set out to try the new Western sport of train robbing, it was my belief that New Mexican trains were a lot more cooperative than they actually are. In the East, trains stop every few miles to let people with tickets get on and off, and somehow that had given me the notion that if you showed up beside the tracks with the proper hardware the train would stop and let itself be robbed.

In the East, where trains are civilized, that approach might have worked, but in New Mexico Territory trains were as hard to manage as anything else. When I stood up on the track below the Fort Stanton mines and tried to stop an ore train I had to dive off the embankment to keep from being squashed. I stood in the middle of the tracks and shot off my pistol, but the train just kept on coming.

The next time, I determined to try the thing on level ground—there was plenty of *that* available in the eastern part of the state. I picked out a train, and Rosy and I raced up beside the engine and I shot off my pistol a few more times, thinking that the engineer would soon realize a robbery was in progress and shut things down. Of course, I just shot in the air—I had no desire to injure anyone.

But the engineer just laughed and waved his cap at me and kept on engineering. Maybe it was his birthday and he thought I was giving him a send-off, or maybe his wife had a baby and he thought I was congratulating him—I'll never know.

I don't give up easily, though. I raced along beside that train for several miles, thinking that sooner or later the engineer would realize I was serious. I shot twenty or thirty shots up in the air—but then I dropped my pistol, trying to reload on the run. The engineer was still just as cheerful as ever—once in a while he'd wave his cap at me and toot his whistle.

It annoyed me a little, that engineer's sunny humor. I was ready to chase the damn train all the way to Kansas City, but Rosy was of a different mind. After six or seven miles she decided the whole thing was ridiculous and pulled a spectacular balk. She stopped and didn't move a muscle for about three hours. I could have done her portrait if I'd had a paintbrush and an easel. My threats didn't impress her; my blandishments failed to appease her. It was slap dark before she decided she was ready to travel. I never did find my pistol, either.

The next day, riding back along the tracks toward Las Cruces—it was the one place in southern New Mexico that had a decent hotel, and I was definitely in the mood for a few days in a decent hotel—I came upon three Mexicans working on the rails. They had pumped their way far out on the plains on one of those little handcars. I feel sure I could have robbed them—I still had my Winchester and my derringers. It would have been a train robbery, of a sort; I would have had something to show for three weeks of anxiety.

But I was hungry and depressed and ended up giving

them fifty cents for a few tortillas. Instead of robbing them, I guess I made their fortune, for they soon packed up their tools and headed for town to invest the fifty cents.

A low mood seized me. I couldn't think why I had supposed I could be a train robber anyway—or any kind of owlhoot, for that matter. It wasn't in my breeding.

I said as much to Billy Bone and Joe Lovelady after trying to explain to them, as best I could, what had gone wrong in my efforts to rob trains.

Billy thought the story of me and Rosy chasing the train was the funniest thing he had ever heard. He nearly rolled off his blanket laughing. Even Joe Lovelady, who was not comfortable with hilarity, chuckled a time or two.

"You have to race up and shoot the conductor if you want to stop a train," Billy explained, when he had got himself under control. "You don't need to kill him—if you just wing him he'll usually pull the brake.

"Me and Joe don't go in for robbery, though," he added. "Joe'd rather punch cows."

Joe Lovelady looked at me thoughtfully. He had done a perfect job of cooking the hens and had even provided salt and pepper, which he kept in a pouch in his saddlebag.

"You talk like you're homesick, Mr. Sippy," Joe Lovelady said.

"Oh, that's why you cotton to him now," Billy said. "You figured out he's homesick, like you."

I expect Billy's words were true. For there we were, by a little flicker of campfire, on a plain so vast you couldn't even think of the end of it, under a sky as huge as time. It was a place to make you homesick, if you'd ever had a home. Joe Lovelady and I had had one, but the notion had little meaning for the orphan boy, Billy Bone.

"You had a ma," Joe said to Billy kindly. "You told me you remembered her."

It was not the last time I would hear Joe Lovelady try to persuade Billy that he'd had a life like the rest of us.

"Oh, I remember her, Joe," Billy said quietly. "She used to catch me between her knees and pick lice out of my hair. I remember that much."

Joe Lovelady looked at me again. I think we both regretted that the subject of mothers had ever come up.

"What brought you out here, Mr. Sippy?" he asked me as a way of getting off a painful subject.

"Dime novels," I said. It was true, true, true.

But Billy and Joe looked blank. It confused me for a moment. I would never have expected to find myself in the company of two people who had never read a dime novel. In fact, I was in the company of two people who couldn't even read. Neither one of them could have read any of the hundreds of newspaper stories that would soon be written about them.

Well, if the West taught me anything, it's that there's different kinds of education.

We were all of us wakeful, in spite of the long day. Billy and Joe seemd to be in the mood to listen, so I talked to them as the sparks flew upward, and, once the fire died, under the freckling starlight, tried to explain why I had left the safe life in Philadelphia to become a laughingstock in New Mexico.

5.

_____

The curious truth is that if I hadn't chanced upon that first half-dimer at a cigar stand—it was *Hurricane Nell, Queen of Saddle and Lasso*—I might never have become an actor in this wild play. I would have gone on living the comfortable life in Philadelphia, suffering nothing worse than any man suffers who has nine young daughters and a disenchanted wife.

I doubt anyone has caught a worse case of dime-novel mania than I had. First I read them, then I had to try writing them. The fever they aroused in me was a kind of mental malaria. Even now, with all the characters in the story long since dead—unless Bloody Feathers is still alive, up there in his black country by the river of Souls, or Katie Garza still fomenting revolution in Patagonia or somewhere—occasionally the old fever flares up again.

It seems astonishing, thinking of it now, that a little trifling half-dimer such as *Hurricane Nell* could change a man's life so. Yet it did. Without it I would never have known Billy Bone, or Will Isinglass and his tall killer, Mesty-Woolah. I would never have set foot in Greasy Corners or made the acquaintance of Des Montaignes and Tully Roebuck. I would not have picked prairie flowers with the brilliant Lady Snow, or ridden with the fearless Katerina Garza. Someone else, not I, would have been left to heap the sod over Joe Lovelady, and over Simp Dixon and Happy Jack Marco and most of the other sweethearts who died in the Whiskey Glass war.

But *Hurricane Nell* led to *Mustang Merle's Mandate*, and *Mustang Merle* to *The Kansas Kitten*. Within a year I had written *Sandycraw, Man of Grit*, a character so popular that someone, somewhere, is probably still churning out his adventures. On days when I wasn't in the mood for the Man of Grit, I wrote about *Orson Oxx, Man of Iron*, a somewhat more sensitive specimen, and no less popular.

I had been a Philadelphia gentleman, reasonably attentive to the duties of my station; but in a matter of months I became wholly distracted, descending each morning into the sea of my daughters with prairies in my head.

Our butler was required to present himself at the local cigar stand at 8 A.M. precisely; by eight-fifteen I expected him to race in the door with whatever new adventures were available. A day that brought no *Mustang Merle* or *Saul Sabberday (The Idiot Spy)* was a day of emptiness and gloom, followed, invariably and rapidly, by sodden, unhappy inebriation. Why wouldn't the damn writers write faster? Had they no inkling of the painful needs they aroused?

"What's a butler?" Billy Bone wanted to know. His folks had brought him West to Trinidad, Colorado, as a six-weeks-old baby, and his only notion of a city was some little place such as Santa Fe. Joe Lovelady had grown up in Texas and was no better informed.

I tried to explain about butlers—of course I was still miserable about what happened to ours. But Billy had a fine curiosity. He'd ask a hundred questions, as any kid will.

"Sounds like a slave that's not a nigger," he concluded. "If I was ever a butler I'd probably shoot the whole family the first day."

"I don't think you need to worry about becoming a butler," I assured him.

"You never know, though," Joe Lovelady put in. "You just never know."

I later learned from Billy that it was the death of Joe's young wife and month-old baby that had so ingrained in him a sense of the uncertainty of life.

6.

I tried to explain to the boys how much I grew to hate writers in the time of my mania. Many a day I cursed their laziness, their irregularity. Finally, driven almost to despair by the four-month absence (never explained) of *Solemn Sam, the Sad Man from San Saba,* I decided to effect his return myself, which I did. If I couldn't buy adventures, I would simply have to write them; nothing less than my sanity hung in the balance.

Fortunately I soon discovered that I could write as rapidly as the next man—a good deal faster, in fact, than the sluggard responsible for keeping the nation informed about *Mustang Merle.* For a while I sailed along fairly happily in the broad wake of my own pen.

But only for a while. The more I read and wrote, the more I burned. For hours each day—having read all the available adventures and written till my hand stiffened and my arm cramped—I would sit in a kind of agitated lethargy, staring out my study window at the familiar lawns of Chestnut Street and seeing in my mind a horde of gaudy figures streaming across an endless plain. Cowboys, Indians, buffalo, stagecoaches blew through my vision like leaves.

At night I tossed and turned and dreamed of Black Nick, a bandit and lecher with rotting teeth whose adventures must have been composed by a human snail, so slowly did they reach the newsstands.

"He sounds like Des Montaignes," Billy observed, when I described Black Nick—and when I met the old beaver man I had to admit that the resemblance was striking.

It was obvious to me, in the month or so when the fever was highest, that I was passing up the Dim Trail toward the Plain of the Crazed—insanity, in less flowery words. I was, at the time, one of the most popular dime novelists in the nation: Orson Oxx was plodding into his seventeenth adventure, with Sandycraw just ahead in his twenty-first. It didn't matter: I was racing toward madness on an uncheckable steed, as a dime novelist might have put it.

"Men don't go crazy just from reading books," Billy observed skeptically. "You was probably crazy anyway, Sippy."

7.

On that point, Billy never changed his opinion. Of course I had a few ragged *Mustang Merle*s in my saddlebags, and when the action was slow in Greasy Corners, or when we weren't chasing anybody, or being chased ourselves, I read them to Billy and Joe. They came to like dime novels fairly well, giving the stories close attention and making astute criticisms of the impulsive Merle's many errors in judgment.

But Billy remained firm in his conviction that the yarns, as he called them, could not have been the cause of my derangement.

"I'd say you were crowded up in the house with too many females," he concluded.

Be that as it may, what finally brought me to my senses was the sudden death of our butler, whose name, I learned, was Chittim. I had never been quite solid on the man's name, and had had to ask Dora to please inquire of Cook. J. M. Chittim, we were informed.

Poor Chittim dropped dead one morning on his way

back from the cigar stand. While we were waiting for the van to come from the mortuary I had a good look at his corpse and saw to my astonishment that he was thin as a rail. I was simply amazed! I felt sure Chittim had been fat—or at least solidly plump—when Dora and I had hired him some twenty years before.

Dora and I were newlyweds then; perhaps we were happy. One doesn't pay a world of attention to a butler in the morning of one's marriage, though I do remember that Dora's dreadful mother, a violent hand with servants, advised against him because of his inexperience. Young Chittim could not have been more than a year or two out of his teens at the time, and I'm quite certain he was plump.

But he died thin as a rail. The death shocked me, and for a few days I gave more thought to J. M. Chittim than I had, I'm afraid, in the twenty and more years he had served me faithfully.

"That shows you were crazy already," Billy said. "There's no reason to think of dead people. They're gone. If you let your mind drift like that, somebody that ain't dead will sneak up behind you and steal your wallet."

Billy liked to suppose he was the practical man, all business. He didn't like to be reminded of how superstitious he himself really was.

"You don't have no fresh dead, Billy," Joe Lovelady observed with a note of sadness in his voice. He was whittling a stick; now and then he would brush the little curls of wood into the fire.

"It's when they're fresh gone that your mind gets stuck on them," Joe said, the thought of his baby and his young wife, Nellie, no doubt too fresh for comfort.

Billy had no comment on that. Joe's abilities might irritate him a little, but he was usually respectful of the older man's opinion.

We watched the little wood curls flare in the fire.

8.

As to J. M. Chittim, my rueful conclusion was that he had become the first martyr to dime novels. I might have been going crazy, but Chittim stopped on the sidewalk and died—and who can say that it wasn't because he hated to walk in, for perhaps the hundredth time, and tell me, No sir, very sorry sir, no sign of the new *Mustang Merle* this morning?

I can't say it, and he was my butler. For a time I stopped feeling crazed and just felt guilty.

Now you might suppose that since my butler died as the result of my mania, my family must have suffered agonies just as acute, if not as final.

Not a bit of it! No happier bunch of females than Dora and those girls resided on Chestnut Street—or in the whole of Philadelphia, for that matter. There they were, and there they flourished, ten firm impediments to the freedom of the imagination, and to most other freedoms as well.

I include Dora in the account, for Dora and the girls

only differed in degree. In kind they were as alike as ten turnips, and could have been no more indifferent to the doings—much less the feelings—of dear old Dad. The larger girls concerned themselves mainly with beaus and tea dances, while the smaller ones made do with birthday parties and ponies.

No, the Sippy girls were fine; popular all over town and happy as peaches.

And Dora? I suppose Dora was happier still, if it's possible to be happier than a peach. Dora had Society, a source of complete happiness to a woman of her leanings.

Billy Bone seemed to feel he knew all about Society. "I saw a picture of it in a newspaper once," he informed us.

Joe Lovelady was interested in Dora. "Did your wife ask a lot of questions?" he inquired.

Is water wet? I might have replied. Dora was never one to suppress a question. She didn't suppress the hard ones, or the easy ones either.

"Why are you lying on top of me, breathing in my face?" I remember her asking, early on.

"Oh," I said, and got off. Of course I didn't mention that one to the boys.

Over the years, Dora modified that question a bit. "Why are you still breathing, no more than you do?" she asked, a few days before I left home.

I mentioned that one to Joe and Billy—I was just trying to be humorous about the little vagaries of married life—but Billy flared up at the thought that any woman would ask a man such a question.

"Was she a brunette?" he asked, and when I confirmed that indeed Dora had a fine dark head of hair, he muttered and looked at Joe—evidently I had confirmed some theory he held about the questioning nature of brunettes.

"If he had nine children he must have been right fond of his wife," Joe said. Billy still looked sulky at the thought that a man's own wife would ask him why he was still breathing.

"Fond of her!" Billy said indignantly. "If a woman asked me why I was still breathing I'd show her some fondness all right. I'd fondly whack her with a big bed slat."

9.

Was I fond of Dora? At this distance I hardly know. There's the fact of the nine girls, and yet I can't recall that Dora and I ever shared what a happier man would think of as a warm embrace.

Certainly it was early on in our married life that I had ceased to breathe in her face. Or in her bedroom, either. Or in the hall that led to her bedroom. Or on the floor of the house where her bedroom was situated. Indeed, I would almost rather have had myself strangled than risk wafting a breath in Dora's direction—and yet, somehow, despite our rather polished avoidance of one another, little girls kept coming. The first I would suspect of their arrival was when I heard a new baby squalling in the nursery.

Of course, Dora was an accomplished and efficient Philadelphia woman, quick to exploit any opportunity, but, in the matter of the little girls, I can't help feeling that she must have exploited some that arose in total darkness, while I was drugged or drunk. I really can't explain it otherwise.

It wasn't easy to get a new butler in Philadelphia, I can tell you; there was fierce competition for every competent man. While we were working our way through a number of unsatisfactory applicants I was forced to develop a measure of self-reliance, at least as regards the procurement of dime novels.

I soon formed the habit of clipping downtown in my buggy to meet the early-morning train from New York. In those days dime novels were baled more or less like hay; I took to haunting the freight platforms, and the second a bale of the precious booklets dropped, I was on it. The news vendors rather resented this at first, but I was a wealthy man, and it took no more than a few gold pieces to convince them it was in their interest to let me paw through the books at once.

"Des Montaignes is like that about whores," Billy said. I was curious as to why someone with a fine French name would be living in Greasy Corners, New Mexico, so I asked.

"Because it's the one place where everybody is as pure a rascal as he is," Billy said.

"Most places they'd just shoot him down like a dog," Joe explained.

"Philadelphia must be a curious kind of a place," Billy said. "You wouldn't catch me getting up early just to go buy yarns."

"It's hard to get you up early to do anything," Joe said —it was a bone of contention between them.

"The sun itself don't get up as early as you do, Joe," Billy said.

"The early bird gets the worm," Joe remarked.

"Yeah, but who besides a bird would want a dern worm?" Billy replied.

I guess he had heard enough about the Philadelphia life because he yawned, as a kid will, rolled his blanket around him, and fell asleep long before I had finished the story of why and how I had come to be sitting on that rock in the Hidden Mountains where the three of us met.

10.

Billy was right about Joe Lovelady's penchant for an early start. The stars were still bright above me when I heard him stirring the fire—as bright as opals against a black velvet choker.

By the time the stars had melted into the coming light, Joe had his horse saddled. He made what noise he could while he went about it—it was as if he hoped we'd hear him and take the hint.

Well, I took the hint—I had not made much progress at learning to sleep on the ground, anyway. The earth might be my mother, as the red men believed, but that didn't mean it was much of a mattress. I had spent fifty years sleeping on feathers, and atop a high bed at that. On a high bed, nothing much worse than Dora was apt to crawl over me—the same could not be said for the great bed of the plains, particularly if there was nothing between you and it but a saddle blanket.

I sat up and picked hairs out of my mouth for a while —evidently my beard was shedding. Joe Lovelady handed me a tin cup of bitter coffee. A sip of it dissolved the rest of the hairs, and what sleep was left in me as well.

"We don't travel with no sweetening," Joe said apologetically.

It was just coming light. The sky above us and the grass around us were the same color, a dim gray. Then the coyotes began to yip. A herd of antelope grazed to the east of us. When the sun began to edge from the ground it seemed for a moment as if the antelope were walking along the rim. It was still and nice.

I didn't mind the plains so much in the morning stillness. It was when the wind came searing across the long emptiness, snatching at every weed and seed, that I felt a little exposed.

Billy lay flat on his back, his mouth open, snoring lightly. Asleep, he looked about twelve. And he was supposed to be the great killer of the West!

I saw that the horses were ready. Joe had even saddled Rosy—a remarkable thing. Often I had to spend an hour paying her insincere compliments before I could get her to accept the saddle.

"How'd you come to know Billy?" I asked. From the manner of their intercourse I assumed they must have been friends for years.

"Why, we just met up," he said, as if surprised that anyone would care to inquire. "He doesn't have no folks, and I don't either, now—we thought we'd see if we could get on with a cow outfit."

He sipped his coffee for a bit. "But I don't know that Billy's going to make a cowboy," he said, with a sigh. "I guess it just ain't his line."

It was Joe Lovelady's line, though. I soon came to see that if there were such a thing as the perfect cowboy, Joe was it. He had the skills to perfection—and more than that, he had the temperament. Joe asked for no more than horses and cattle, ropes and saddles, grass

38

and sky. It was his misfortune—well, better say his tragedy—to fall in with the gunmen.

If I had realized that still morning how fast the old wheel of fate was spinning I would have wired for some money and bought Joe a ranch in Nebraska or Montana or somewhere as far from New Mexico as I could get him. I liked him the minute I set eyes on him, and I had the money, too. But I suppose there's no likelihood Joe would have ridden away and let Billy fall. Call them sidekicks, *compañeros,* or what you like, I doubt they could have been separated, except by the one thing that did separate them, finally.

"He snores even worse when he sleeps on his stomach," Joe remarked in a tolerant way. You could tell from the way he said it that the man was a true friend to Billy Bone.

11.

We rode all day at a fast Joe Lovelady clip but got nowhere—or nowhere that one could rightly call any-
where, at least. We must have traveled seventy-five
miles, but seventy-five miles is no more than a breath
on those plains. When we made camp that night we
could still see the mountains where we had been the
day before—the air was that clear.

I had been around the edges of the great plain for the
past month, but I would never have dared just strike off
across it—not unless I had a competent fellow such as
Joe Lovelady to follow.

It was such an immensity of sky and grass! And when
you've said sky and grass, you've said it all: there was
nothing else within reach of human vision except the
faint bulge of the mountains far to the west.

I had the feeling I could ride on across that plain all
through my life and never get across it. I knew there
were places across it—Philadelphia was across it, for

example, and St. Louis and a number of other cities—but so endless were the plains that it seemed I would be lucky to arrive at any of those cities much before the hour of my death.

I felt the plains had caught me in some way; when I finally did make my return to the Eastern cities, it was a burden to have to resume life under such small skies.

"You might as well pull that hat down to your chin, Sippy," Billy Bone said to me—he was amused at my habit of lowering my headgear down to about eyebrow level, the headgear being a floppy hat I had purchased in El Paso.

Billy didn't realize that the Western light was an altogether different species from the thin, manageable light of Philadelphia. A full day of drinking it in gave me headaches as severe as if I'd spent the same amount of time guzzling a ripe wine.

"Oh, this is fine," I said. "I don't need to see past the ears of this mule, anyway."

"If Old Whiskey and the tall nigger were to lope out of one of these gullies you'd need to see," he informed me. "You'd not only need to see, you'd need to fly."

He was referring to Will Isinglass, owner of the Whiskey Glass ranch—his cowboys referred to him as Old Whiskey because of his habit of strapping a quart jar of whiskey to his saddle before he left his headquarters each morning. He had had a well-padded pouch made to protect his quart—and if he happened to chance back by his ranch house around the lunch hour, he'd secure himself another quart for the afternoon.

Of course Isinglass and Mesty-Woolah—his African warrior—didn't lope out of any gullies that day, but I believe in the course of that long ride Billy Bone decided to adopt me, more or less. The peculiar way I had of wearing my hat seemed to convince him that I couldn't possibly take care of myself.

"Why'd you ever come out here anyway, Sippy?" he

41

asked that evening, as we were watching our second campfire die. There were no prairie chickens to feast on that night, either—just a couple of stringy jackrabbits.

"You should have hit that brunette you married with a bed slat," he told me. "Then you wouldn't have to be out here trying to stay alive in a place you don't know nothing about."

12.

In fact, it was a slow day in the dime-novel trade that concluded matters between Dora and me.

Inevitably there came a morning when no bales of booklets were dropped. I rode home with a heavy heart, oppressed by the knowledge that not a single new dime novel was likely to enter Philadelphia that day.

Once home, I trudged miserably up to my study, thinking I might reread a few chapters of an old favorite, *Boiled in Yellowstone; or, Mustang Merle Amid the Geysers*. My own hero, Orson Oxx, had somehow strayed into Africa and was about to be boiled himself, though in a cannibal pot rather than a geyser. I thought it might be best to revisit a tried-and-true favorite, so that I might better bring my own adventure in progress to the boiling point itself, in a manner of speaking.

And then, calamity! My study had been stripped! The thousands of dime novels, so neatly stacked in sequence, were gone. Not one remained, not even the

43

half-read *Saul Sabberday* left on my desk the night before.

Ashen, I raced down to Cook, who was up to her elbows in bread dough.

"Oh, yes," she confirmed. "The scrap-paper man came by and Missus told him to take them all. She said your color had not been good lately and it might be because of the dust from them old books."

My color! Dear God! I raced to the scrap-paper dealer, but too late. As dust goes to dust, pulp had gone to pulp.

Had I hurried home then, I might have murdered Dora and left our nine cheerful turnips motherless. Instead, I went to my bank, secured a substantial letter of credit from an astonished officer, and took the train to New York, burdened by not even so much as a shaving mug.

I didn't need it, for that day I ceased to shave, or to be the Benjamin J. Sippy who had resided so unobtrusively all his life on Chestnut Street in Philadelphia.

The next afternoon I settled myself in a small cabin on a boat bound for Galveston, Texas. I had meant to book for New Orleans, but the Galveston boat was ready to lift anchor, and I took it.

"You may meet with some brashness in Texas, but you'll like it," the captain said. He was a thin little Yankee with the worst-fitting set of false teeth I had ever encountered—if the seas were even moderately rough they clicked like a telegraph key.

"They can keep their talk of Saint Louis," he said. "I say Texas is where the real West begins."

"Then I made the right choice," I said. "The real West is exactly what I'm looking for."

"Oh, it's real, mighty real," he said briskly, before the sea surged and his teeth began to click out a code of their own.

13.

"But won't your family wonder what became of you?"
Joe Lovelady asked. It shocked him that I had left Dora
and the turnips without so much as a goodbye.

"Sippy's like a lot of people out here," Billy said. "He
don't intend to be found."

"His wife's probably worried, though," Joe insisted.

"Well, let her!" Billy said. "She asked him why he
was still breathing."

A little later, though, he softened a bit toward Dora.
"She's probably crying fits, all right," he said. "Women
ain't very tough."

I was to remember that remark the morning he lay
dying. Long before then, I think he had been forced to
revise his views on the toughness of women.

What did *I* think? Was I being missed and worried
about in the big gray stone pile on Chestnut Street? Had
the family noticed that old Dad was no longer moping
feverishly in the study, his head in a pamphlet? Was
Cook still setting my place at the table? Had anyone

observed that I wasn't turning up to sip my terrapin soup?

The questions troubled Joe Lovelady a good deal more than they troubled me. Joe had been married only a little more than a year when his wife and baby were taken—he could not conceive of leaving them over such a trifle as *Mustang Merle*.

How could I explain—to a man who had never seen a butler—that in Philadelphia gentlemen of my station leave their wives every day for parlormaids? Joe had never seen a parlormaid, either; perhaps he had never even seen a parlor. Among the many worldly things he had no grasp of was the fact that there are some very decent parlormaids.

There seemed no point in trying to explain to him that from Dora's point of view it was probably better that I left her because of books. *That* she could simply put down to lunacy, whereas a parlormaid would have called for a rather more ticklish interpretation.

In fact, my only serious familial responsibility had been to see that our excellent servants were punctually paid, but that was not a truth easily conveyed to two young men whose only schooling had been the raw frontier.

"I had a wife, too," Joe said. Then he stopped and asked me if I had enjoyed my sea voyage. I believe he had started to raise the question of longevity—to ask me what it was like to have a wife, not for the brief year that he had had his Nellie, but for the more than twenty years that I had had my Dora. But the question choked him. Billy Bone saw it as clearly as I did and gave me a worried look.

Joe Lovelady wanted to believe in happiness. He needed to feel that things could be the way they were supposed to be, that life would yield its ripe sweet fruits to competence and application.

But he had stuck himself with two skeptics, Billy Bone and me. Perhaps he realized that we would rip his

46

nice hopes to ribbons, so he switched to a question about boats.

"I won't cross much water," Billy said nervously. "You can't see through it. How would you know if a big fish was waiting to bite you?"

"A fish couldn't bite you on a boat," Joe pointed out.

"No, but the boat could sink," Billy said. "Then where would you be? If I have a bad dream tonight it'll be your fault, Joe. I've had more than one bad dream about big fish."

Not wishing to increase his risk of scary dreams, I waited until he was snoring to describe my little boat ride down to Galveston.

14.

I boarded that boat with high hopes, thinking I was free at last—free of Dora and her disquieting questions, free of the boring lawns and dilute light of Chestnut Street, and, perhaps, even free of dime novels.

Why would I need cheap tales, once I was bound for the real—even, by some standards, the mighty real—West? I had jettisoned my sedate habits; why not also jettison my gaudy dreams?

Fortunately the boat—it was called the *Texas Moon*—was more seaworthy than my hopes. A slow cruise to Galveston was not necessarily the best cure for dime-novel mania. We had barely cleared the harbor before I was ransacking the ship for reading matter, cursing myself for my own high-minded neglect of the many excellent newsstands I had passed in New York.

The *Texas Moon* was not exactly a floating library. It was an old cattle boat, returning empty to Texas with only her crew, myself, and a light load of dry goods. I turned up a sea tale called *Sailor Dan; or, The Water-spout*, but most of the crew sailors just looked confused when I asked them if they had any reading matter. The first mate rather grudgingly loaned me a well-thumbed copy of *Rose, the Frontier Angel,* and the little Yankee captain yielded up three *Red Charlie* adventures; but unfortunately, *Red Charlie (The Chippewa Scout)* was one of my own inventions, and not one of my favorites, either.

So, once I had gobbled down *Sailor Dan* and *The Frontier Angel,* there was nothing to do but to write. The Beadle and Adams firm had just started a series of half-dime domestic tales, and I decided—since I'd left it forever—to have my say about married life.

I flashed out a trifle called *Wedded but Not Won; or, Did She Care?* in which—I admit it—I settled a few long-standing scores with Dora. She had a simpering admirer named Waddy Peacock, a man, by my reckoning, even more boring than myself, though I suppose it's just possible that Dora's reckoning was more favorable than my own. This speculation gave verve to my pen, and in the tale that resulted Dora was given the energies, as well as the inclinations, of a Lola Montez.

Two days and I was finished; but the *Texas Moon* was still only inching its way past the Carolinas. My thoughts kept turning to Chittim. I felt I owed him something, but how to pay it? The man was dead. I had left money to his widow, but still I had a sense of the debt.

Had anyone ever been kinder to me than Chittim? I couldn't recall that they had. Being far from home, hearth, and newsstands, sentiment made easy prey of me. I had scarcely ended *Wedded but Not Won* when I began *The Butler's Sorrow; or, Chittim's Trek.*

It was the story of a loyal butler who crossed the Sonoran desert on foot in order to deliver an important document to his beloved young mistress, a rich girl soon to be richer, but presently taking the waters at a spa in California. The document informed her that she had just inherited a vast ancestral estate.

The loyal butler, knowing that he could aspire to nothing more, hoped that at least the young lady would take him with her to her new home and keep him as her butler forever, but the heartless vixen, annoyed by his shabby appearance—there had been the usual scrapes with Apaches and Gila monsters—sacked him on the spot. The poor man's despair was such that he lost his way, drifted south, and was eventually eaten by cannibals in Ecuador.

We stopped in New Orleans for a day and I posted the two stories, little suspecting that I had just mailed off the most popular dime novel ever written: *The Butler's Sorrow.*

Wedded but Not Won may have struck a chord with a few embittered husbands, but *The Butler's Sorrow* circled the entire globe in a matter of months. It became known as the book read by four Presidents; and besides the four Presidents, the young Czar read it, the old Queen read it—virtually everyone who could read in the whole world read it. It even outsold *Ragged Dick*, and I've heard it reported—though this may be spoofing —that when Livingstone was finally found, he inquired of Stanley if he had thought to bring a copy with him.

I suppose it merely means that more people than one might think secretly harbor the feeling of having mistreated the butler.

15.

That night a dry storm rumbled across the plains a few miles to the north of us. Thunder cracked and lightning slit the darkness. Joe Lovelady slept right through the worst of it.

I was somewhat nervous, but Billy Bone was terrified. "Now lightning's something I *really* hate," he informed me. "They say it cooks you into black bacon if it hits you. I'd give a million dollars if we was inside so we could hide under the bed."

Since we definitely weren't inside, he hid under his saddle.

"Throw the saddle blanket over me, quick, Sippy!" he said. I draped it over the saddle, so as to make a kind of curtain, but Billy was shaking so much it soon slipped off.

"I'd rather be dead than go through this," he said.

"Oh, that's extreme," I said. "It's not that bad."

"You'll think so when you're black bacon!" he said bitterly.

Then he saw something that made him even more frantic. He gave a cry, threw off the saddle, and yanked both pistols out of his coat.

"Did you see him?" he asked, which gave me a bad scare. I assumed he had seen an Apache in the lightning flash. But it hadn't been an Apache, it had been something that frightened him even worse. Before Joe and I could even figure out what we were being attacked by, Billy had emptied both pistols into the darkness, and when I say emptied, I mean emptied—twelve shots.

Even Joe Lovelady couldn't sleep through twelve shots. He rolled over, pistol in hand, just as the lightning flashed again; but so far as either of us could see, the plain was empty.

"What was it, Billy?" Joe asked, puzzled but not really alarmed.

"It was the Death Dog," Billy said. He was so scared his teeth were chattering, and he was dropping bullets, trying to reload.

"There ain't no Death Dog, Billy," Joe said. I believe he was a little exasperated at having been so rudely awakened from a sound sleep.

"It was the Death Dog!" Billy insisted. "He was standing not thirty feet away, grinning at me. It means I'm a goner for sure."

"It was just an old lobo, coming to eat those rabbit guts," Joe said firmly. He lowered the hammer on his pistol, rolled over, and soon went back to sleep.

But Billy Bone was a long way from sleep.

"There's no worse luck than to see the Death Dog in a lightning flash," he assured me.

I knew Joe Lovelady was right—if a wolf had been there he was probably only after the rabbit entrails. But I wanted to do what I could to reassure Billy; he still flinched every time the lightning tongued toward us.

"He was probably looking at *me*, Billy," I said. "I'm the only one old enough to be eligible in this crowd."

52

"No, you didn't see him," Billy said. "I seen him. The Death Dog only lets you see him if he wants you."

Neither of us slept the rest of the night, though the storm soon passed so far to the east that the lightning was no worse than the flickering of a lamp. Billy kept his guns in his hands all night.

"It's true you don't know much about staying alive out here, Sippy," he said. "But I know dumber people than you, and they're still alive."

"Luck," I said.

"Must be," he agreed. "You rode on that boat and it didn't sink."

16.

The boat didn't sink, but my spirits did, when I finally arrived in Galveston. The island was just a low, muggy strip of sand whose citizens seemed to spend all their time either sweating or scratching or both.

From researches in my favorite literature—the dime novels, of course—I had formed the impression that the first thing a traveler ought to attend to upon arrival in Texas was the acquisition of a certain amount of ordnance: guns and knives, that is, and the more the better.

Consequently I had not been on the island an hour before I acquired a Winchester rifle, a Colt revolver, two derringers—one for each boot—and several bowie knives. I expected assailants, and soon had my guns loaded and my knives sharpened.

The assailants didn't keep me waiting, either; they arrived in my hotel room at once and in force, unfortunately too small to shoot and too quick to cut.

I was soon to realize that in all my considerable reading about the West, the bug factor had been seriously skimped. Apaches I was prepared for; *bandidos* I might almost have welcomed; but what I got in Galveston was bugs.

In Philadelphia we give as little thought to bugs as we do to butlers. Oh, we might swat the occasional fly, and our summer place in the Muncy hills might tempt the occasional mosquito; but bugs, on the whole, did not loom large in the life we lived there.

They were not exactly a constant presence in dime novels, either. Mustang Merle never scratched, that I recall; Hurricane Nell, though she slept in the prairie grass most of her life, never complained of chiggers, much less anything worse. But I had not been on the Texas shore twenty-four hours before I had to contend with lice, chiggers, mosquitoes, nits, ticks, houseflies, horseflies, bedbugs, beetles, ants, spiders, roaches, centipedes, scorpions, and gnats. And so it was to be in all my Western jaunts. The inventory might vary a little, depending upon the altitude or the season, but the violence of the many Westerners I encountered—and they *were* violent—was seldom as great a threat to my morale as the intense and tenacious appetite of the Western bug.

In fact, the insect population and temperament came to seem to me such an impediment to the winning of the West that I devoted one of my best dime novels to it— my book *The Bug Oracle,* in which a man's fate is foretold by the squiggles a snail leaves in the sand.

I wrote it while acting the part of a male Scheherazade in the great Isinglass castle north of San Jon. Lady Cecily Snow, as precise in all matters biological as she was beautiful, informed me that a snail was not in any true sense a bug. I guess I must have known that; in any case I meekly changed the snail in the story to an ant, for I would not have wanted to increase Cecily's dissatisfaction with me by even such a trifling thing as a literary inaccuracy.

Later, once Cecily Snow had gone where Guinevere

55

is—surely she had; all they found was her sidesaddle—
I got out the manuscript and changed the ant back to a
snail; it seemed to me readers might just accept a snail
as a harbinger of a man's fate; it seemed to me they
might reject an ant.

Billy Bone still gripped his pistols. He showed little
interest in my descriptions of the bug tortures I had
endured on Galveston island.

"I seen the Death Dog tonight," he reminded me. "I'd
rather have a million ticks and lice in my hair than to
see him grinning that old grin of his."

"Who told you there was such a thing as a Death
Dog?" I asked. Of course, dime novels were full of such
legends. I still remember one called *Maria Verlaine; or,
The Werewolf of Quebec*, which had a creature much
like a Death Dog in it.

"La Tulipe told me," Billy said. "You'll meet her tomorrow.

"Joe don't have many nightmares," he added, looking
wistfully at his friend.

The tense look had left his face, but his hands were
still clinched on his guns.

"What's the worst thing that's ever happened to you,
Sippy?" he asked. "Tell me the worst thing. It might
take my mind off that old grinning dog."

"That's easy," I said. "The worst thing that ever happened to me was riding a stagecoach from Galveston to
El Paso."

I meant it, too. It was not too much to say that in the
ten pounding days it took us to pass across Texas I completed a passage of a different sort.

When I got on that stage in Galveston I was still
young, at least in my attitudes. By the time I got off it in
El Paso I was old.

17.

I've often wondered if that terrible trip would have aged me as it did if I could have kept my rightful rear seat in the stagecoach.

It was not my first experience of stagecoaches, though it was to be by far my longest. Wells Fargo had brought a couple to the big '76 celebration in Philadelphia; rides around the park only cost five cents, and I took fifty or sixty cents' worth before the celebration ended.

Even that brief experience was enough to convince me that a stagecoach was a miserable conveyance, useful in dime novels but a pounding torment in real life.

Those bumpy rides around the park also taught me that the only chance one had of escaping spinal injuries, kidney disease, and mental dissolution was to secure a rear seat, facing toward the horses. Stagecoaches tip to the rear; in Philadelphia this was caused by kids piling on at the back; in the West it was the result of a ton or so of mail stuffed in the baggage boot. If you sat in a rear seat you at least had the comfort of something firm to lean back against—i.e., the rear of the coach.

But if fate cast you into one of the dreadful front seats, facing away from the horses, due to the up-tip of the stage, you not only had nothing to lean back against but had to brace yourself desperately hour after hour to keep from pitching forward into the lap of whoever sat across from you.

In this case, the person sitting across from me was a sizable woman named Eliza Bargesley, traveling west with her savage quadruplets to rejoin her husband in El Paso.

Naturally I had reserved the rear seat—Galveston to El Paso looked to be an ordeal no matter how one traveled, and I wanted to give myself every chance.

But a fate almost as malicious as Billy Bone's Death Dog caused Eliza Bargesley and her brats to book on the same coach. Naturally, being a Philadelphia gentleman, I could not let a lady, or even a woman, take the terrible front seat while I lounged in comfort against the back.

With a tip of my new wide-brimmed felt hat to Mrs. Bargesley I politely surrendered my seat.

The two men I then had to wedge myself between, a fat harness salesman named Pope and a weasel of a land speculator with elbows like razors named Brisket, looked at me as if I had lost my senses.

"See, that's a gent, he gave us his nice seat," Mrs. Bargesley said, seating herself directly opposite me. We were to remain thus, locked knee to knee, twenty-four hours a day for the next ten days. Long before I passed into a delirium of fatigue it seemed to me that Mrs. Bargesley and I had become a form of Siamese twins, humans joined at the knees. I realize that she had *chosen* me to lock knees with, rather than the vulgar Pope or the sly Brisket, but long before we reached San Antonio the honor I should have felt was overwhelmed by my urge never to see the woman or any of her get again.

58

Her get—that is, the four brats, all seemingly stout boys—soon developed motion sickness of an intensity I would not have thought possible. We had scarcely cleared the ferry that took us off Galveston island before they began a sequence of violent retchings that were sustained, with few interruptions, for the next ten days and nights. Besides the vomitings, they were soon awash in fevers, diarrheas, and wild seizures resembling convulsions in which they clawed at one another and chewed on one another's clothes. In their few quiet moments Mrs. Bargesley doped them with a thick pink nostrum from a quart bottle she kept handy.

The worst riot that ever occurred in Philadelphia— and we've seen some beauties—was as nothing to the melee inside that stagecoach. Pope, the harness salesman on my right, immediately took to drink, while Brisket, on my left, contented himself with peculiarly foul cigars. The smoke had at least the effect of discouraging mosquitoes.

To me, the coach seemed to bounce over Texas like a huge flying ball. Though disgusted by the Bargesley brats' retchings, I could hardly blame them for it. If I had had much in my stomach I would have vomited too.

Wind was equally hard to contain. During her many naps Mrs. Bargesley farted like thunder; if a similar slip occurred while she was awake, she would blush and slap the nearest boy silly in an effort to transfer the blame.

"You mean she farted right there in the coach?" Billy Bone asked, badly shocked.

The look of fear left his face; somehow the thought of Mrs. Bargesley's farts cleared his mind of the Death Dog.

"I hope no woman ever farts around me," he said nervously. "I wouldn't have stood it. I'd have climbed out and rode with the drivers."

The next day, when we were no more than twenty

miles from Greasy Corners, I heard him telling Joe Love-lady the awful news: a woman had farted in a stage-coach.

"Probably wasn't given nothing but frijoles to eat," Joe concluded. "They will make you blow."

Billy muttered about Mrs. Bargesley's bad manners for weeks. In his mind, frijoles were no excuse. He was delicate about such matters, nervous and delicate; and yet he was just a boy who had been raised scrappy, in the raw mining saloons of Colorado.

18.

In fact, I did try riding with the drivers, but I was soon judged to be a threat to public safety and stuffed back inside the coach. Apparently I woke from a brief nightmare and tried to strangle one of the drivers, almost causing us both to fall off the stage.

I have no memory of that incident at all. The last thing I remember about the trip was wasting the hour we had in San Antonio buying a new hat. Mr. Pope and Mr. Brisket did the same, for of course all our headgear had blown out the window somewhere around Houston.

We were all fools; we should have flopped right down on the street and caught a few precious minutes of real sleep—if we had been run over, our torments would have ended there.

Of course our new hats blew out the window almost at once; it only got windier and more bumpy as we traveled west. I passed an hour or two of time trying to calculate how many hats were lost along that stage route every year: the figure I came up with was fifteen hundred.

At least this made clear to me what might otherwise have been a puzzling fact about the West: why so many Indians and outlaws wore hats made in Brooklyn. If they grew dissatisfied with a particular hat, all they had to do was ride over to the stage road and pick a new one off a sagebrush or a prickly pear.

Otherwise, I spent a thousand miles trying to keep myself from pitching forward through thin air into the broad abyss of Mrs. Bargesley's lap—though I'd have to admit that the farther we traveled the less thin the air grew, thanks to Mr. Brisket's peculiarly foul cigars.

Leroy Pope, the harness salesman, was rarely sober during the trip, but it was he who first noticed that the Bargesley boys were quadruplets. I had averted my eyes so successfully from the retching, clawing brats that I had failed to catch this fact.

"Are those young 'uns all one litter or am I seeing quadruple?" he asked one morning, after awakening from a particularly hard souse. The boys were all clearing their tonsils by spitting at one another.

"Why, yes," Mrs. Bargesley said with a look of motherly pride. "Matt, Mitch, Martin, and Monroe, born six years ago this week."

I was in a bleary state, half mad from fatigue, but it seemed to me I had some vague memory of reading about the birth of quadruplets some years ago. Could it have been in Trenton, New Jersey?

Mrs. Bargesley—it's only fair to allow that she wasn't enjoying this dreadful trip any more than we gentlemen —brightened when I asked if the boys had been born in Trenton.

"Oh, yes, it was all in the papers," she confessed.

My mind, already slipping its halter, was strangely fluttered by this news: for what were the odds that the only dime novelist with a mansion on Chestnut Street would end up losing his seat on a westbound stagecoach to the mother of the only quadruplets ever born in Trenton, New Jersey? A billion to one seemed to me about how the odds would factor out.

"I don't waste no time counting odds," Billy remarked, when I mentioned my calculations. "I just ask the Tulip if I want to know what's happening."

"Just because she's old don't mean she's right," Joe said. "Old folks can be wrong too."

"It ain't because she's old, it's because she's a witch woman," Billy replied, sounding a little vexed.

"It's foolish to waste time worrying about things that haven't happened," Joe Lovelady said. "If they happen, they happen. Then worry about them."

"You and me will never agree, Joe," Billy said, a little sadly. "I don't know why we're even sidekicks."

"There's no why to that," Joe said. "We just are."

There was a sad tone to their talk, at times. It made me nervous when I heard it; I would try to swing them off the subject, even if I had to make up a story or tell a lie.

Usually they would listen brightly, too—and even indulge me in my little exaggerations. I think they were glad to have me along, useless as I was in most respects. Still, I could talk, and I had seen more of the world than they had. They both had some curiosity and were tired of having only their own experience to discuss.

Besides, I *was* a famous dime novelist, not tight with my adjectives. I could splash some color on a story.

I splashed plenty on the story of my stage ride, though in fact I had sunk into a stupor of fatigue just west of San Antonio and could remember nothing about the rest of the trip. When consciousness returned I was lying on the floor of a barroom in El Paso, too tired even to lift my head off the floor. All I could see, when I forced my eyes open, were dusty boots with big silver Mexican spurs attached to them. I have no idea how I got in that barroom; I suppose I fell out of the stage and some kindly soul dragged me inside. I'm told I'd lain there for three days, with no one knowing or caring whether I was alive or dead.

It seemed to me that my sufferings had been lavish, and lavishly was how I described them, but, despite my best efforts, the account seemed to fall flat with Billy and Joe. The hard young men of the West seemed more amused than sympathetic.

"My gosh, Sippy, you should have just got out and walked, if you was that picky," was Billy's only comment.

I felt a little hurt—I suppose I expected more rapport.

But we had crossed the Arroyo del Macho, and were skirting the white scars of the Bitter Lake. The setting sun was like a ball of gold behind us when we trotted into Greasy Corners.

From then on I had little time to brood about old adventures. Neither did Billy or Joe. Within a few hours we had plenty of fresh ones to keep us occupied.

II

The Whiskey Glass War

1.

From the moment we rode into Greasy Corners—it consisted of no more than a dozen crumbling adobe hovels
scattered beside the alkaline Pecos—I knew I had come
to one of the strangest and most forlorn places I would
ever visit in my life.

A pig or two slunk around the hovels and a few dusty
curs scratched in the street, now and then adding their
whines to the whine of the wind. The pigs were as thin
as the dogs, unnerving to a man used to the fine plump
pigs of Pennsylvania.

It looked odd—mighty odd, as the little Yankee captain might say.

"Not much to behold, is it, Sippy?" Billy said, as we
trotted in.

But then he was grinning—he looked excited,
whereas Joe Lovelady only looked depressed.

Of course Billy was the young prince of the town, the
adored boy. He whipped up his horse and loped in,

ahead of Joe and me. Joe looked as melancholy as the dusk which had by then embraced the long plain.

"You don't look too cheerful," I remarked.

"No, I don't enjoy Greasy Corners," he said quietly. "I just come here to humor Billy."

"I can see that it's not exactly a garden spot," I said. In itself that was Yankee understatement. The soil was so alkaline that the tufts of buffalo grass looked as if they'd been salted; the stems of sagebrush were white.

I felt a little apprehensive. "What's the main thing to watch out for?" I asked.

"The people are the main thing to watch out for," Joe said. "Folks that stay in this town are only interested in two things."

"What two?"

"Killing and dying," Joe said.

2.

"I may die eventually, but I'll be damned if I'll allow myself to be disappointed," Will Isinglass said to me in one of the curious conversations we had while I was his prisoner north of San Jon.

He was eating a beefsteak, and he paused to look at me down the length of the long table his dead partner, Lord Snow, had brought from England. Drippings from the meat stained his beard. He looked like an old gray buffalo—a shaggy mane, a great head.

"I've lived eighty-five years and got every damn thing I wanted," he added.

"Except a son with a chin, I suppose," Cecily Snow said, contempt dripping from her voice as the juice dripped from the meat. The English do know how to manage contempt.

Isinglass studied her a moment—her enmity affected him as little as the bite of a flea, though she was a beautiful woman, daughter of a family that had held sway in England for six hundred years.

"Well, a whelp is usually a burden," Isinglass said. "I've found it cheaper to hire my help."

Yet he had had four sons by Cecily's mother, started three in Cecily herself, fathered Katerina Garza, the flame of the cantinas, on a Mexican woman, and Bloody Feathers, hawk of the Jicarillas, on an Apache girl.

All these years later I still wonder about that old man. When the knell had finally rung for all the sweethearts; when Cecily Snow was gone and even Mesty-Woolah had fallen; when the great Whiskey Glass ranch was taken from him and a century weighed upon his shoulders; when Billy Bone had killed his four mute sons, and only the Mexican girl and the Indian brave were left to mark his passage across that huge land—did he know regret?

Even I had regrets about Dora, a woman who used her tongue as a cabbie uses a buggy whip.

The one person I had to put the question to was Tully Roebuck, the sad sheriff, one of the men Isinglass sent after Billy once Mesty-Woolah was dead.

He and I were sitting in the shade of his porch in Lincoln, listening to his little blind daughter croon from her bedroom, when I asked him if he thought Isinglass had known disappointment at the end.

"Doubt it," Tully said, tipping his chair. "Old Whiskey was not a man to question himself."

3.

The extraordinary thing about Will Isinglass was that, to an uncommon degree, he forced life to honor his expectations. Most of us can't do that—I'm a prime example of one who can't. My own expectations are apt to soar and dip, depending on the direction and the stiffness of the breeze.

Ten seconds after Joe Lovelady and I followed Billy Bone into the China Pond, my own expectations took an immediate plunge.

It was just a dim, smoky barroom—why Des Montaignes had chosen to call it the China Pond was never explained. Joe and I had just got through the door and were peering through the smoke trying to spot Billy when guns began to shoot.

I realize that's a poor description; it would never pass muster in a dime novel, but then I wasn't in a dime novel at the time. I couldn't really see the men—the barroom was too murky—and all I could think of was that guns were shooting.

The sound, in the small room, was so loud that it paralyzed me. I meant to run back out the door, but the message could not seem to proceed from my brain to my legs.

Others were luckier in passing the message—there was such a rush for the door that I got knocked completely off my feet. I rolled up against the bar and hid my face in my hat. It was primitive reasoning—if they can't see your face they won't shoot you—but I was badly scared.

Then the guns stopped shooting, which felt better. Still, I decided to stay hidden in my hat for a few minutes, undignified as that might be. I wasn't sure the guns were through with their shooting.

My mind, a spinning top, spun me back to Philadelphia. I lay there in the dust and cigar butts, regretting the fact that I had never kissed Kate Molloy, a very appealing Irish parlormaid, who had shown signs that she might allow it.

No doubt it's always the unkissed girls you remember when you're about to be killed. Kate was so pert, so lively—what had stopped me?

Before I could reflect and grow sorrowful about this lapse, somebody grabbed my pants leg and began to drag me across the dusty floor. It was a short, furious little man in buckskins, with greasy black hair and rotting teeth—the very image of Black Nick.

He was strong and brisk, though. I was fairly whistling across that floor.

Then Billy spotted me.

"Hey, slow down, Dez," he said. "That's my friend Mr. Sippy who ain't from Mississippi. Don't be dragging him out—I don't think he's even shot."

"I'm not," I said meekly, though it was really too early to be sure.

Des Montaignes immediately got huffy. He dropped my legs and frowned.

72

"Stand up if you're alive!" he said with some exasperation.

I guess I had inadvertently wasted the man's time. He marched over to the corner, where he soon found a man who *was* dead. As I was getting to my feet, he dragged him out.

"Dez is all business," Billy said. He seemed in unusually high spirits. His young eyes were dancing.

Soon the people who had knocked me down on their way out came trooping back in—an eclectic mixture of retired buffalo hunters and leisured gunmen. Billy made a fine joke about Des Montaignes mistaking me for a corpse, so I got introduced to the sweethearts of Greasy Corners while they were having a good laugh at my expense.

4.

Hill Coe, Pleasant Burnell, Wild Horse Jerry, Simp
Dixon, Happy Jack Marco, Moss Kuykendall, Ike Pumpelly, and Vivian Maldonado were the principal gunslingers operating out of Greasy Corners in the time
Billy and Joe and I were there.

Among the buffalo hunters present were Nute Rachal,
Jim Saul, Hank Leedy, J. C. Smurr, and Zack Stuckey.

I met them all and came to like most of them, but I
admit I was nervous at first. Billy and Joe had impressed
upon me the absolute necessity of keeping people
straight as regards profession and reputation. It could be
fatal, they assured me, to confuse a buffalo hunter with
a gunslinger. A buffalo hunter might slap me on the back
and buy me a drink if I promoted him to gunslinger, but
it wouldn't work the other way around. Were I to casually ask a prominent gunslinger how many buffalo he'd
killed, rude treatment would be the best I could expect.

"Most of them would just pull out a gun and plug

you," Billy said matter-of-factly. "Hill Coe and them others, they got reputations to keep up."

Hill Coe, the famous marshal of Abilene and Dodge, had the coldest eyes in town, and a big standing among the locals. Only the Italian dandy, Vivian Maldonado, who had quit a life as a trapeze artist in a circus to seek glory with the gun, ever seemed disposed to challenge him.

The rest were frankly just the journeymen of the owl-hoot trail—a jolly lot when jolly and a sullen lot when sullen.

All of them—even Hill Coe—were careful of Billy Bone, a boy with little experience, but with a reckless eye.

"They don't know what Billy might do," was Joe Love-lady's analysis. "They don't, and he don't neither."

5.

It seems that Greasy Corners owed its existence to the reactionary nature of buffalo hunters. Like most humans, they were reluctant to strain themselves learning a new trade.

I gathered that Jim Saul and Nute Rachal and their crowd had stuck it out to the end at Fort Griffin, Texas, the last big shipping point for buffalo hides.

"Then one day we skint the last buffalo and there was nothing to do," Jim Saul said, with a sad, weary look in his eyes. He had hunted the southern herd in the days when it strung out over the plains for hundreds of miles.

"None of us is smart enough to make no living gambling," Hank Leedy said. "You got to have them quick hands to play cards."

"I just don't know where all them big critters went to," Nute Rachal said—the buffalo hunter's melancholy song.

They were all large men—ripping the hides off dead bison takes muscle. They would sit around all day in the shade of an old hide shed in Greasy Corners, whittling and spitting, looking sadly again and again across the empty plain, like old tired bears whose coats had worn shabby.

A few hundred buffalo from the southern herd had grazed down the Rio Pecos. Jim Saul and the others had come over from Texas and killed them. The hides were so poor that in the end they decided it wasn't even worth it to ship them—a huge pile of hides still lay just south of town. When the wind shifted the smell was strong enough to gag you.

Rumor had it that there were still some buffalo in Montana, but the Greasy Corner professionals didn't go north.

"I'd rather just think about them being there," Jim Saul said. "If we go kill them then it'll just be the same story."

They had lost their hope, and everybody knew it.

"Somebody ought to just shoot them," Billy Bone said. "I don't know if they'll fight."

But when Mesty-Woolah swept down with the hard riders, they did fight. And Isinglass did kill them, to the last sad man.

6.

_____

What had occurred when I had first stepped into the China Pond was a sharp disagreement between Vivian Maldonado and a stranger who had been slow to adapt to local ways.

It was the stranger Des Montaignes dragged out the back door, once he became disgusted with me.

Billy walked me over to the card table where the fracas had occurred and gave me a brief lecture. Napoleon was no keener student of battle tactics than Billy—and yet Billy's fighting was all impulse; it was only after the bodies were removed that he liked to pretend he had had a plan.

"The stranger's mistake was to sit too close to the table," he explained. "Everybody knows you don't sit too close to the table with Viv—if he loses two hands in a row he's apt to go for you with a pigsticker. Now look at Hill Coe, he's positioned perfect. He can reach his cards, but he ain't in range of no knife."

Hill Coe, of the cold eyes and fine reputation, dressed

like an old saddle bum. He was dealing cards to Simp Dixon, Happy Jack Marco, and Vivian Maldonado. The latter sported an elegant white buckskin vest and had pomaded his hair.

"Beely, take a hand," Maldonado said. I had seen his type in Naples, when Dora and I did the tour.

"No, I ain't in a mood to be stuck with a knife today, Viv," Billy said in a joking way.

Happy Jack Marco, a jolly-looking fellow with bright blue eyes, also sat well back from the table. "I'm thinking of hiring a nigger to handle my cards when Viv's hot," he said in a drawl as slow as molasses.

Happy Jack had a pistol in his lap—it seemed he had actually shot the stranger. Vivian Maldonado had lunged across the table in a fit of temper and slit the man's throat, but instead of just dying quietly the stranger managed to get a gun out and pump off several wild shots.

"Happy Jack cut him down neat," Billy said with admiration.

"Yeah, Dez, don't I get a free drink for restoring public order?" Happy Jack asked.

Des Montaignes had returned and was kicking dirt from the floor over a puddle of blood.

"Go poke a pig," Des Montaignes replied. Such rough talk was commonplace in Greasy Corners.

"Why, the dern shoats won't have me," Happy Jack said. It got a general laugh. Even Hill Coe managed a smile.

Then I heard a crooning from a dim corner near the bar. The noisy crowd heard it too, and at once grew silent. The crooning came from an old yellow woman, rocking on a little stool near the end of the bar. She was a heavy woman, and heavy-voiced too; and she wasn't merely crooning, she was singing in the French tongue:

O fleuve profond,
O sombre rivière ...

"That's La Tulipe," Billy said. "She knows the past and the future."

The old woman's singing got louder—it seemed to surge from her throat. Jim Saul and the other buffalo hunters stood listening with tears in their eyes—maybe La Tulipe's hoarse voice reminded them of the lowing of the animals they all missed. Then the song died back into wordless crooning as the old woman rocked back and forth on her stool.

Before anyone could stop him, Des Montaignes rushed over and kicked La Tulipe off the stool. She was his wife—he felt he had the right, I guess. He started to kick her again, but before he could, Billy Bone stepped over and stuck a pistol against his scraggly jaw.

"Don't be mistreating the Tulip," Billy said. "If you do I might decide to blow your brains out that back door."

Des Montaignes was a violent, filthy old man. But he had trapped beaver in the country of the Blackfeet and the northern Cheyenne; he had lived with the Shoshone and the Yankton Sioux, sold slaves to the Comanche and the Kiowa, eaten dog with the Mandans. They say he made a fortune on the Red River of the north and lost it on the Red River of the south. He was said to know every stream and campsite from the headwaters of the Missouri to the mouth of the Rio Grande.

In short, the man had had time to acquire a little common sense. He did not kick his wife again.

"These sad tunes are bad for business," he said, by way of excuse.

"Not as bad for it as me shooting you in the head," Billy remarked dryly.

Then he put away his gun and helped La Tulipe get back on her stool.

"A wolf will eat you and shit you out as a green puddle," she said to her husband, in clear if husky English.

Adjusting for the difference in circumstances, it was not unlike the kind of things Dora used to say to me.

80

7.

_____

After Des Montaignes gave up kicking his wife he went back and kicked some more dirt over the blood the dead stranger had bled. He had fairly drenched the floor along one wall. None of the cardplayers got up to help.

It may be that the easy life produces a little too much sensibility. I don't consider myself to be unusually squeamish, but the sight of all that fresh blood made me feel so sensible, all of a sudden, that I hurried out to seek a breath of fresh air.

Joe Lovelady had already gone out. He was squatting by a wall, having a smoke.

"I wish Tully would show up so we could get out of here," he said.

Tully meant Tully Roebuck, a man Joe and Billy sometimes cowboyed with. They had even once cowboyed for Isinglass, but Billy was a dud as a cowboy, and when he got fired Joe and Tully left out of loyalty.

Isinglass, of course, recognized that Joe Lovelady was the genuine diamond, when it came to cowboys; he offered to make him range boss of the Whiskey Glass ranch, and that was when the ranch covered some three million acres—most of eastern New Mexico and a lot of western Texas.

To be selected as foreman of the largest ranch in the world was quite an honor, but Joe Lovelady politely declined it and rode off with his reckless young friend, Billy Bone.

"Besides, I don't like to be bossing men who are older than me," Joe later explained.

Perhaps I seemed a little wobbly in the legs when I stepped out of the saloon. "You act like you're sick," he said.

"Well, it was a little close in that barroom," I admitted.

The prairie dusk was fading but it was not yet completely dark. I squatted down by the wall in an effort to imitate Joe—he had become my model in matters of Western etiquette and deportment.

"That old woman sings songs that make you feel like you have to die soon," Joe said. It was a fair description of La Tulipe's music.

"I don't suppose I'd settle in this place if I was planning a long life," I remarked.

"No, but it's ideal for gunfighters," Joe said. "They ain't got no plans."

8.

When I got to know the gunslingers better, I saw that Joe had a point. The majority of them never looked farther ahead than the next hand of cards. On the whole, their prospects were as dim as those of the buffalo hunters.

The dime novelists might portray gunfighters as a confident, satisfied lot—I've been guilty of that myself—but the truth is they were mainly disappointed men. They spent their lives in the rough barrooms of ugly towns; they ate terrible food and drank a vile grade of liquor; few of them managed to shoot the right people, and even fewer got to die gloriously in a shoot-out with a peer. The majority just got shot down by some bold stranger, like the drunk who killed the great Hickok.

A cowboy such as Joe Lovelady might not have firm plans, but at least he had dreams. I expect Joe saw himself running a small ranch in a peaceful valley somewhere, with a wife and tots and hay in the barn, and a good cow horse to love. Greasy Corners didn't figure in his plans—he just felt he had to allow Billy a little holiday.

I had barely settled into my squat when we heard the crackle of gunfire and the sound of hooves, many hooves. The noise came from the south, toward the Bitter Lake.

"That could be your man Tully," I suggested.

"No, that ain't him," Joe said. "Tully Roebuck mainly travels alone. I don't know if he'll even show up. Sometimes Tully just gets out of the mood for company."

I was still trying to get adjusted to the sound of gunfire —you rarely hear it in Philadelphia, at least not on Chestnut Street.

"I expect it's just *los Guajolotes*, coming in for a little frolic," Joe said, perfectly calm.

"Los what?" I asked.

"*Guajolotes*," Joe repeated, crediting me with more Spanish than I have.

I was reluctant to expose my ignorance, but the gunfire grew louder—it sounded as if a small army was racing toward the town.

"What's *guajolotes*?" I asked, hoping the word meant militia or something official and benign.

"Turkeys," Joe said. "The turkeys. It's what Katie Garza calls her gang."

9.

It's often occurred to me that the Wild West would have been a safer place if fireworks had been more generally available a little sooner.

Nothing elaborate would have been needed—just firecrackers and Roman candles, the usual Fourth of July stuff. No one realizes the lengths people would go to in the West just to hear a little noise.

So much of the country was silent and empty, you see —men in the lonely line of cabins strung out around Isinglass's ranch could go for months hearing nothing but the wind's howl or the coyote's cry. They made what noise they could, yelling and whooping at the livestock. They scratched at fiddles and blew into harmonicas— Lady Snow even taught Billy to play one, though he never really learned a tune.

But the silence of the huge plain carried more resonance than such puny sounds.

I'm sure a few Roman candles would have contented most of the caballeros who rode with Katerina Garza;

perhaps that would have satisfied many of the gunfighters too. Their lives were bleak and boresome; the
livelier among them liked to hear noise once in a while,
and see sparkles in the night. And the only noisemakers
or sparklers they had were guns.

Before I could inquire of Joe Lovelady why a lady
bandit would call her gang the Turkeys, the gang itself
came racing right up to the China Pond, shooting at the
heavens. The horse in the lead was a white mare—I
guess the race into town had excited her because she
fought the rein and pranced when her mistress stopped
her.

A cur yelped, causing one of the bandits' horses to
pitch. The horse threw the bandit, who pulled a gun and
shot repeatedly at the dog.

The young woman astride the white steed—I still
think of them as steeds; it's the dime novels again—
seemed annoyed that the caballero had tried to shoot
the dog that caused him to get thrown.

"If you hit that dog you're going to cook it and eat it,"
she said. "It ain't the dog's fault you can't ride."

I'm not sure the caballero heard her—he was stomp-
ing around in a pet, shooting at nothing.

"Let's shoot him and take his horse, he can't ride anyway," another caballero suggested. There was a general
laugh, which didn't improve the furious bandit's humor.

"No, save your bullets, we might need to shoot some
of these white people," Katerina said. She swung off the
white mare with a confident motion—it reminded me of
the way some ladies rise from the bed of love.

Then she noticed us.

"Joe, could it be you?" she asked in a softer tone.

"Hello, Katie," Joe said, standing up.

Then, to my surprise, he gave the bandit queen a good
long hug.

10.

While Joe and Katie were hugging, Billy Bone walked out—probably he was curious about the shooting. He was that way: he would go to violence wherever he found it, and that was his doom, as I tried to show in my novelette *Billy the Kid; or, the Wandering Boy's Doom*, written after it was all just history.

It was my tale that produced his nickname, Billy the Kid—certainly nobody in the New Mexico Territory would have been fool enough to call him a kid while he was alive and well armed.

But when he walked out of the China Pond that evening, he didn't find violence. He found his friend Joe Lovelady hugging a woman, and I think it shocked him more than if the seven or eight caballeros had been lying dead on the ground. It shocked the caballeros too. The one who had been thrown stopped shooting at the long-gone dog, and they all just stood around.

"I didn't know Joe had a mistress," Billy whispered to me later in the evening. Somehow he had picked up the term. We were standing at the bar in the China Pond, watching Katie dance with Viv Maldonado.

Oh, but Katie was a looker, with raven hair and eyes to match. Her vest was buttoned with little silver nuggets, given her by an admirer, and she had splashed her shirt with sequins, which glittered as she danced. La Tulipe, the old yellow Creole woman, played the castanets for the dancers as they danced. Vivian Maldonado, perhaps remembering the applause of the crowds from his days on the trapeze, was mighty acrobatic, but his step was never too quick for Katie Garza.

"I don't know that just because he hugged her it means she's his mistress," I said, as we watched the dance.

"It does so!" Billy said, firmly convinced on the subject. "That Joe, he's all secrets—you never know what he's really thinking," he added. It was clear he was having to revise his opinion of his friend, who was outside, still squatting by the wall. Joe Lovelady didn't enjoy barrooms, even with Katie Garza there to rouse up the crowd.

She roused it up, too—she had such animation! In Philadelphia they would have soon had her running the biggest balls. Hill Coe and Pleasant Burnell and some of the other gunfighters sat up a little straighter and tried to shine; but of course for plain American gunmen to try and outsparkle an Italian circus hand is hopeless in itself; and anyway, Katie was merely making use of the fact that Vivian knew how to dance.

Her eyes were only for Billy, the awkward boy who didn't really know what a mistress was, although the whores of the Colorado mining saloons had been the only aunts and nannies he had ever had.

"That Joe, he's tight with his talk," he muttered, as irritated by his friend's reserve as he had been by his competence the day I met them.

"I guess the next thing, he'll be getting married," he said gloomily. "Then I won't have nobody to pal around with except you, Sippy, and you and I will starve to death without Joe to rustle the grub."

He was right on that point, but wrong about Joe and Katie—when it came to love, he had no experience to draw on, just his boyish fancies. He thought love all happened in capital letters, but I knew better. I had Dora to teach me that it was mostly fine print.

"I don't think they'll be getting married, Billy," I said. I had already seen the glances Katie was casting his way. Women *will* tend toward the man with the reputation, a fact I've often noted in Philadelphia.

"Oh, they'll marry for sure, Joe Lovelady can't wait to get settled down agin," Billy said, in a misery of gloom.

The buffalo hunters and the caballeros stood around stiffly, trying not to bump into one another or anger Des Montaignes; the gunfighters went on with their formal cardplaying, although Katerina's mere presence had taken much of the interest out of the cards.

"That Joe Lovelady, he don't tell you much, does he?" Billy said, still bothered by that hug.

89

11.

It was in that stinking barroom, to the music of castanets, that the great love story of the West began. For Katie Garza was Billy's true love, and Billy was hers. Katie had come up as scrappy as he had; kill or be killed was her way, just as it was his.

I won't say Lady Snow shouldn't have had a role in the play—you can't keep a sad boy such as Billy from wanting such a dream of beauty as she was that day he came upon us in the little prairie creek.

But Cecily Snow was more of a fascination: she offered, in the short time they shared, a brief escape from the ways of the rude country where Billy lived his life.

"He liked her because she was white and clean," Katie Garza said in her bitterness. It was Tully Roebuck who reported the remark.

Heartbreaking words, though Tully didn't notice—he just passed the remark along as he might any other. Katie Garza lived hard in a dirty place—it must have nearly killed her to think she lost Billy to a woman who had servants to press her dresses and change her fine sheets.

I didn't figure in the play, really—I call it a play, but as the dead piled up on the plain, it began to seem like one of those great old poems of war, Homer or Roland or Horatio at the bridge.

I just followed along with Billy as he rode the bloody trail—a wandering boy one step ahead of his doom.

12.

The romance the whole West was soon talking about started with a friendly shooting match between Billy and Katie, the morning after they met.

A night's activity at the China Pond would generate a good number of empty bottles. La Tulipe's job every morning was to load up a little cart with these empties and haul them about a quarter of a mile out of town, where part of an old adobe wall still stood. She had a sluggish donkey named Bonaparte who pulled the cart —no one in Greasy Corners could figure out where she came up with such a name.

La Tulipe would line the bottles up on top of the old wall if it was a still day, or on rocks in front of it if the wind was blowing stiff. Then she would sit and smoke her long pipe and sing little songs in French to Bonaparte, the donkey.

One by one the gunmen would shake off the effects of their hangovers and stroll out to the wall for a little practice.

Billy and Joe and I camped on the Rio Pecos, not far out of town. Katie and *los Guajolotes* had bedded down nearby—three or four of the caballeros whooped and sang until nearly daybreak.

At breakfast, while Billy snoozed, I sipped bitter coffee and asked Joe how he came to know Katerina Garza.

"I helped her once," he said. "She rides them spooky horses. I found her hurt up in the white sands—her horse had thrown her and kicked her in the head."

I waited for more story, but none came just then. As Billy said, Joe was tight with his talk.

A month later Joe let slip another few words of remembrance.

"When Nellie and the baby were dying, Katie came and stayed with us," he said. "She helped me dig the graves."

He said no more about it, but it was clear from those few words that his hand would always be there for Katie Garza.

The sound of the gunmen's morning practice woke Billy, finally, He sat up and hugged his knees and yawned. His hair in a cowlick, he looked very young.

"Let's go watch," he said. "It won't hurt to know which of these fools can shoot."

"Hill Coe can shoot," Joe said.

Hill Coe might look like an old saddle bum, but he took his morning practice seriously. They say he shot fifty practice rounds a day, every day of his life. I like to do little calculations. As we strolled over the pistol range I pointed out to Billy and Joe that that added up to 18,250 bullets a year, not counting what he might fire in life-or-death situations.

"Eighteen thousand bullets a year!" Billy said. "Think of the cost! You couldn't put that many bullets in La Tulipe's bottle cart."

More than most, Billy lived in a world of his own. Joe Lovelady seemed to be the only person he was really curious about—at least until Katie came along.

But my little calculation impressed him: eighteen thousand was probably the highest sum he had ever heard mentioned in his life.

"Let's hurry," he said, hiding his cowlick under his old hat. "I'd like to see if he's getting his money's worth out of them bottles."

Katie Garza fell in with us as we were strolling along the riverbank. She seemed a little grumpy, but, though her skin was a bit roughened by the wind and the sun, she still had a glow. She carried a pistol and had a cartridge belt thrown over her shoulder.

"They better let me shoot," she said, in something of the tone of a little girl, not sure the boys were going to let her join their play.

Pleasant Burnell and Happy Jack were shooting when we arrived. Wild Horse Jerry, a mean little ferret, was taunting them, and indeed they were missing more bottles than they cracked. Occasionally a bullet would clip the wall and sing as it sliced on across the grass.

"If this was a battle you'd both be in hell by now," Jerry pointed out.

Pleasant Burnell, who was rarely pleasant—at least in my company—spat a wad of tobacco juice at his critic.

"I'll be glad when the tall nigger comes and cuts your head off," he said—a reference to Mesty-Woolah's favored method of execution.

"That tall nigger's gonna eat a lead breakfast if he comes near me," Jerry replied.

They finished their turn and Hill Coe walked over to the wall and carefully lined up some thirty bottles along the top.

No one so far had said a word to Katie Garza—they just quietly ignored the fact that they had a woman at their practice session.

Katie was not one to curb her impatience long. Hill Coe came walking back to the firing line, carefully pulling on his shooting glove. The gunfighters, most of

94

whom had been spitting and hawking, tried to compose themselves a little more respectfully.

Billy Bone looked amused—he had no very high regard for any of them.

As Hill Coe got ready to shoot, Katie Garza spoke. "Mr. Coe, you're a gambler," she said. "I'll gamble you."

Hill Coe seemed startled. Few women spoke to him so boldly.

"What would be the gamble?" he asked in surprise.

"I think I can outshoot you," Katie said. "I've got a hundred dollars that thinks so, too."

The gunfighters mainly looked embarrassed, though Wild Horse Jerry favored us with an evil smirk. Katie's challenge was taken as an affront—a young bandit girl, with only a local reputation, had challenged the great marshal of Abilene and Dodge.

But Billy Bone looked at her with new eyes. It was just the kind of thing he would have done himself, whether he had any chance of winning or not, just to show his spunk.

"Why, Miss, it would hardly do to take your money this early in the day," Hill Coe said rather formally.

"I don't think you can beat her, Hill," Billy said loudly.

Joe Lovelady watched the little scene calmly, just as he watched the rest of life. But the gunslingers were upset. They were testy men at best and resented any threat to their routine.

"I think she'll skin you, Hill," Billy said, knowing full well that he had just hung the old gunman on a hook he could not get off of.

"The Tulip can hold the money," he said. "Me, I'm putting mine on the lady."

Hill Coe looked dismayed; but after a moment he nodded politely to Katie and finished adjusting his glove.

13.

The rules for the match were soon agreed upon: each contestant to shoot twenty bottles; in the event of a tie they would then shoot bottle by bottle until someone missed.

"Why, Hill can shoot all day and not miss," Happy Jack said. "Unless Katie slips up we'll have to race over to Roswell and get some more bottles after a while."

La Tulipe gave a hearty laugh. In the daylight she looked mulatto, or high yellow, as it's called in the South; it was clear she had been a beauty in her day.

"What are you laughing about, you old slut?" Pleasant Burnell said. There was no friendship between him and La Tulipe.

"I'm laughing at the thought of how quiet you'll be when you're dead," La Tulipe retorted.

Katie Garza shot first. She sat down, crossed her legs, rested her pistol across her forearm, and proceeded to shatter twenty bottles. It was as cool a performance as you'll ever see—for of course all the gunfighters were expecting her to miss.

When she stopped to reload, after cracking the eighteenth bottle, there was a fair amount of tension among the men—not including Billy.

"She don't mean to miss, does she?" he whispered. He was no shot himself, and I think it astonished him that a woman could shoot so well.

Katerina calmly cracked the last two bottles, shook out the two empties, reloaded, and stood up.

"I'm satisfied with the first round," she said.

"Pretty shooting, Miss Garza," Hill Coe said, perfectly amiable.

He stepped up to the line and waited confidently while Happy Jack lined his twenty bottles along the top of the wall. He even had a bit of a shine—perhaps he supposed that Katie had taken a fancy to him and had offered the challenge as a way of attracting his interest.

Then he raised his pistol, as he had some eighteen thousand times a year for many years—and missed clean with his first and only shot.

14.

A hasty move, the twitch of a finger, the smallest of miscalculations—I suppose we all stand no farther than that from ruin.

Did Chittim know he was going to lie down and die on the sidewalk, while going, as he so often had, to fetch my morning dime novel?

I doubt that he knew—no more than Hill Coe could have known that on that sunny, still plains morning, in perfect shooting light, the arc of his life would break.

But there it was: he missed. The bullet cut the prairie grass, fifty yards behind the wall. The twenty bottles still stood there, untouched: Katerina Garza had won the gamble.

It was so unexpected that for a moment none of us could quite believe it had happened. Had he really fired the gun and missed the bottle, or were we all in a dream?

The gunfighters were simply dumbfounded; not a word was uttered. Hill Coe glanced down at his pistol, a look of faint puzzlement on his face—it must have been hard for him to believe that the wild shot which sliced the grass had come from his own reliable gun.

I believe even Billy was embarrassed for the old marshal.

"That sure didn't take long," he said, looking at Joe with a crooked grin.

Pleasant Burnell came out of his shock and whirled on La Tulipe.

"This old yellow nigger caused it," he said. "She witched Hill. We ought to drown her."

La Tulipe smiled.

"There ain't water enough to drown me in this country," she said. "There ain't wood enough to hang me, either."

"You could die just as dead from a bullet, though," Wild Horse Jerry pointed out. "And there's plenty of dirt around here for making graves."

He looked around as if he expected to be applauded for his wit.

"If there's any graves made, you'll be the first to get cozy in one, Jerry," Billy Bone said. "I consider you a card cheat anyway."

"Why, Bill, that's a black insult," Jerry said in an unfriendly tone.

I had a sense that a fight was looming, though no one had actually moved. Katie Garza still had her pistol in her hand. Billy motioned for me to step back, out of the field of fire.

"Don't anybody shoot this old Yankee, now," he said. "He's not armed."

Probably he had seen me take my derringers out of my boots that morning. I had never had the occasion to fire one, and they raised terrible blisters.

I don't know what might have happened, or who might have fallen in the coming fray, if Simp Dixon hadn't chosen that moment to wake up.

Simp, a short, fat man who could never keep his shirt-

99

tails in, had been napping on a warm spot not far north of the wall. Target shooting evidently didn't jolt his slumbers much.

Simp suddenly popped up and sauntered into our midst, his shirttails out and a bleary, hung-over look in his eye.

"Boys, if it's my turn, I'm ready," he said.

Nobody said a word. Simp took it as encouragement. He yawned, pulled out his pistol, and casually let fire. His first shot exploded the bottle the great Hill Coe had just missed.

"I always hit the first one, but then my aim gets jerky," Simp said. He proceeded to demonstrate the truth of his statement by missing the next five shots—part of the trouble may have been that he was trying to tuck his shirttails in with his free hand.

One shot ricocheted off the wall and came so close to Happy Jack that he swatted wildly at it with his hat. Then he looked sheepish.

"I thought it was a bumblebee for a minute there," he explained.

But the fact that Simp Dixon, half-asleep, had hit the very bottle he had missed finished poor Hill Coe. He seemed almost too weary to drop his gun back into its holster—I saw him fumble twice before he got it in.

The gunfighters, primed for battle, all looked at him, but he wouldn't help them. They had followed him from town to town; had deputied for him, fought at his side, taken their cues from him—some of them for years. His pride supported their pride, such as it was, and now his pride was lost, with that one errant bullet.

"Pretty shooting," he said again to Katerina Garza, handing her two fifty-dollar gold pieces.

"Thank you," Katie said, careful not to rub it in.

Hill Coe still had a look of faint puzzlement on his face as he headed down the path for Greasy Corners, walking like a man who had just turned ninety.

One or two of the gunfighters would have liked a fight,

but Simp Dixon's behavior gave the whole thing a silly twist; and then, Hill Coe left. He had been their pillar, but he had crumbled.

Pleasant Burnell maintained his dark look, but he left without another word, and the others followed.

"You'll answer for that insult someday, little Bill," Wild Horse Jerry said as he was leaving.

15.

"I should shoot that Wild Horse Jerry," Billy muttered, once the gunfighters were out of sight.

"I've known him to be ill-tempered," Joe Lovelady admitted.

"Would you call him out or shoot him in the back?" Katie Garza asked in a tone of light curiosity.

Questions involving ethics always made Billy uncomfortable, and Katie's was no exception.

"Well, I hate a card cheat," he replied.

"Do you approve of shooting them in the back?" Katie asked bluntly.

La Tulipe chuckled—I think she enjoyed the two youngsters.

"A killer can't be particular," she said.

"It's what I maintain!" Billy said, happy to have an ally. "A man shot face to face is just as dead."

Katie watched Billy thoughtfully. Her quiet scrutiny seemed to make him nervous.

"Kill your man and get the job done," he said. "Best not to waste time worrying about front or back."

"Shoot with me, *chapito*," Katie said, grinning. "Mr. Coe didn't give me no contest."

Chapito means "little Shorty," but Katie said it with a lilt in her voice, and Billy didn't take offense.

"Let's shoot," he said, and even swaggered a little—I doubt such a pretty girl had taken an interest in him before.

Joe and I and La Tulipe sat by the donkey cart and watched the two of them play. Katerina shot another round of twenty bottles and hit eighteen. Joe later said he thought she had missed two on purpose to let Billy think he had a chance.

Then Billy stepped up and *missed* eighteen—and of the two he hit, one was barely chipped. On some of the shots he would aim for two or three minutes, and the bullet would still sing away.

Joe Lovelady was deeply embarrassed for his friend. "He can't shoot a pistol," he said. "I don't know what makes him think he can.

"I hope it don't put him in one of his surly moods," he added.

I wouldn't have thought Billy would tolerate losing that badly either—but Katie sat down by him and flirted so charmingly that his mood was far from surly. He soon grew amused at his own bad shooting and began to giggle. He loaded both his pistols and blazed away at the bottles with both hands without hitting a thing. That struck him as so funny he had to stop and wipe tears out of his eyes.

"You shoot, Joe," Katie said, still in a lively mood.

Joe Lovelady performed respectably, breaking twelve bottles of twenty.

"I hate being beaten by a dern cowboy," Billy said, but he was just joshing. With Katie Garza laughing at his side, he kept a carefree attitude.

103

"Could I try?" I inquired.

"Oh, try, Sippy, show us your style," Billy said, giggling. He handed me one of his guns.

"This'll be rich," he said, smirking at Katerina.

Katie had taken little notice of me, but she looked me over thoughtfully when I stepped to the line.

"I guess he knows how to shoot," she said, though I don't know what she based her conclusions on.

"Sippy?" Billy said. "Why, he don't know anything. He chased a dern train nearly to Kansas and couldn't stop it."

Imagine his surprise when I cracked seventeen straight bottles. It takes a fair selection of hobbies to get a man through a year with Dora, and target shooting had once been one of mine.

16.

I was shooting confidently, and I feel sure I could have shattered the next three bottles and beaten Katie Garza, but while I was drawing down on number eighteen, the thunder of hooves was heard and *los Guajolotes* came racing up to the shooting range, one of them leading Katerina's white mare.

"*Señorita, los caballeros!*" the man leading the horse exclaimed. It was clear he was eager to be leaving, as were the rest of the *Guajolotes*.

Katie and Joe were looking north. I looked north too and saw a dust cloud on the uttermost rim of the prairie.

I don't think Billy noticed—he was still lolling on the grass, his mind on Katerina.

"Here comes Old Whiskey," Joe said. "And not only that, here comes Tully, too."

He pointed to the west, where a lone horseman was racing toward the Pecos at breakneck speed.

Billy Bone stood up and reclaimed the pistol I had been about to fire.

"That Tully, he's always in a hurry," he remarked, knocking the empties out of his gun. He dug some loose bullets from his pocket and began to reload.

"Tully's a little jumpy," he added.

Katie Garza hung her cartridge belt over the saddle horn and swung onto the white mare. She allowed the mare to prance for a bit as she studied the dust to the north.

"I'm getting in the mood to go to Mexico for a while," she said. "You boys want to come?"

"Well, we told Tully we'd wait," Joe Lovelady said. "I don't want to leave until I hear what Tully's got to say."

"How about you, *chapito?*" Katie asked, looking down at Billy.

"Why, I can't go off and leave Joe, not with this army coming," Billy said.

"I thought Joe was a grown man," Katie said.

Billy was looking a little flat—often after a long laugh or a temper fit he seemed to lose all energy. Katie's remark surprised him—I doubt that it had occurred to him until that moment that he could travel the world with Katie Garza instead of Joe Lovelady. The thought startled him so much that he promptly changed the subject.

"Tully's running that horse flat out," he said. "Now that can't be good for the horse."

Indeed, the approaching horseman was fairly flying over the grass.

I think Katie Garza knew Billy wasn't quite ready to ride off with her, but it amused her to press her point, anyway.

"Come see the world, *chapito,*" she said. "We'll go down to San Isidro and eat a fat goat."

Billy looked to Joe for help. He was obviously not accustomed to having women try to lure him away.

Joe Lovelady was watching the large dust cloud to the north. He didn't appear to be alarmed—just observant.

106

Perhaps he had not even heard Katie invite Billy to Mexico; but if he had heard, he obviously had no interest in ruling out the invitation.

"I think your pa's coming, Katie," Joe said.

17.

That was when I learned that Katie was Isinglass's daughter.

"Señorita, it's nice weather in El Paso today, I bet," one of the caballeros said.

"Pa won't bother us," Katie said. "He's probably just looking for strays."

Billy Bone stood there looking shy, awkward, ugly, and small. He seemed to be on tenterhooks: on the one hand, he wished Katie would go away; on the other, he wanted her to stay.

"That damn fool Tully Roebuck, why *will* he run that horse?" he said. It was the only topic of conversation he could come up with, and it didn't last long, because a minute later Tully Roebuck yanked the lathered horse to a stop right between Joe Lovelady and Billy Bone.

He was a lanky fellow, Tully, with a charming smile and sweet brown eyes.

"Hello," he said mildly, as if he had raced like fire across the prairie just to invite us to tea.

"Why, Tully," Joe Lovelady said. "How's your health?"

"My health's dandy," Tully said, lifting his hat to Katerina, "but I admit I'd be more relaxed if we was up in Santa Fe drinking toddies."

"You can get toddies right here in Greasy Corners," Billy said. "Dez makes toddies that'll take the feathers off an owl."

"Dez is gonna wish he was an owl when Old Whiskey gets here," Tully said. "If we ride off right quick maybe we won't get implicated."

"I bet you'd like it in San Isidro," Katie said to Billy. "Those fat goats are mighty tasty."

Billy looked embarrassed. He was at a loss for a reply. "I expect I'll visit soon," he said politely.

Katie knew when to let be. She laughed and wheeled her mare.

"Joe, don't let Pa provoke you," she said, and a moment later *los Guajolotes* were raising their own dust cloud as they headed down the long plain toward Mexico.

18.

_____

"What's the news?" Joe Lovelady asked, once Katie and her men loped off.

"Isinglass means to clean out Greasy Corners—that's the news," Tully said.

Billy immediately took offense. I think he realized that he had not acquitted himself too brilliantly with Katerina, and he seemed inclined to make others pay— the others being anyone he met who rubbed him the wrong way.

"Clean it out! What business is it of his how dirty it is?" he asked.

"Well, it's on his ranch," Joe said. "He owns all this. I guess he figures he can do what he wants with it."

"I say it's too much land for one man to own," Billy said hotly. "He oughtn't to be allowed! Why, they say he owns all the way to Kansas. They say he owns Texas, or a lot of it. Now that's a disgrace—why should one ugly old bull get to own everything?"

Tully Roebuck dismounted. He seemed mildly taken aback by Billy's passion.

"Why, Bill, he just bought it," he said. "Once you pay money for something, you own it."

"I'd like to know who he paid this money to," Billy said. "You and me and Joe live here. Did he pay us? Did he pay the dern Apaches? If the old son of a bitch owns this whole part of the world, then I'd like to know who he thinks he bought it from."

La Tulipe got off her cart and began leading Bonaparte, the donkey, back to town.

"Maybe he bought it from Texas, Billy—I can't remember the details," Tully said. "The Whiskey Glass has been a ranch ever since I can recall."

"I bet he just took it, the rough old fool," Billy said.

Tully Roebuck looked somewhat dismayed. I believed he felt the point was being missed; and, indeed, the dust cloud to the north was no longer blurring the far horizon—it was curling rapidly south, toward Greasy Corners.

"It don't really matter if he bought it or took it," Tully said. "The point is, he's got it and he don't want the buffalo hunters and the gunfighters interfering with him anymore."

"Interfere? Why he don't even know them," Billy said.

"I've heard he suspects them of rustling," Joe said. He, too, seemed a little surprised by Billy's sudden vehemence.

"Rustle? It's just his excuse," Billy said. "Hill Coe and that crowd wouldn't take a cow if you gave them one."

"Bill, it's hard to find a word you agree with today," Tully said, cutting himself a chew of tobacco off a plug he took out of his chaps pocket.

"Is Isinglass coming to warn them or is he coming to kill them?" Joe Lovelady asked.

111

"Why, I wouldn't know," Tully said. "I guess it depends on how brisk a mood he's in."

The dust cloud to the north was coming steadily closer. I had no idea how many riders it represented or how brisk their mood might be, to adopt Tully's phrase.

"I was thinking we'd drift on over to Van Horn," Tully said. "Some of the ranches down there might be looking for hands."

"Okay," Joe said agreeably. "That's nice airy country. I like it."

"I ain't going," Billy Bone said bluntly. "I ain't, and that's it."

19.

Joe Lovelady was a patient man. He seemed no more than mildly stirred by Billy's stubborn ways, though they caused him not a little aggravation—and worse than aggravation—in the time I knew the two of them.

"You don't even like those gunhands, Billy," he pointed out. "Half the time you're ready to spit in their faces."

Billy shrugged. He disdained anything resembling reasoned argument.

"I ain't going, and that's it," he repeated. "I won't be run out of New Mexico by Isinglass or anybody else."

With that he started back to town, grabbing my arm as he passed.

"Come on, Sippy, lets go have a drink and brace up," he said. "These two cowhands probably want to get their milking done, or something."

We soon caught up with La Tulipe, who was having difficulties with Bonaparte.

The donkey had stopped to meditate, much as Rosy

was apt to do. La Tulipe was tugging on the headrope, but her tugs were having as little effect as if la Tulipe were a bird flying overhead.

As Billy passed by, he grabbed the donkey's tail and gave it a sharp twist, inspiring Bonaparte to such an unexpected burst of speed that La Tulipe had all she could do to escape being run over. She dropped the headrope, and Bonaparte and the cart raced on toward the settlement—to call it a town would be flattery.

"You don't start a donkey at the head end," Billy remarked. "You start a donkey at the tail end."

"That Katie wants to take you to Mexico," La Tulipe said to Billy.

"Katie's pretty," Billy admitted. "I never expected to see a girl so pretty."

"Death lives in Mexico," La Tulipe said.

Billy had been indulging in some pleasant reverie about Katerina, I imagine. When La Tulipe spoke he went white. Any mention of death turned Billy white unless it was a death he was preparing to cause.

"Oh, now," he said, in a shocked tone.

La Tulipe's hair was white and her heavy body slow, but her skin was unwrinkled and her eyes a clear blue.

"You got to watch out about rivers, Billy," she said. "If you cross the North Canadian a horse will fall on you and you'll be crippled."

"I'll never go near it," Billy said quickly.

"Don't cross the Rio Animas either," the old woman warned. "If you do your soul will fall into the water and be carried away. And if you cross the Rio Grande you'll die."

"Shoot, I wasn't planning to travel much anyway," Billy said. "What's my luck if I just ride up and down the Pecos?"

"Bloody luck," La Tulipe said. "But the blood will not all be yours."

We stopped in camp to get our horses, and the old woman hobbled on.

Billy looked as white as a sheet. He sat down on his blanket, shaking as he had when he saw the Death Dog.

"I almost went off to Mexico," he said in a weak tone. "If Joe hadn't wanted to wait for Tully, I'd have gone."

"Well, Miss Garza's a pretty girl, as you pointed out," I said.

"Not pretty enough to die for," Billy said.

20.

To everyone's surprise, Isinglass trotted into Greasy
Corners alone. The twenty riders who had helped make
the dust cloud crossed the Pecos north of town and rode
on east, toward Texas.

The appearance of one old man on a scrubby black
horse was a considerable letdown for the gunfighters
and the buffalo hunters, all of whom had been working
themselves up for a glorious last stand. A huge amount
of weaponry was quickly assembled, and many bracing
toddies were gulped down.

Joe Lovelady and Tully Roebuck rode in and sat quietly on their horses, a little apart from the mob.

Billy Bone lounged against the hitch-rail in front of
the China Pond. His horse, Chip, always hard to saddle,
had been particularly difficult that morning. Though I
held Chip's ears and tried to soothe him with an Irish
ditty, he still kicked Billy twice before he accepted the
saddle. This had the good effect of making Billy furious.

116

He soon forgot Mexico and death and everything else except how much he disliked Chip; by the time we got to the Pond he was in ideal fighting spirits.

He seemed coolly contemptuous of the buffalo hunters' solemn preparations for battle.

"Look at these fools, they're ready to die roaring, ain't they?" he said, watching Jim Saul blow dust out of the sights of his buffalo gun.

The gunfighters emerged from the saloon in a nervous cluster. Hill Coe was walking unsteadily—he was already on his way to becoming the shaking drunk he would be for the rest of his life.

Vivian Maldonado had drunk till dawn, as was his habit—he had not had time to perfect his toilette, or even to slick down his hair; obviously he would have preferred to delay the annihilation until a more civilized hour—that would have been the style in Naples.

Billy was peeved at Joe and Tully for showing more reserve than the rest of the crowd. They sat quietly on their horses, a little way down the street—the very models of decorum.

"Now look at them!" Billy exclaimed. "They're too fine to join the rabble, them two."

He insisted I take one of his pistols—the one I had used to shatter the bottles.

"Don't be polite, now, Sippy," he said. "Shoot a few cowboys, if the chance arises."

"You seem to have it in for cowboys, Billy," I said.

"I consider them dull fools, for the most part," he replied.

"But your best friend's a cowboy."

"Yes, because he's stubborn," Billy said with some irritation.

Then, to everyone's surprise, the dust cloud veered to the east, missing Greasy Corners by a couple of miles.

"They're circling," Happy Jack Marco said. "Maybe they're Indians."

117

"Maybe they're angels, but I doubt it," Billy said, slightly bored.

Then the old man trotted in on his nondescript black plug.

21.

It was clear that fear formed no part of Isinglass's makeup, for he trotted casually up to the very door of the China Pond, ignoring the arsenal that had been assembled to stop him.

"Look at the way he rides, the dern old sack of oats," Billy said, as the slouching old man arrived.

Indeed, Isinglass did not cut a graceful figure in the saddle. He slumped as if the horse were a kind of open-air stagecoach; he had not even bothered to adjust his stirrups correctly—his feet dangled, only now and then touching a stirrup rung. I have seen farmers in Pennsylvania look as awkward in the saddle; but the farmers had not crossed and recrossed the endless prairies as Old Whiskey had done constantly in his long life.

Des Montaignes, looking as furious and filthy as ever, had come outside carrying a rusty 10-gauge shotgun. He was squinting a little in the bright sunlight.

Isinglass was intent on undoing the leather strings that held his quart jar in its pouch; he practically rode over Des Montaignes—would have, had the horse not stopped of its own volition.

Isinglass lifted the empty quart jar from a bulky, well-padded leather pouch, and handed it down to Des Montaignes.

"I'll take a refill, Mister, if you stock whiskey," he said. "I'll caution you not to drop it—it's my only jar."

He seemed scarcely to notice the crowd of men, all bristling with arms, who stood in the street.

Des Montaignes, to everyone's surprise, propped the shotgun against the adobe wall of his saloon and went inside with the jar.

Isinglass didn't seem to find the man's compliance surprising—no doubt, to him it appeared quite natural that any man he came across would do whatever he requested.

He seemed to feel no need to make light conversation, or heavy conversation either, merely sitting in a restful indifferent way on the scrubby black horse until Des Montaignes reappeared with the jar full of raw liquor.

"Obliged," Isinglass said politely, not offering to pay. He lifted the jar and took a long swallow. Then he wiped his mouth thoughtfully, a few amber drops of liquor spotting his full, graying beard.

"Are you the man with the yellow wife?" he asked.

"Yellow," Des Montaignes admitted.

"I've heard a story about you," Isinglass said. "They say the last time you washed was when a horse pitched you into the Missouri River eight or ten years ago. Now that I've had a look at you I see the story's accurate."

He took another long drink and then carefully eased the jar back into its pouch.

"They say that wife of yours tells fortunes," he said when he had resettled his jar to his liking.

"She knows the past and the future," Billy Bone said loudly. Sometimes he would simply burst out, as if seized with the need to call attention to himself.

120

Isinglass's eyes were so deep-set you could hardly see them, but when you did they flashed a hard glint.

"I thought I fired you off this ranch a while ago," he said, looking at Billy. "You don't look crippled, so why ain't you left?"

"You mean this sand hill is part of a ranch?" Billy asked with a smirk. He loved being the center of attention.

Isinglass didn't answer immediately—he was tying the leather throngs that held his jar in its pouch.

"I fired you off it and you would have done well to leave," Isinglass said, when he looked up.

"I tried, but my horse gave out," Billy said. "You have to ride dern near to the ocean to get off your property, anyway. Seems like everything's your property, and I don't consider that fair."

Isinglass turned in his saddle and surveyed the crowd of armed men.

"Is that the opinion, then?" he asked.

"It's my opinion," Billy said hotly. He took the fact that Isinglass had turned away as a slight to himself. No one was as touchy about small things like that as Billy.

"It's a hundred miles to that big house of yours," Billy said. "A hundred miles is far enough to ride off, I say."

"You're a brash boy and will very likely meet a bad end," Isinglass said. "I despise wordy talk so I'll just deliver the facts of the matter. My north line is above the Cimarron, and my south line is not much shy of the Guadalupes. I own what's in between, hide and hair. This settlement here is an illegal settlement within the bounds of my ranch, which I've let be up till now because I had other things to attend to. We've got the Commanche reservationed off, and the Apache reservationed off, although that Jicarilla whelp of mine will still fight you if he likes the odds. The Pawnee and a few other bands are pretty well settled. You men have been well-behaved up to now, but a barroom community like

121

this can easily breed rustling, and I am not such a fool as to encourage rustling of any sort. I saw a brochure the other day about Arizona—there's lots of space in Arizona and plenty of fine dry sunlight. I recommend a move in that direction within the next few days. Or if that direction don't suit you, a couple of hundred miles in any direction will pretty well put you clear of me."

He stopped and smiled, evidently pleased with himself. "I doubt the governor himself could render a cleaner speech," he said.

"What you mean is get out," Billy said. "That's all you meant. You might as well have just said it plain."

Isinglass looked again at the buffalo hunters and the gunfighters, all of them as silent as stumps.

"I find this peculiar," he said. "Here I sit amid a dozen grown men, and no one except this brash boy has a word to say."

"The trouble with Arizona is that the Earps are already there," Happy Jack Marco said. "We've all seen enough of the dang Earps, I guess."

"I've no doubt they're surly," Isinglass said, "but it ain't likely they're as surly as Mesty, when he's bent on war."

He looked down the street. We all looked down the street, and not since Cook informed me that J. M. Chittim had just died have I had such a shock.

A red camel stood there, and on the red camel sat the tallest black man anyone in Greasy Corners had ever seen.

22.

In my novelette *The Negro of the Nile; or, Son of the Mahdi* I made up a good deal of nonsense about Mesty-Woolah, and the history boys later mixed some of it in with the truth, which in this case is easily related.

Lord Snow, Isinglass's partner, had been a great one for expeditions; he took one to the Nile with the notion of acquiring some camels as breeding stock, his plan being to get the U.S. Army interested in a camel cavalry of some sort.

Mesty-Woolah was not the son of the Mahdi, but he *was* the greatest camel thief in his part of Africa. When Lord Snow met Mesty-Woolah, Mesty's youngest son was at the point of death with a fever, which Lord Snow promptly cured with some good English medicine. In gratitude Mesty-Woolah agreed to accompany Lord Snow to Texas to handle his camel herd; they had scarcely arrived when Lord Snow, who was forever wandering off without his coat, got caught in a plains blizzard, developed a pneumonia which was beyond the reach of even the best English medicines, and died.

Neither the army nor Isinglass had any patience with the notion of a camel cavalry at that time. I believe the army later tried it down in the Geronimo country, with poor success.

Most of Lord Snow's camel herd went wild—I'm told there are still wild camels in the Texas desert. Mesty-Woolah owed no debt to Isinglass, yet he stayed on at the Whiskey Glass ranch, becoming far and away the most feared man in the West.

"Mesty stayed for the warring," Isinglass informed me during one of those grim dinners at the castle, with him dripping meat drippings as Cecily Snow dripped contempt.

"I would have thought he could find plenty of war in Africa," I said.

"Not enough to suit Mesty," Isinglass said. "He says the A—rabs and the bush niggers have about lost their ginger. He thought highly of the Comanches as fighting men, and he compliments the Apache, up to a point."

"What about you?" I asked.

"Oh, Mesty has no respect for me, or any white man," Isinglass said. "I just provide the targets."

"Living targets, of course," Cecily said lightly.

"Once Mesty chooses you for a target, the living is brief," the old man replied.

It was precisely that point that he wanted to make to the citizens of Greasy Corners.

23.

Mesty-Woolah stood seven foot tall, and wore a white turban. A long rifle was propped against one thigh. The red camel he rode was not the sort of animal you expect to see standing in your little American street on a fine summer morning. Mesty and the camel towered over the low adobes of Greasy Corners—you felt, seeing them for the first time, that there should have been a pyramid in the background or maybe the Sphinx.

But there was no pyramid behind them, and no Sphinx, just the great open plain.

"He's a sight, ain't he?" Isinglass said amiably. "He's a fine shot with a rifle, but he'd rather slice than shoot."

The gunfighters and the buffalo hunters were speechless, which annoyed Billy.

"Why, this old man's treating us like white Indians," he said. "He wants to reservation us off in Arizona, or someplace where there's nothing to do."

Isinglass looked around the settlement with its thin pigs and rough men.

"I can't see that there's much to do here, either, other than die," he remarked.

"We'll see who dies, if we're bothered," Billy said.

Isinglass turned his horse.

"I hope you men will use some good sense," Isinglass said. "Visit the depot in Roswell, the sooner the better —there's a nice selection of brochures there to tempt people who want to emigrate. This could be a case when giving way to temptation would be the healthy thing."

He rode slowly up the street toward Mesty-Woolah; then, after riding a few steps, his mood seemed to harden; he stopped for a moment and looked back.

"I rarely give advice of this sort," he said. "I could have just ridden in and killed every malingering one of you, and I have little doubt that that would have been the efficient course."

"You better ride a swifter horse than that when you come to kill me," Billy Bone said.

The old man didn't answer or look around.

Wild Horse Jerry jerked a pistol out of his holster, surprising everyone.

"This is a dern solemn kind of jubilee," he declared. "I'd rather kill niggers than play cards, and a nigger that big would be hard to miss."

He promptly fired three shots, and all missed. Isinglass angled his horse toward the side of the street, but he didn't look around and he didn't quicken his pace. Mesty-Woolah didn't move.

"What a fool," Billy said. "You shouldn't talk about how easy it is to hit something unless you can hit it."

Wild Horse Jerry ignored Billy's taunt and walked up the street, holding his pistol above his head as if he were the starter in a horse race.

The red camel began a swift stride toward him, but Mesty-Woolah had disappeared. One moment he was in the saddle, tall as a tower, and the next moment he wasn't.

It confused Jerry, and you can't blame him—the long-legged camel was upon him in a few strides, but the long-legged rider had vanished. Dust from the camel's hooves blurred the action briefly; then Mesty-Woolah reappeared atop the camel, a long sword shining in his right hand.

Wild Horse Jerry doubled over as if he had been seized by a stomach cramp; then he fell face down. A second later he scrambled to his hands and knees and gave a chilling shriek.

"That tall nigger spilled his guts with the big sword," Billy said, stunned. "Look, they're hanging out beneath him. But how'd he do it?"

They were certainly hanging out, more of them than you would think a small man could contain.

The sight of his own innards shocked Wild Horse Jerry so much that he died after that one shriek.

The red camel nearly strode into the gunfighters before Mesty-Woolah turned him. His face beneath the white turban was coffee-colored; his age was hard to guess.

Isinglass rode over and looked down at the dead man —no doubt he had seen far worse sights during the Indian wars.

"Mesty learned that trick from the Comanches—lean under your mount and slice," he said. "It's easier on a camel than on them short ponies, I guess, but it still helps if you have long arms."

He left, Mesty-Woolah slightly behind him.

Des Montaignes, acting as if he were the mayor, grabbed Wild Horse Jerry by the pants leg and dragged him off to the little graveyard just beyond the China Pond.

"It's the grave for Jerry," Billy said with no great feeling. "That threat he slung at me this morning didn't amount to much, did it?"

24.

Wild Horse Jerry's disembowelment promptly brought my own stomach up, though I had had no breakfast and there was nothing in my stomach except fear. I stepped around the corner of the China Pond and heaved away violently for a time.

Des Montaignes squatted nearby, picking through Jerry's pockets. A couple of skinny whores who occupied a shanty behind the saloon came out and helped him. The state of the corpse made scavenging messy, but the whores were in no position to be fastidious, and Des Montaignes evidently had a considerable tolerance for mess.

The sight of them stripping Jerry hardly soothed my fluttering stomach—I was so weak and dizzy by the time I stopped heaving that I propped myself against a wall of the saloon and shaded myself with my hat. I was sitting there feeling blank when Joe and Tully finally found me.

"We thought you might have run," Joe said.

"I don't think I could run," I said. "I might be able to crawl, though."

"Well, there's gonna be a war," Joe said, no more excited than if he were predicting showers.

"I don't believe that old man will wait no few days," Tully said. "I expect him back any time."

"You ought to go home, Mr. Sippy," Joe Lovelady said. "You're an educated man."

What he meant, I imagine, was that no educated man ought to risk dying in a squalid hole such as Greasy Corners; he was a well-intentioned man, though a little romantic about advantages he himself had never had.

But I shook off his advice—I saw myself, for the moment, as Russell of the *Times*: the Whiskey Glass war would be my Crimea. Russell had probably seen hundreds of men disemboweled before breakfast in the course of his work.

"Oh, I'll stay," I said. "I've taken a fancy to this country—and perhaps I can be of some use to Billy."

"The best use you could be would be to talk him out of fighting," Joe said. "That tall nigger is a scratch too rough for Billy."

"A scratch too rough for me, too," Tully Roebuck said. "Did you see how he hid behind his camel? That was slick."

There was a thunder of gunshots from inside the saloon. The whores, who were trying to get Jerry's boots off, looked up hopefully. Des Montaignes had gone inside.

"That sounded like Billy's gun," Joe Lovelady said.

"Yep, the debate's begun," Tully said.

129

25.

We crowded into the China Pond, where a stormy scene was in progress. Billy had become enraged at Nute Rachal, the meekest of the buffalo hunters, and had fired at him twice, but Nute, adopting my own tactics, had dropped to the floor and the bullets had only chipped the wall of the barroom.

"Get up, you dern possum, and die," Billy said. He was pointing both pistols at Nute, who still lay on the floor.

"No, Billy, I've never enjoyed falls," Nute said with surprising calm. "I guess I'll just die flat."

"What's the dispute?" Joe Lovelady inquired.

"Why, the coward favors moving to Arizona," Billy said.

"Now, Bill, be fair," Happy Jack Marco said. "All Nute said was we oughta go kill the Earps—now that can't hurt."

"Yes, and as soon as we've killed them Old Whiskey will buy Arizona," Billy said. "He owns New Mexico now, what would keep him from buying Arizona if we remove the Earps?"

"We'd have to remove Doc Holliday, too," Ike Pumpelly remarked. "Doc's a little firecracker."

Billy, abrupt as ever, lost interest in Nute Rachal and stuck his guns back in his coat pockets.

"Every possum-hearted one of you can go, for all I care," he said. "I won't turn tail to that old cud myself."

"I'll stay with Beely," Vivian Maldonado said. "In Arizona you can stick to the trees."

"They ain't trees, they're cactus," Simp Dixon said.

"We whipped some rough Comanches here," Jim Saul said. "Maybe we could whip Isinglass."

He was referring to the famous battle of Greasy Corners, in which forty buffalo hunters had held off three hundred Comanches some years before. Jim had been among the forty.

"Hell, yes, they're just cowboys," Billy said.

"The tall nigger's no cowboy," Joe Lovelady reminded him.

"Besides, the old man won't be coming with no cowboys," Tully said. "The word in Lincoln is that he ordered a trainload of gunmen to do the chore for him."

"I don't believe it," Billy said. "Where would that old fool get a trainload of gunmen?"

"South Texas," Tully said.

"Pshaw, that's just a rumor," Billy scoffed. "When's this train supposed to arrive?"

"It arrived in Tucumcari two days ago," Tully said. "That's what I rushed over to tell you, only you wasn't in the mood to listen."

"Well, I'm still not," Billy said.

"That old man's a sight," Ike Pumpelly said. "Why would he ride in to warn us if he had his army with him?"

La Tulipe chuckled. "Big Whiskey didn't come to warn you," she said. "He came to make corpses of you."

Fear blew through the dark barroom like wind

131

through an open window. The thought that Isinglass's visit had simply been a distracting ruse, meant to disarm them, sobered most of the drinkers instantly—only Hill Coe, his disgrace still fresh and smarting, went on consuming whiskey.

"That dern old man," Simp Dixon said, with a moody look. "What a damned old liar he is."

Nute Rachal scrambled nimbly to his feet and hurried to the door.

"I felt the ground shake," he said. "I guess they're coming. *Adiós*, boys, if we don't all make the fort."

26.

Nute was speaking metaphorically, I assumed: there was no fort to make anywhere near Greasy Corners.

But the men, if not brilliant, were very quick. No doubt all of them had been required to hurry many times in their life on the plains. They poured out of the barroom like bees and, with no more than a glance at the line of riders racing toward the town from the east, made some lightning choices. Those who planned to fight hastily gathered weapons and ammunition, while those who preferred to run even more hastily flung saddles on their horses.

I was confused, and no doubt would have been the first man lost had not Tully Roebuck taken firm control of me, virtually pitching me on my mule.

"Let's get!" he said. "Flail that mule!"

It was probably the general excitement, and not my flapping and flailing, that roused Rosy from her customary lethargy; she took off so rapidly that I almost lost my seat, but even so, Tully and I were far to the rear of the crowd. All the gunmen seemed to be ahead of us, including Billy and Joe.

I noticed, as we raced off, that none of the buffalo hunters were mounted yet—they were all standing moodily in the middle of the street, watching the hard riders come.

"What about *them?*" I yelled at Tully—something about their big glum faces shook me.

"They ate their horses, it's *adiós*, I guess!" Tully yelled.

We had scarcely passed the wall where the shooting contest between Katie and Hill had been held, when a far more deadly contest was joined in Greasy Corners. I didn't look back—I was just trying to hang onto my panicked mule—but I heard the first booms of the big buffalo guns, and the more rapid pecking of the Texans' rifles.

Russell of the *Times* might have stayed and got the story firsthand—I just flailed the mule and ran for my life.

27.

Years later, in a little half-dimer called *Nute Rachal; or, The Deadly Fight,* I tried to do justice to the heroic stand the buffalo hunters made in Greasy Corners that day.

They did make a fort of sorts, hastily taking cover behind the moldering, smelly piles of unshipped buffalo hides at the south end of town; from there they held the Texans at bay until sundown, losing only two men in the course of the long fight.

Several times the Texans tried to rush them, but their horses could not take the smell of the putrid skins. They bucked and quivered, but would not charge into the fort of hides; six Texans were killed while trying to encourage their frightened steeds.

"Shabby fighting," Isinglass told me later. "I should have just let Mesty whittle the community down in his own good time."

The gunfighters, and Joe and Tully and Billy and I, did not realize immediately that the buffalo hunters had checked the Texans. We raced on across the naked plain for twenty miles or more; not until it became necessary to rest our winded mounts did we notice that the only dust being raised was our own. The prairie behind us was empty.

Billy Bone was abashed and vexed when he saw that no army of gunmen was in pursuit.

"Why, we're only cowards," he said indignantly. "Why did we run? If the dern buffalo hunters beat the Texans we'll all be laughingstocks."

"It seemed like a lot of Texans, Bill," Simp Dixon said. "Just because they ain't here yet don't mean they won't show up."

When the horses were fully rested we rode on into the shadows of evening, arriving not long after dark at the broken gullies of the Arroyo del Macho.

The strategists in the company felt that the Arroyo was an ideal place to make our stand.

Billy Bone only got more sulky. He felt that he had been startled into an unnecessary and undignified flight, and he held Joe Lovelady responsible.

"It's a disgrace to run like that," he said. "We'll never live this down."

"The war's just starting, Billy," Joe said, not much agitated by his friend's ill-temper.

"That's my view, too," Tully said. "That old man gets more contrary every year."

"I'll stop his contrary if he comes near me agin," Billy said. "I'll put him where the tall nigger put Jerry."

The Arroyo del Macho offered few comforts to the traveler, but the panic of the morning and the hard flight had exhausted me; I slept deeply for a few hours and awakened unwillingly because of some commotion around me. I assumed we were under attack and tried to spring up, but my joints wouldn't respond; the syrup of my heavy sleep seemed to have stuck them together.

"That's all right, Sippy," Tully Roebuck said reassuringly. "It's just Hank Leedy—he made it through."

Hank Leedy was an earnest young buffalo hunter, inclined to solemnity. Back East his type was common in the Presbyterian ministry. It seemed he had tumbled right into the gully where we slept.

He had ridden across the prairie on Bonaparte, who stopped at the head of the gully and commenced a loud braying, to the annoyance of several of the men.

"Shoot that damn donkey, he's ruint my dream," Happy Jack Marco said.

"What was it a dream of?" Simp Dixon asked.

"It was a dream of a whore," Happy Jack replied.

Hill Coe and Joe Lovelady were more interested in Hank Leedy's story than in Happy Jack's interrupted dream.

"I stole the Tulip's donkey, that's why I got through," Hank said.

"Where's the rest of the boys?" Tully asked.

"Dead, I'm sure," Hank Leedy replied simply. "We thought we could make it across in the darkness, but the tall nigger trailed us."

"That devil—how many did he get?" Billy asked.

"Why, Bill, he got us all, for don't you see I'm dying?" the young man said calmly.

"Dern, I didn't—it's pitch-dark," Billy said apologetically.

"I seem to see a light—I suppose it's heaven," Hank said. "Would you ask that feller who can write to pen a note to my sister? Just tell her my luck held—she's quite religious."

"I don't seem to recall where your sister lives, Hank," Joe Lovelady said.

"Oh, Little Rock, Arkansas—just Jenny Leedy," Hank said. "I hope you'll bury me well, boys, so the critters won't disturb me."

He died a little before dawn. When it grew light we saw that he had been shot through the lungs. La Tulipe's donkey was covered with his blood.

The Arroyo del Macho was rocky, and we had only

knives to dig with; the grave we scratched out for Hank Leedy might not have met his standards, and the funeral we skipped altogether. The plains around were empty, but there was a menace to the emptiness. No one knew where Mesty-Woolah was, or the Texans either. Before the sun broke on the horizon we had dispersed and departed.

28.

Billy and Joe and I headed due west, toward the mountains. Tully Roebuck traveled with us for an hour or so, being eager to detach himself from the fraternity of gunfighters, several of whom had been rather pettish that morning.

Vivian Maldonado had been particularly discontented.

"No bed, no breakfast, no whore!" he exclaimed testily, making it clear that he was accustomed to better accommodations than the Arroyo del Macho could provide.

"Where's a town? I'm hungry," he added.

After some discussion, the gunfighters decided to make for Lincoln, the nearest place offering the amenities they required.

"Viv may go for Hill Coe before the day's over, now that Hill's disgraced," Tully said as we rode off.

"Well, let him," Billy said. "I suppose old Coe could still drop Viv—he's a larger target than a beer bottle."

"I don't see why it wouldn't be smart to go to Texas," Joe Lovelady said. No doubt he still had hopes of getting Billy to adopt some safe profession.

"It might be smart, but it would sure be dull," Billy replied. "Let's go to Tularosa—Katie Garza comes to Tularosa once in a while."

I reminded Billy that he had not even cared to lunch in Tularosa the day we met.

"It's true there are unkind sons of bitches there," he said. "If they interfere with me I'll just kill 'em."

When we were well distanced from the gunfighters, Tully decided to leave us. He lived on the Rio Hondo with his wife, who was with child. She had not wanted him to leave her side, but Tully had been determined to warn his friends.

"Guess I'll go back to Bess, she's the worrying kind," he said.

Billy had been leading La Tulipe's donkey, an animal not inclined to rapid travel.

"Dern, it's like dragging an anchor across the prairie," Billy said. "You take him, Tully. I'll tell the Tulip he's safe in your care when next I see her."

Tully accepted the responsibility for Bonaparte, but seemed reluctant to go. The prairie was sunlit and fair; the meadowlarks were singing and the hawks circling high. The beauty of the country was unsurpassed, with antelope frolicking near and the grass so endless.

Yet, within a day, I had seen three men meet their deaths. I was beginning to have to reckon with the fact that I was riding around in a place where it was rather hard to last.

Tully Roebuck, more experienced than I, seemed to be reckoning too, perhaps along the same line.

"I don't know when I'll see you boys again," he said.

"Oh, the breeze will blow us up your way someday, Tully," Billy Bone said lightly.

"That old man's a troublesome neighbor," Tully said.

"He don't let up. If I were you boys I'd scat for a while. Maybe a horse will fall on him and slow him down."

"If not, I'll put five or six bullets in him—that'll slow him down," Billy said. He was impatient to be off.

"Say hello to Bess. I hope to come by and sample her pudding once she's had the baby," Joe Lovelady said.

"Come if you can, we've a shanty you can bunk in," Tully said, and rode off in the sunshine.

"I like old Tully, but I suspect he's lazy," Billy said as we started on toward the mountains.

It seemed an odd remark, since the man had just made a long ride to warn us; neither Joe nor I replied.

I would have said happy, not lazy; Tully Roebuck seemed serene—and perhaps he was, as he loped off toward the Rio Hondo, dragging Bonaparte behind him.

But Bess, his wife—Joe Lovelady said she made excellent puddings—caught a fever and died in childbirth; the little girl lived, but soon went blind. Tully Roebuck would never be serene again, or happy; the next time I saw him he was sheriff of Lincoln County, and his gun was at the service of Will Isinglass.

29.

Two days later, as we were filling up on chiles and frijoles in a somewhat inhospitable bar in Tularosa—Billy was right about the town—Katie Garza blazed into legend by robbing Governor Lew Wallace at gunpoint as he sat in a buggy with his wife outside the Mission San Miguel.

The whole territory had a laugh at the expense of old Lew, in my opinion no more than an inferior dime novelist himself—for what was *Ben Hur* but a fat double-dimer set in Roman times?

Katie turned her white mare, the Dove, and raced down through the terrible wasteland known as the Jornada del Muerto—she knew of a secret water hole that enabled her to go where a posse wouldn't dare follow. Of course, Governor Lew had to get up a posse—I'm told he rather liked Katie's spunk, himself, but his wife took being a governor's lady seriously, and was not amused. He convened the posse mainly to save face: some old chiefs from the Bosque del Apache, with whom he had been parleying at the time, thought it hilarious that a girl could rob a governor, so he had to do something.

By the time we heard the story in Tularosa, Katie was already back in Mesilla, buying drinks for all comers in her favorite cantina.

"Now that's sass!" Billy said, when he heard of the adventure. He had been in a low mood; if he spoke at all it was only to mutter about killing Isinglass, or Mesty-Woolah, or the Texans.

"Let's go, boys," he said. "I've eaten the last dern bean I ever intend to eat in ugly Tularosa."

"Go where, Billy?" Joe inquired.

"Go see Katie," Billy said. "I want to hear all about the robbery."

Joe had just worked out an arrangement with a local horse trader to break forty rough colts the man had acquired—he had been looking forward to it, horses being one of the chief pleasures of Joe's life.

"I told that man I'd work his colts," he reminded Billy.

"Then stay and work 'em, I'm leaving," Billy said. "It's too ugly around here for me. I'll just take Sippy along to protect me. When you get tired of having horses kick you and bite you you can find us down the river."

He looked perky for the first time in days. It was the hope of seeing Katie Garza that had changed his mood.

"I expect I can have those colts polished up in about two weeks," Joe said.

"Why hurry? Take a month," Billy said. "Katie and I might rob a few banks, or maybe the President will visit and we can rob him."

"I doubt the President will journey this far west," Joe said.

I think he questioned the wisdom of letting Billy out of his sight, but he had given his word to the horse trader and didn't like to renege.

"Try to keep him moderate, Mr. Sippy," he said, as we were mounting.

"Why, old Sippy's the one who's apt to need watching," Billy said with a grin. "He might see a train and chase it to California, or take some other wild notion."

Joe Lovelady looked skeptical, but we left anyway.

"It's always a pleasure to leave Tularosa, ain't it, Sippy?" Billy said as we rode out of town.

30.

Traveling with Billy Bone was a slower affair than traveling with Tully or Joe. The passage of time didn't weigh on him as it does on some men. If we crossed a creek he might remember that he needed to wash his socks, in which case he'd stop, pull off his boots, and wash them.

He'd acquired an old Winchester during our stay in Tularosa, and while his socks dried he practiced riflery, shooting at anything in sight, from soaring hawks and drifting buzzards to jackrabbits, prairie dogs, and even lizards. Before we got halfway to Las Cruces, his socks were clean but he was out of ammunition for the Winchester. He hadn't killed any game, either—I never saw him hit anything with the Winchester. We lived on some jerky Joe had insisted we take.

"Katie probably remembers I couldn't hit those bottles," he said as we sat around the campfire the first night. We had piled so much wood on the fire we had to sit fifty feet back from it or else be scorched.

"I doubt she'll hold poor marksmanship against you," I said.

"I wish I'd hit at least five or six bottles," he said. "I can't do nothing right, Sippy. I never could do nothing right."

In a trice, a sadness took him.

"Nobody ever has liked me, except Joe, I guess," he said.

"Why, I like you, Billy," I said. "Tully likes you, and Katie must, or why would she have asked you to go to Mexico with her?"

"I don't know if she meant it," he said. "She might have just been joshing."

"Billy, she asked you three times," I reminded him. "She wasn't joshing."

"She don't know me much, though," he said. "When she gets to know me I doubt she'll like me."

His spirits seemed to sink lower and ever lower, a surprise to me, for he had been jolly all day.

"I'm just alone," he said. "I'm just alone. I guess that's how it will be."

"Billy, what about me?" I asked. "I thought we were friends."

He looked at me like a boy whose pup had just been run over by the milk wagon—sad enough to die.

"We are, but you'll go off one of these days," he said. "It don't mean I ain't alone.

"Besides, you're crazy," he added.

"I may be, but Joe isn't," I said. "A man who has Joe Lovelady for a friend can't claim to be completely alone."

"Oh, Joe would help if he could," Billy said. "But he's a cowboy. He's got his place in this world."

It seemed a curious remark, since when I met them they had been riding the western trail together. But there was no doubt that Billy had sunk into a bog of sadness.

"There's no place in this world for me," he said, in a tone that would break your heart.

"Billy, I just can't understand why you feel that way," I said.

He didn't answer. We sat and watched the ridiculous fire we had built throw sparks into the dark heavens.

"Well, Hank Leedy didn't mind dying much," Billy said, in a tone of resignation. "Maybe I won't either."

"Billy, you're young—you're just starting to live," I said, though the look on his tight little face made the words seem hollow.

He was fiddling with one of his old pistols, clicking the chamber and testing the hammer. To my surprise he suddenly blazed away—six rapid shots—at the campfire itself.

That was to be his style to the end—six shots at least, if not twelve; volume, not accuracy, was Billy Bone's skill.

The campfire was unaffected, but the shooting seemed to relieve his spirits a little.

"You may think I'm starting—I think I'm finishing," he said. Then he yawned and curled up, his head on his saddle. In a moment he was asleep, exhausted by his own mood.

When the fire died and the night grew chill, I covered him with his saddle blanket. I guess I felt a little lonesome for my girls.

31.

_____

By the time we got to Las Cruces the news was that Katie had ridden on down to El Paso. I wanted to linger in Las Cruces a day or two—I thought I might introduce Billy to the pleasures of decent hotels—but he was in a fever to catch up with Katie Garza, and wouldn't pause. His bleak mood had passed, and he was primed for action.

"She keeps on the move, that's good," he said. "That's the way I am—don't like to be stopped too long. If you stop too long, people will figure out where to find you."

So on we went to El Paso, where the dust was swirling disagreeably through the famous pass of the north.

"My eyeballs feel like they've been sandpapered," I remarked.

"Shut your eyes, then," Billy said. "There's nothing to see here except these murdering Texans."

He seemed to regard Texas as a far more barbaric place than New Mexico, though to my untutored eye the two places seemed much alike.

148

"Texans are speedy and mean," Billy insisted. "If they don't kill you standing they'll kill you running."

The citizenry did not have an easygoing look, I admit —but we managed to pass a few hours safely in a flytrap barroom, whittling on beefsteaks that must have been carved from some well-exercised beeves.

"The steak is tougher than the knife is sharp," I complained. My taste for decent cooking still reasserted itself from time to time.

"You Yankees are tiresome complainers," Billy remarked.

That afternoon, having heard that we were looking for her, Katie Garza came loping up to the bar.

Billy had been brashly surveying the saloon's clientele, muttering hot death threats when anyone unruly did anything he didn't approve of. But when Katie stepped in the door he began to fidget and look shy. He quickly took off his old filthy hat, and then put it back on.

"Hi, Katie," he said meekly, like a lad greeting his aunt.

"Hi, Bill," Katie said, a sparkle in her eye. "Let's ride off and leave this place to the flies."

We rode some twenty miles south beside the river, which was high but not very wide. Across it, a few miles farther south, we could see a little adobe village.

"That's San Isidro," Katie said.

"Where's your gang?" Billy inquired. He was looking slightly more relaxed.

"Oh, here and there, getting drunk or chasing girls," Katie said. "Sometimes I ride with my turkeys and sometimes I don't."

"Here we'll cross," she went on, turning the white mare toward the water.

Billy started to follow, but suddenly stopped. His face turned white. Katie looked back at him, puzzled.

"Ain't you coming?" she asked.

"I can't," Billy said, very tense. "I can't go over there."

149

"Why not?" Katie wanted to know. "We'll eat some *cabrito* and shoot at bottles."

"La Tulipe warned me," Billy Bone said. "She says I'll die if I cross the Rio Grande."

Katie Garza looked slightly vexed. "Why'd you ride all the way down here, if you didn't mean to do anything I want to do?" she asked.

"I forgot what the Tulip said," Billy replied, embarrassed.

"It's just a river," Katie said. "People cross it every day and they don't die from it."

"No, but I would," Billy said. "The Tulip said so."

"That old woman's jealous," Katie said bluntly. "She don't want me and you to have no fun.

"I guess she fancies you for herself," she added, her black eyes grown cold.

"The Tulip?" Billy said, shocked. "It's nothing of that sort, not a bit. It's just that she can see the past and the future."

"She can see a pretty boy, is all she can see," Katie Garza said. "Old women are full of lies."

She deliberated for a minute, while Billy looked miserable. Then her cold black eyes fixed on me.

"What do you believe, Mr. Yankee?" she asked. "Do you believe that old yellow whore?"

"No, I'm not convinced by fortune-telling," I said.

"See, Mr. Yankee don't believe it, either," Katie said. "A river is just a river. It don't want to kill nobody."

Billy was in an agony—I doubt he had ever angered a woman before, and he was new to the fire and the ice. So far Katie had only applied the ice—but I felt the fire might not smolder much longer.

Billy just sat on his tall horse, Chip, looking worried. He was scared to go nearer the river but also scared of what Katie might say next.

What she did then stunned him even more than her cold words. She shook her head in vexation a time or two and then got off her horse and began to undress.

"What's wrong?" Billy said, shocked as she shucked her silver-nuggeted jacket and began to undo her skirt.

Katie smiled, as if her little pet was forgotten.

"Why, nothing," she said. "The river's up and I don't want to get these clothes wet. You ought to strip off too, if you're coming."

Then she grinned at us like a child who had thought of some playful dodge that the grown-ups would have trouble coming up with an objection to.

Soon she had stripped to her birthday suit and made a bundle of her clothes—she had a fine young figure, too.

I thought Billy Bone might die from embarrassment without so much as dipping a toe in the Rio Grande— but if Katie Garza felt the least confusion, she didn't show it. Her only problem was what to do about her boots, which didn't fit in the convenient bundle she had made of her clothes.

"Wet boots are worse than wet clothes," she said, mounting. She managed to squeeze the boots in between herself and the saddle horn, balancing the bundle of clothes on top of them.

"Now, come on, Billy, strip off," Katie said, grinning. "There'll be no one to see you but me and Mr. Yankee, and we won't tattle."

Then she rode into the brown river. Soon the white mare was swimming, the water flowing over Katie Garza's legs. Katie's long black hair hung down her back, the ends almost in the water.

"Ain't she a peach?" Billy said.

He looked a good deal more comfortable now that the object of his awe was out of hearing.

In the middle of the river, Katie turned to beckon us —we saw the white flash of her smile.

It didn't strip Billy of his clothes, but it did remove some of his caution.

"She's just a peach!" he said. "Let's go, Sippy."

I may have looked startled. Fear had had such a grip

on him only a moment before that I doubted anything—
even a glimpse of a naked woman—could dispel it.

"They'll shoot me down anyway, let's go see the
world," he said, urging Chip toward the river.

Rosy rolled her eyes in annoyance when she took the
water, but once in she swam like a shark. Five minutes
later we were shaking the water off ourselves in sunlit
Mexico.

III

On the Pecos Stream

1.

So Billy and Katie Garza fell in love in San Isidro—and
in the same dusty town, by the same slow river, under
the same soft moonlight, I slid into despair.

Why? Well, I can't say why. I have not the penetration
it would take to dig down to the roots of the sadness I
felt in those weeks.

I suppose the sere tree of my sadness might have
sprouted from the fact that I had forever missed my
chance to kiss Kate Molloy, our lively parlormaid. Some
might think it a small lapse, or no lapse at all; and yet it
did seem to give life rather a downward tilt, for Kate was
very winning and I was swiftly aging. No such fine nature might welcome my kiss again.

Old men forget, the Bard says; but I have not forgotten
the puzzled look in Kate's gray eyes, or the cloud of
disappointment that crossed her face, the day I muffed
our chance.

Not long after, she gave notice and married.

Still, I mustn't falsify the ledger by making all my

sadness the debt of that failure with Kate, fine as she was.

By the time we reached San Isidro I had been gone from home long enough to begin to feel foolish and low —after all, I had deserted a flourishing family just because some few hundred dime novels had been scrapped.

Having recently seen a living man disemboweled and two others shot dead, the loss of my little collection had shrunk somewhat in import.

Now I had come to a land where I had no ties and no skills—and for what? Was I happier? It didn't seem so.

Worse, the one skill I had acquired through boredom, in Philadelphia—the ability to write dime novels—had atrophied almost completely in only a matter of weeks.

I parked myself each day under the shade of a fine old mesquite and scratched miserably at a little half-dimer, but I knew it was wretched work. The command I had shown in *The Butler's Sorrow* and *Wedded but Not Won* had evidently been lost as I wandered the llano.

What the rest of my life would be I couldn't imagine. All day I sat in gloom under the mesquite, filled with a sense of having missed something—something precious, something I would never be offered again.

What was it that I had missed? A sprightly woman, of course; and with her might have come a sense of fullness that I—though a born describer—cannot even describe, or really imagine. I could only miss it.

At any rate I felt more hopeless in those weeks in San Isidro than I had any right to, for the mesquite cast a fine shade, and the goats were as tasty as Katie had claimed, and no one was shooting at me—a luxury that could not always be assumed in our great Western lands.

2.

_____

The historians come to me now with their questions about Billy and Katie, for I am the only living witness to the springtime of that famous love.

The *federales* destroyed old San Isidro when they were after Villa, or perhaps it was another of their bandits; when it comes to Billy and Katie, the Mexicans who live there now just know what they hear in their songs.

So the historians come to see me, but they go away annoyed, for my main memory of that time is how sad I felt, and how hard I found it to write that miserable half-dimer which I called *Black Beans; or, The Texan's Defeat.*

Billy and Katie I scarcely saw. Some days they would ride off on their horses; other days I heard the pop of their guns as they shot at targets by the riverside. Sometimes late at night I would see them pass the cantina on their way to Katie's little hut, where I suppose they went to play the old common game.

But when the historians or the newspapermen ask me for the texture of those times, I've not much to say. Did Billy and Katie kiss? Did they sigh? I'm sure they kissed, and I expect they sighed; for that sighing follows kissing has ever been been the way of love.

But their words and their looks, their whispers and their laughing, the little joys they may have shared or imagined or looked forward to—all the sweet interchanges of happy young hearts—all these I missed.

I don't know what wiles Katie employed to overcome Billy's shyness—he started mighty shy—and I didn't want to know; those who have taken their leave of *l'amour*, as I have, don't care to be spectators at the bower.

The historians think I just want to keep the story for myself, but they're mistaken. Some things I know; others I can made a shrewd guess at; but the main things the professors and the newspapermen want to know about the romance of Billy and Katie, those things have floated on down the stream that makes no turning.

I know Billy loved Katie, for he was a quick-hearted boy who could never conceal a feeling for a second. He was in love, and he bubbled with it. I'd be rich if I had a dollar for every time he looked at Katie and said, "Ain't she a peach!"

Katie, though, was a woman—which is to say, complicated. She cast a shawl of chatter around her feelings, and the shawl had a fine weave. I couldn't penetrate it, and I guess I didn't realize how deeply Katie Garza loved Billy Bone until that dark morning in Chavez County when I heard her speak her words of heartbreak over his grave.

3.

Joe Lovelady, ever a man of his word, polished up those Tularosa colts in just two weeks. He came trotting into San Isidro on a day so hot and still you could hear a watch tick from thirty yards away.

I know, because I owned the only watch in town, a sturdy pocket model with far too healthy a tick. Being in an irritable state generally, I often thought of smashing it with a rock just to gain a little peace and quiet. Once I stuck it in the crook of a tree, and a big Mexican woodpecker flew in and watched it for nearly an hour as if it were a small, round bird with an unfamiliar call.

Joe rode up to the table where I was struggling to compose my half-dimer.

"I never thought Billy would consent to cross that river," he said. "I guess he got over his superstition."

Billy immediately popped out of Katie's hut—he had heard Joe's voice. Having a girlfriend had put a little shine on him. He walked with a good deal of swagger, and sometimes even brushed his hair with an old horse brush he had found somewhere.

"Ain't it bully down here in Mexico?" he said to Joe.

"It's sunny, but I do miss the plains," Joe said. "I'm fonder of the grassier places myself."

Katie came skipping out then, in a fine humor.

"Here's that tall broncobuster," she said, giving Joe a big hug. It was clear she really liked Joe Lovelady.

Billy watched them with some suspicion—he was a jealous boy—but was in too good a mood to fuss.

"What's the news from Tularosa?" he asked. "We don't hear much down here."

"Oh, there's still a war on the Whiskey Glass," Joe said. "The Texans chased the gunfighters out of Lincoln."

"Was there much slaughter?" Billy inquired.

"No pitched battles yet," Joe said. "But Moss Kuykendall and Ike Pumpelly are dead. They were headed for Santa Fe and ran into a posse of Texans."

"Those men are regular roadrunners, ain't they?" Billy said, with some contempt. "Where'd they let themselves get chased to now?"

"Anton Chico," Joe said. "It's north up the Pecos stream. I expect the old man will send his tall nigger to clean them out any day."

"That old fool should let people alone," Billy muttered.

"I wouldn't call him a fool," Katie said. "Pa's old, but he ain't a fool."

"Well, I can't get comfortable with a man like that, even if he is your pa," Billy said. "I don't know that I can tolerate his damn sass."

"Just let him get old and die, *chapito*," Katie said mildly. "He's too rough to fight."

Billy just bristled the more when she said it. Something in her tone pricked his vanity. He was an untried boy who had acquired a big reputation from doing little

160

or nothing, and now no one could persaude him he didn't deserve the reputation.

"Why's he too rough to fight?" he asked. "He looks like a damn old farmer, and that old horse he rides wouldn't even make good soap."

Katie saw her mistake and let it pass, but Billy just grew hotter. I believe he wanted us all to agree that he had more ginger than any man in the West.

"What makes you think he's too rough to fight?" he asked again.

"Because all the people who fought him are gone," Katie said. "The Comanches fought him, and they're gone. I don't suppose you're as tough as a Comanche."

"You're just a girl, you might be a poor judge of tough!" Billy snapped, before he thought.

I think he wished immediately that he hadn't said it. Don't we all, when we throw some quick insult at a woman?

"Why, I'm proud to be a girl," Katie said. She was not reluctant to argue.

"At least I can shoot a pistol," she added. "And the only man in this country who can shoot one any better is the man who taught me how."

"Who would that be? Some sweetheart I ain't met?" Billy asked, quite defiant.

"No, Pa taught me," Katie said.

"What? That farmer?" Billy scoffed.

"You may think he dresses odd, but he can shoot your eye out at forty feet," Katie said coolly. "You'd be lucky to hit an elephant at the same distance, from what I've seen."

With that and a flash of her eye she turned and walked back to her hut, leaving the three of us to stand there under the fine mesquite tree.

Billy Bone was shocked, but Joe Lovelady and I just felt slightly embarrassed.

4.

"Well, what now?" Billy asked, finally.

Neither Joe nor I spoke. We had no idea what to say. He had provoked his lady, and his lady had walked off in a temper, if only a mild one.

Billy was no judge of such little contretemps, though. I am sure he had begun to suppose that he and Katie would enjoy perfect bliss forever, with never a cross word said.

Though swaggering a moment before, he now looked pale and sickly.

The truth is, Billy Bone was delicate, a prey to sick headaches and sudden spells of weakness. He had survived a hard boyhood, and it's commonly assumed that such trials toughen a person—but Billy Bone's health, in the time I knew him, put the lie to that assumption.

His rough childhood hadn't toughened him: it had weakened him. When a headache or a bad spell seized

162

him he could quickly look so wan you'd hardly expect him to survive.

That happened as we stood around, nervous and embarrassed, in front of the little cantina in San Isidro. Billy suddenly turned so white and faint-looking I had to jump and urge him to take my chair.

"It's all right, Billy, it's just a tiff," I said. "Sit down before you topple."

He sat, his hands trembling.

"I wish we hadn't eaten all those good pills, Sippy," he said. "I'm getting one of those old headaches."

Joe Lovelady walked over and soon fetched Katie back. At the sight of Billy's wan face her annoyance at once gave way to concern.

"Just look at you, Billy," she said. "Can you walk?"

"I feel somewhat wobbly," Billy said, in the formal way he was apt to speak when he was deathly sick.

"You worry me, Bill," Katie said. "Now come lie down inside, it's cooler there."

"Oh, I'll be well in a while," Billy said. "It's just a spell."

When he felt a little better, Katie coaxed him across the scorching plaza to her hut. She was soon back to draw water from the river, and after that we saw them no more that day.

"I hope he don't go take on Old Whiskey on a day when he's likely to get a spell," Joe said. We idled through the long hot afternoon at my table under the tree.

I guess we were both worried—Billy had sunk so fast. "I hope he doesn't go after him, anyway, well or sick," I said. "What was Katie's mother like?"

"Oh, I never knew her," Joe said. "She's been dead for years. She must have been a beauty, though—they say Old Whiskey offered to marry her, but she refused."

"I'm surprised anyone could refuse him," I said.

Later, in the castle, when I asked Isinglass about her,

163

he looked sad for a second—it was one of the few moments of emotion I ever caught him in. But he told me nothing.

"I've shut my mouth on that, Mister," he said. "And when I shut my mouth I shut it for good."

5.

There was little to tire a man in San Isidro except carousing. I was never any good at carousing and seldom attempted it; consequently I was usually awake by daylight, or soon after. The mornings were lovely and quiet —someone had belled a nanny goat, and you'd hear the bell tinkling as the nanny wandered around; the doves fluttered and the wrens conversed, but it was a quieter place, by far, than Philadelphia.

I had formed the pleasant habit of taking myself an early morning stroll by the Rio Grande. I liked to watch the flare of colors over the mountains to the east as the sun rose—the fresh air and the clear light brought a brief exemption from the sadness I was struggling with.

The morning after Joe Lovelady arrived I was strolling back toward the village, trying to avoid snakes— they were hard to spot at that hour—when I came upon Katerina Garza sitting by the river in a long white nightdress.

She had drawn a bucket of water and had then sat

down beside it to cry. She looked around at me but made no effort to hide the fact that she was crying.

"Why, Miss Garza," I said—we were still on formal terms—"you seem distressed. Is Billy worse?"

"He's not worse, he's fine," she said, wiping her wet cheeks with the hem of her nightdress.

I was brought up not to pry, and I searched for some safe word of encouragement I could mutter before passing on. But before I could find the word, Katie abruptly pulled aside the shawl that usually hid her feelings.

"He's leaving!" she said bitterly. "He won't stay."

"Oh, perhaps that's just his mood of the moment," I said. "He's changeable, I've noticed."

Katie shook her head grimly.

"No, he's going," she said. "He won't stay for me, and now I wouldn't let him if he asked. If people want to go it's best to let 'em."

I had come to that judgment myself, but I was in my fifties. For a girl scarcely twenty to arrive at it struck me as remarkable.

"If you'll tolerate my inquiring, where does he plan to go?" I asked.

"Why, to Anton Chico, to get killed, of course!" she said. "He's no reason to go! He don't know those gunfighters, and he don't know Pa, either. He's no business in that fight, but he thinks different."

"Maybe Joe can talk him out of it," I suggested. "Joe's practiced at handling Billy."

Katie Garza's tears were gone, but in her eyes was a look beyond tears.

"Joe can't," she said. "They're already saddling up. Joe can't and you can't and I can't—and we're the only three people he's got.

"He thinks he's got to make a reputation," she added. "That's all it's about—as if he ain't famous enough already."

She reached for the water bucket, but I was quicker. I carried it for her as we walked back along the silver

166

river. Her look had the sadness of a woman, also the sadness of a child.

"I've not had the opportunity to compliment you on your shooting, back in Greasy Corners," I said, merely searching for a safe subject that might cheer her.

Katie Garza was not fooled. "You shot just as well," she said. "I wish my pa had been there, though. My pa could beat us both."

"I was much impressed with your father, the little I saw of him," I said. "I'm surprised he taught you pistol shooting—it's not a common skill in a young woman."

"It ain't common in a young man, either," she said, with justice. "Joe can only shoot fair, and Billy can't shoot at all.'

"That's a point," I admitted.

Katie sighed—it was clearly one of those days when life's a heavy weight.

"Pa likes me,"she said. "He don't come to see me as much as he did, but he likes me. He said I'd get no help from the law, so I'd better learn to shoot. He said the law would be my enemy, and I already see he's right."

"Miss Garza, that's a harsh view, surely," I said. "Why would the law be your enemy?"

She looked at me as if I were God's own fool.

"Because I'm brown," she said. "And that's Texas, across the river."

6.

Billy Bone turned into quite a chatterbox that morning in his efforts to convince Katerina Garza that his departure was just a trifling thing.

"It's just that I've never been to Anton Chico and I'd like to see that part of the country," he said, as we were standing by our horses. "Besides, I'd like to josh those dang gunfighters for a day or two and maybe win some of their money before your pa runs them clean out of the country."

He looked at Joe and me in appeal, hoping we'd help him drum up convincing reasons for hurrying off an hour before breakfast. But Joe and I both felt sorry for Katie, who made no effort to conceal how forlorn she felt. We didn't provide any help.

Billy himself didn't believe what he was saying—nor do I imagine he understood why he had awakened so determined to leave. Billy Bone was just a puppet to his instincts, jerked this way and that by strings whose pull he couldn't predict. He *had* to go: he just didn't know why. Joe and I were puzzled, and Katie in tears, so he tried to make it better by talking, and, of course, he failed.

"I doubt we'll be gone but a week or a little more," he said awkwardly. "I'm in the mood for some fast traveling and I've got Joe here to lead the way.

"I don't care how long you're gone," Katie said. "A year can't hurt no worse than a day."

She said it in a muffled voice and turned and walked back to her hut, to cry alone. She didn't look Billy's way again.

Billy looked pained, as he always would if another person refused to look at life as he looked at it.

"I don't know what's the matter with Katie," he said. "I guess she's just gonna cry and carry on no matter what I say."

Joe Lovelady did not appear to be enthusiastic about the coming journey, but he was mounted and ready.

"Are we going to New Mexico?" he asked. "Or do you prefer just to sit here and jaw?"

No one had asked me if I cared to participate in a range war, but Joe Lovelady had thoughtfully saddled my mule.

Billy tried to act as if I was the one who was delaying the start. "Well, are you coming to the fight, Sippy? Or had you rather sit here and scribble?" he asked.

"Oh, I'll come, if my mule can keep up," I said, taking the reins from Joe.

The Rio Grande's cold waters stung like ice when we swam the river.

7.

Billy Bone chattered all day as we cut through the
Hueco Mountains and crossed the desolate land that lay
beyond them. It was a plain, but a poor plain—for hours
we saw nothing living except a colony of thin prairie
dogs and the occasional soaring buzzard.

He chattered—and got little in the way of response
from Joe and me.

I supposed I had hoped to feel more cheerful once we
got moving, but the country was of a bleakness not designed to lift one's spirits. Life had seemed pointless in
Philadelphia, but was there noticeably more point to
riding a difficult mule up and down the New Mexican
plain in the company of a rash boy such as Billy?

I couldn't see that there was, and I was not the only
disaffected traveler along the trip. Joe Lovelady was as
out of sorts as I'd ever seen him. He managed to kill one
of the thin prairie dogs, which was all we had to eat that
night.

Billy had been so anxious to rush off before Katie could shame him with her emotion that we had left unprovisioned.

"There was a time when I had more to show for a day's work than a dern prairie dog," Joe Lovelady said.

Indeed, the meat was greasy and half raw; we had barely been able to scrape up enough brush to cook it.

"We can stuff when we get to a town," Billy said, trying to sound nonchalant.

He was aware that we were both somewhat unimpressed by him at the moment. It may be that the abrupt departure from San Isidro was a reaction to his sense that Katie and Joe and I had come to regard him as ever so slightly ridiculous. I believe he intended to show us that he was every bit as dangerous as he was generally held to be. Any discomfort that might be encountered on the way to battle he was prepared to ignore.

"You did say you'd try Texas, Bill," Joe reminded him —it was a promise I'd not been aware of.

"I will, too—we'll just lope right over there after we josh those roadrunners a little," Billy said. "Maybe I'll win enough at cards to buy you a spread."

It seemed a farfetched hope, and Joe said so.

"You won't win nothing at cards, Viv will just skin you," he said. "We're just a nod from the Texas ranches now. Why don't we leave the warring to the warriors and lope over to San Antonio? You could land a slick job in the city, since you don't care for livestock."

It was a long speech for Joe, and well-intended, but hearing it immediately depressed Billy Bone.

"I hate Texas," he said bluntly, "and I ain't going to San Antone. If you want to go, go, and take Sippy with you. I can make Anton Chico on my own, or anywhere else, for that matter."

Joe said nothing; he was prepared to let it drop. But Billy went on sinking.

"You don't know what I'm like, neither one of you

171

do," he said in his sad voice. Then he turned his back to us and put his head on his saddle.

"Nobody knows what I'm like," he said with some bitterness, without looking around. "Nobody knows— but they will before I'm through."

8.

The next morning Billy was sullen. He didn't utter a word when he got up, and he ignored the cup of coffee Joe offered. He flung his saddle on Chip and rode off north.

Joe Lovelady and I were faced with a decision. Texas, offering peaceful occupation for Joe, at least, was within easy reach. Billy Bone was rapidly becoming a dot on the prairie. Should we be sensible or loyal?

I had already seen enough violence to know that I had neither the taste nor the capacity for it. I liked Billy and felt somewhat fatherly toward him; a man with nine daughters will usually welcome a son. But I had been badly scared in Greasy Corners, and was more than half inclined to visit Texas.

"He may be bluffing," I suggested. "If we call it and go on to Texas, don't you think he'd come, eventually?"

"Nope," Joe said. "He won't. A crowbar bends oftener than Billy does."

"You're a cowhand," I reminded him. "Do you really want to wade into this fight?"

Joe picked up his saddle.

"Nope," he said again. "But I don't want to lie awake all night worrying about Billy, either. He don't know these old plains. If he strikes a wrong angle he could find himself a hundred miles from water. Half an army nearly starved to death out there, you know."

He was referring to the ill-fated Texans who tried to capture Santa Fe—their failure was the subject of my half-finished half-dimer, *Black Beans.*

"I wouldn't want that on my conscience," Joe said.

So, reluctantly, we saddled up—and reluctantly we followed Billy north.

Neither of us was in any particular hurry to catch up with him; we were trotting along, two or three miles to the rear, each of us thinking his own rather sober thoughts, when Joe Lovelady, ever alert, spotted two riders far ahead.

"Why, there's the Fay brothers," he said cheerfully.

I looked, but except for Billy, himself just a speck on the grasslands, I saw no one. My eyes, trained on vistas no more spacious than a fine Philadelphia lawn, had yet to adjust to western distances. We rode on for some three miles before I was able to discern the Fay brothers, two specks even more minute than Billy Bone.

"How can you be sure it's them?" I asked. "They're just dots. They could be anybody."

Joe grinned, amused by my amateur ways.

"I'd recognize that pacing mare of Elmer's any-where," he said. "I once owned that mare myself."

We swung into a lope. I gathered from his smile that the Fay brothers were friends. I discovered that I *was* feeling a bit more cheerful at last. It was a fine morning; company might even lift Billy's mood.

I had scarcely a minute to enjoy my improved morale when there was a crack; the sound of a gunshot rolled across the empty plain. We were no more than a quarter

174

of a mile from the riders then. There was another rolling crack, and I saw the flash of sun on Billy's gun barrel.

Billy and the two riders were stopped only yards apart. Then one rider slid off his horse; the other fired a wild shot before he turned and raced away.

Billy shot four more times at the fleeing man, to no effect.

"Good Lord, Billy's shot Elmer," Joe said, kicking his horse into a run.

The fallen man had managed to cling to his bridle rein. The mare spooked and dragged him thirty or forty feet before Joe could stop her.

That didn't matter, for the man was dead.

Billy Bone had not dismounted. He had an empty gun in his hand and a look of cold satisfaction on his face.

9.

Joe Lovelady was too shocked to speak, at first. He knelt by the body of Elmer Fay, looking as if he expected to see the man open his eyes and talk, though he knew as well as I did that the man was dead.

"I believe he's gone, Joe," I said, dismounting.

"I hope he is, the Texas son of a bitch," Billy Bone said. He knocked the empty shells out of his pistol and began to reload.

"If this was a better gun I might have kilt the other one, too," he added.

"It's Elmer Fay," Joe said in a shaken voice. "I knew him well. Why did you have to kill Elmer?"

I think Billy had expected nothing but praise—he was startled by Joe's tone, and perhaps by the looks on our faces.

"Why, he said he was from Texas—I supposed he was one of those killers," Billy said. "There was two of them. I wanted to be quick and get off the first shot."

"You were too damn quick," Joe said. "Elmer and

176

Jody were just horse traders. You might have asked before you shot. Now you've killed a fine man and ruint a family."

Billy Bone looked disgusted—he had expected a hero's greeting, and did not enjoy being criticized.

"Well, of course you'd take his part, you're a Texan yourself," he said. "What was he doing in this country if he wasn't one of the killers?"

"I expect they were just going back to Texas for more horses," Joe said.

Elmer Fay's hat had fallen off his head. Joe walked over and retrieved it. Then he put it carefully over his dead friend's face.

"You were far too quick to shoot," he said. "Elmer Fay was a steady fellow. It's a big pity that he's dead."

"Oh, you've got to be a regular preacher," Billy exclaimed.

Joe Lovelady ignored him. He took the bedroll off the dead man's mare and spread it on the grass.

"Would you help me, Sippy? Let's wrap him up," he said.

I took the end that Des Montaignes usually took—the feet—and helped Joe lift the corpse onto the bedroll. Joe rolled him up neatly and tied him with his own rope. Then we placed the body across the nervous mare.

Billy Bone watched us silently, but I think he was as nervous as the mare. Something had gone wrong. Luck had brought him what seemed a legitimate chance to become the killer everyone fancied him to be. But there was a dark side to the luck. He had killed his friend's friend, and an innocent man at that.

I believe he would have welcomed a hot argument, but Joe Lovelady offered him none. Joe looked grave, and went on tying the body across the saddle his friend had been riding only a few minutes before.

"Are you planning on a church funeral?" Billy blurted, unable to stand the silence. "Why not just scratch out a hole and plant the man here?"

177

"Why, I know the family," Joe said. "I'd be remiss not to take Elmer home."

"How long since you've seen the man?" Billy asked. He could not stand to be thought in the wrong.

"I believe I saw Elmer last year," Joe replied.

"Well, then you don't know so much, after all," Billy insisted. "He could have got tired of horse trading and gone to killing for Isinglass. I might have been the one shot down if I hadn't fired quick."

"No, Elmer Fay was steady," Joe said. "Jody was the one with the wild streak. You'll have to keep an eye on Jody from now on. I expect he'll be wanting to revenge his brother."

"Him? Why he ran like a jackrabbit," Billy said.

"I've no doubt he was surprised," Joe said. "That don't mean he won't come back for you, once he's thought about it."

Then he mounted and looked down at me.

"I've got to be taking Elmer on home," he said. "Do you want to accompany me, Mr. Sippy?"

It's hard to describe what was in my mind at that moment. Elmer Fay had been a skinny fellow—his corpse reminded me of Chittim's, although Elmer Fay had fallen on the open prairie and Chittim on a Philadelphia sidewalk. I hadn't really known either man and had no honest claim to grief, but in both cases the closures were so sudden that it left me numb.

I suppose all death is sudden, if you think about it: the luckiest among us still must pass between one breath and the next; but to reason it out is not so affecting as to see it occur.

No doubt the late Mr. Fay had seen a boy approaching and had merely thought to say good morning; now he was dead.

Even Joe Lovelady was numb, I believe, though it didn't reduce his competence.

Only Billy Bone, the wrongdoer, still had all his nerves exposed. He saw that his friend Joe Lovelady was about to ride away. Though he offered no apology, I think the fact troubled him almost to despair. He looked bleak and pinched and hopeless.

Perhaps it was the boy killer's hopeless young eyes that curdled my judgment—I don't know.

"Thank you, no," I said, to Joe Lovelady. "I believe I'll ride along with Billy. Maybe I'll see old Texas another time.

"Why, I hope so," Joe said, as he left.

10.

"Why, Billy was the storied one, and you're a storybook man," Tully Roebuck said to me, years later, as we were discussing the old troubles along the Pecos. I was speculating about my decision to follow Billy on to Anton Chico, although I had just seen him slaughter Elmer Fay.

"Joe Lovelady was just a cowboy," Tully added. "I doubt he would have made any of the write-ups if he hadn't given the tall nigger such a chase."

"But that chase was the finest thing in the story," I protested—for the Texas cowboy on his cow pony had led the African warrior across the badlands and the hilly lands all the way from the upper Pecos to the Mogollon Rim.

To me Joe Lovelady's ride was as fine as Roland at the pass, and the histories and the stories did give it some recognition; but of course, from then till now, it was Billy Bone and his hot gun that got the most space.

"Joe Lovelady never killed a soul," Tully said, to sum the matter up.

Scarcely a month after our conversation Tully himself was ambushed by Brushy Bob Wade, leaving the little blind daughter, for whom he grieved so deeply, to be raised by a sister in Oklahoma.

11.

It's true that when I watched Joe leave for Texas with Elmer Fay's body, I was passing through the feeblest phase of my career as a dime novelist. The half-finished *Black Beans* was a clear failure. My old hero Sandycraw, who had foolishly joined up with the brash Texans, seemed to have lost all force of personality; he had allowed himself to be trapped by some scoundrelly Kiowas and was awaiting a terrible fate with unaccustomed passivity.

Indeed, I had no more to show for two weeks of scribbling than a hodgepodge of travel notes, none of them likely to arouse cheers from the benumbed editors at the house of Beadle and Adam.

Was Tully right? Did I ride north with the boy killer in order to become the Buntline of the Whiskey Glass? Am I such an opportunist as that?

I dispute it. I went north because I couldn't stand to leave Billy Bone, as he sat there looking so low—just a little Western waif, with such a lonely look stuck on his ugly young face that you'd want to do anything for him.

I stuck with him out of sympathy—not admiration. None of us admired his killing; but none of us could stand to desert him either.

Joe Lovelady veered off in shock at the killing of Elmer Fay, but he was back in time to play the decoy, else Billy would never have escaped from that jam in Skunkwater Flats.

Katie Garza turned away in misery in San Isidro, but it was Katie who managed to slip Billy the gun that kept him from being hanged in Lincoln County.

He had the sad boy's appeal—and yet the minute you succumbed to it he'd make you wish you hadn't.

Joe Lovelady was scarcely out of sight with Elmer Fay's corpse before Billy wore through his bleak mood and became cocky as a rooster.

"Joe, he's just finicky," he said, and he rode along all day singing ditties in rough Spanish that I suppose Katerina had taught him. He was in perfect spirits.

That night we were so far out on the llano that I could not find a single stick of wood, and we were forced to make a smoky campfire from a pile of cow chips I assembled. All we had to eat was a piece of jerky that had been in my saddlebag since our visit to Tularosa, washed down with a little canteen water from the Rio Grande.

My mood, not high to begin with, had sunk during the course of the day, but Billy's was soaring.

"The Tulip must have read the cards wrong on me," he said. "I crossed the Rio Grande and came back and got in a gunfight, and I'm still alive."

"I'd remain a little humble if I were you," I said. "Tomorrow you might meet a gunfighter instead of a horse trader."

Billy looked disgusted.

"I wish you'd gone with Joe, if you're so finicky about

killing," he said. "You've been gloomy all day over one dead Texan, and I call that ignorant."

"I suppose Mr. Fay had a life, the same as you and I," I said. "He may have enjoyed a good meal, or liked to dance. He may have been a comfort to his family. But that's all lost now, and for no reason."

Billy clearly didn't see the point of such a comment.

"Why, he can dance in hell, if that's his pleasure," he said. "I'll send that brother of his to join him, next time we meet."

I had thought to draw a little picture, describe the dead man's life a little, hoping to draw from Billy at least a drop of remorse for the life he had so brusquely ended —to get him to consider them the moral aspect of murder, I suppose.

But my hope was misplaced. Indeed, it was foolish; the only regret Billy felt was that he had not managed to kill Jody Fay too.

"I think I ought to buy a big old shotgun" he said.

"Why, for the prairie chickens?" I asked, mindful of my hunger.

"No, not for prairie chickens," he said. "All you Yankees think about is food. I just need the shotgun because I'm no good with a pistol at moving targets. If I'd had a loaded ten-gauge, that dern Jody would never have escaped."

The first thing he did when we arrived half starved in Anton Chico was borrow fifty dollars from me, all of which he promptly spent on a shotgun and a sackful of buckshot at the general store.

12.

Billy decided at once that he didn't care for Anton
Chico, a community little more imposing than Greasy
Corners had been.

"Too chilly," he said, as we were shivering over our
coffee the morning after we arrived. Dark clouds were
rolling down from the Sangre de Cristo, not far to the
north. Billy was taken with a sneezing fit that left him
dizzy. He blamed it on the chill.

The gunfighters had also found the town not to their
liking; the only one still there was Vivian Maldonado,
who had conceived a grand passion for an Apache girl.
The rest had drifted back down the Pecos to Puerta de
Luna.

"There they will die, but not me," Vivian said. "I'd
rather be in love."

He had acquired a heavy serape and sat most of the
day drinking tequila with his back against the adobe
wall of the little store where Billy bought the shotgun.
If a crack of sunlight pierced the clouds and lingered for

a minute, Vivian would scoot over to take advantage of it.

"If you're so in love, sell me your pistol," Billy said. "My best one will hardly ever hit where you aim it, and my other one's plumb worthless."

"No, I don't sell you no pistol," Vivian said, with a Neapolitan sigh.

The object of his passion, a comely if somewhat rotund Apache girl of no more than fourteen, was grinding corn across the street from where we sat. She worked for the *alcalde* of the village, an old Spaniard who also owned the general store, the only commercial establishment in town.

"But if you're in love and have quit the battle, you don't need an expensive gun," Billy argued. He was intent upon raising the quality of his arsenal, though it seemed to me he was deadly enough with what he had.

Vivian ignored him. "I see cows," he said.

He was right. Three cowboys were approaching the town from the south, driving forty or fifty head of cattle before them.

"I got worse news than that," Billy said. "I see Indians."

Sure enough, three Indians on small horses were loping in from the northwest.

"I don't like this place much," Billy said. "I wouldn't have come if I'd known it was Indian country."

"It's just three, we can kill them," Vivian said.

"Maybe and maybe not," Billy said dubiously. The sight of the Indians had clearly left him feeling subdued.

"The Tulip always said not to drift too far north," he said. "She said the meanest Spaniards and the toughest Indians live up toward the north part of the Territory."

The cowboys were evidently not too cheerful about the arrival of the Indians, either. They stopped their little herd about a half mile south of town and held a quick discussion among themselves.

Then one spurred his horse and came racing into town lickety-split, leaving the other two to hold the cattle. He raced right up to the wall where we were sunning ourselves and yanked his horse back on its haunches.

"Tell Bloody Feathers there's his beef," he said.

The name had an electric effect on Vivian Maldonado —he jumped to his feet at once.

"Bleedy Feathers, is that him?" he asked.

"We don't speak the Apache language," Billy observed to the cowboy in the formal tone he was apt to adopt when disconcerted.

"Why, Bloody Feathers speaks American as good as you do," the cowboy said, obviously impatient to be leaving.

"He's Old Whiskey's son," he added. "The old man sends him fifty beeves a month so he won't be scalping the cowpokes."

"Well, if he ain't gonna scalp you, why are you in such a raving hurry?" Billy asked.

The cowboy was a lanky fellow with a big mustache whose temper was evidently unstable.

"Because, goddamn you, I ain't an idjit!" he exclaimed. "I ain't betting my hair on no loose deal like this. Bloody Feathers might decide he wants the beef and a few white scalps to boot."

With that he loped off down the Pecos, soon to be joined by his companions. The beeves walked slowly on toward the town—it was as if they felt compelled to deliver themselves.

Bloody Feathers rode into Anton Chico with an air of relaxed indifference, much as his father had ridden into Greasy Corners. He was more darkly complexioned and far better mounted—he rode a pretty roan gelding—but the family resemblance was evident: the same stocky build, the same huge head as his father. He carried a Winchester in a fringed scabbard and wore a black headband across his forehead.

187

"Go shoot him!" Vivian whispered to Billy.

But Billy Bone was watching Bloody Feathers as if hypnotized—it was clear that in this instance gunplay was not on his mind.

The two Indians with Bloody Feathers trotted on through town and circled the approaching cattle, but Bloody Feathers, without a glance at us, rode over to where the Indian girl was grinding corn—though by then she had stopped her work and was staring fearfully at the man, no less hypnotized than Billy.

I admit I was awed myself. Though dressed simply and not apparently hostile, Bloody Feathers seemed to fill the town, or at least to seize the eye. It would not have been easy to go casually about one's business with such a presence there.

He stopped near where the girl was working and said a few words to her in low tones. The girl immediately put down her grindstone and climbed on the roan behind him.

"Look here, Viv, he's stealing your girl," Billy said. "I guess you'll have to be the one who'll have to shoot him."

You have to give Viv Maldonado credit for some fire. Before his dusky Helen was well settled on the horse, he was crossing the street in protest.

"Stop! You can't take her!" he said loudly. I believe he might well have tried to for a shot, but his pistol was somewhere beneath the heavy serape, and not easily extracted. Not for nothing, though, had Viv been a star of the circus; he marched across the street with a reckless stride, ready to do battle for *amore*.

Bloody Feathers grinned—being challenged by an Italian acrobat in a run-down village on the Pecos evidently held some comedy for him.

"Why do you grease your hair with that skunk grease?" he asked. Vivian, of course, was as pomaded as ever.

"This woman is my betrothed! I must take her to my

188

homeland!" Vivian Maldonado said, like a regular Manzoni.

"Come to *my* homeland and we'll let you try some good bear grease," Bloody Feathers said amiably, ignoring Vivian's declaration.

"I love her, she's my sun and my moon," Vivian declared. Even Billy had to smirk at that way of putting it, though Bloody Feathers didn't seem to regard it as anything out of the ordinary.

"I want to marry her!" Vivian exclaimed—I suppose he thought that would be the clincher.

"Not today, señor," Bloody Feathers said, turning his horse. "Her grandmother needs her at home to help out with the goats."

He started to turn his horse, but Vivian Maldonado, the passionate acrobat, reached out and grabbed the bridle.

"I'll give you money!" he said. "I'll buy you cows."

Bloody Feathers lifted his rifle—it was still in the fringed scabbard—and rapped Vivian on the wrist rather sharply, causing him to turn loose the bridle.

"Please don't interfere with my horse," Bloody Feathers said. "He might run away. Smelling that skunk grease you put on your hair has already upset him."

Vivian had worked himself into a hot Neapolitan rage —a vein stood out on his forehead. He flung off the serape and went for his gun, a fine pearl-handled Colt, the very weapon Billy had been so anxious to trade for.

I had to admit he was quick, too—but the Apache was quicker. Before Vivian could shoot, he leaned over, caught him by the ear, and lifted him off the ground. Vivian was a light, agile fellow, but the ease with which Bloody Feathers lifted him off the ground and simply held him kicking is something I'll never forget.

It must have been painful to be held by the cartilage of one's own ear, for Vivian let out such a shriek that the departing cowboys, already far down the Pecos, stopped for a moment to look back before racing on.

189

Once he had him lifted, Bloody Feathers turned Vivian just enough that the pistol was pointed in our direction.

"You can shoot those Americans if you need to shoot somebody," he said, in the same amiable tones.

Vivian, though, had lost all thought of murder; his face was stretched almost beyond recognition and he continued to emit piercing shrieks.

Bloody Feathers appeared to be under no strain, and could probably have held Vivian Maldonado a foot off the ground indefinitely, but the two Apaches who had come with him were back with the cattle. They were in a high good humor, grinning at the little sport their chief was having.

Bloody Feathers jiggled Viv a time or two, producing some prodigious shrieks and causing him to drop the fancy pistol, at which point Bloody Feathers dropped him. Viv rolled around in the dirt, as if he had been set on fire, as Bloody Feathers leaned far off his horse and picked up the gun.

"What a pretty little gun," he said. He looked at Billy when he said it, and grinned in rather a challenging way before sticking the pistol in his pants.

Billy looked quite subdued—at times he seemed to shrink an inch or two in size—and ignored the challenge, if that is what it had been.

The plump beauty who was the cause of it all kept her eyes modestly lowered as Bloody Feathers trotted past us and took his place beside the cattle. The man who had so recently aspired to her favors was still moaning in the dust.

"I wisht I hadn't seen that," Billy said, when the Indians were out of earshot. "It's the kind of thing that makes me have them shaking dreams," he said. "I'd almost rather see the Death Dog than a thing like that."

For the moment, he seemed anything but a dangerous boy.

13.

Vivian Maldonado spent the rest of the day holding a sockful of hot corn mush against his sore ear and grumbling and complaining.

"If you are a big killer, why didn't you shoot?" he asked Billy several times.

"I don't have to shoot a man just because he's holding you up by the ear," Billy replied.

But his tone was subdued—I believe he felt he had come off badly in his brief meeting with Bloody Feathers.

Now and then Vivian pitched the sock over to the old Mexican woman who worked in the general store, so she could reheat the mush. While it was being warmed he spent his time looking in the mirror. He looked just as he had before the incident except that his ear was as red as a beet.

"Grow your hair," I suggested. "Then nobody will notice that you have a red ear."

"Now I'm deformed," Vivian said gloomily, though he

191

wasn't. "If I go back to the circus they'll put me in with the freaks."

"You shouldn't have stood so close to the horse," Billy remarked—he was already ready to criticize technique.

"Besides that, you made them speeches," he added seriously. "If you need to shoot, shoot—don't make speeches."

"Now I'll never see my Rosanna again," Vivian said, remembering that he was heartbroken as well as deformed.

"I've never met an Indian named Rosanna," Billy said unsentimentally.

"That's what I called her," Vivian said, with a sad shrug.

That afternoon he rode off toward Puerta de Luna, still holding the sock of mush against his ear.

I suggested a trip to La Glorieta, the village where the invading Texans had been captured. I thought a visit to the site of their defeat might revive my interest in the half-completed *Black Beans*.

Billy came along without protest. "Sister Blandina lives over that way," he said. "She's one of the few people who likes me."

A chill was blowing down from the Sangre de Cristo as we rode west. Billy always hated to see the temperature drop below eighty degrees—he moped along all afternoon with his blanket wrapped around him, looking shivery and depressed.

Fortunately we were back where there was wood. That night we built a fire that would have cooked an ox. Billy sat so close to it that sparks kept popping into his blanket, causing it to smolder.

"It wouldn't be easy to kill that Indian," he said, his mind still going over the encounter in Anton Chico.

"But you've no reason to kill him," I pointed out. "He wasn't hostile. He just came to get his beeves."

"He made Viv look silly," Billy said. "And Viv's fast.

"None of these gunfighters amount to much," he said,

a little later. "Hill Coe missed that bottle, and Viv let himself get picked up by the ear. They're said to be the two best—if that's so, the rest of them won't last no time."

"They could take up a profession," I suggested.

"What, be cowboys for thirty dollars a month?" Billy said. The notion clearly struck him as ridiculous, and I suppose it was.

"It's good enough for Joe Lovelady," I remarked.

Billy thought that over for a long time, a sad look on his face. I believe he truly missed his friend.

"Well, Joe's gone along," he said finally. "If we let the Apaches steal these horses, like they did the last time I came up here, we'll just have to try and get them back ourselves."

14.

Sister Blandina, Billy's friend, was a tiny little nun. She stood about donkey-high and was sassy as a banty hen. When we rode up, she was on the roof of the little church, supervising some repairs to the adobe.

"Why, Billy, where have you been?" she called down. "And where'd you get the Yankee?"

"He was lost, I just happened to find him," Billy replied. The sight of the active little nun seemed to cheer him greatly. She hurried down a ladder and soon supplied us with heaping bowls of *pozole*, a hominy stew much favored in certain parts of Mexico.

Sister Blandina was not accomplished at keeping still. While we ate she climbed up and down the ladder a few times to see that the adobe was being set right, assisted in the butchering of a sheep, and swept the floor of the church's little kitchen, all the while peppering Billy with questions.

"Have you earned an honest dollar lately, Billy?" she

inquired as we were eating. She was about my age and had snapping black eyes.

"Ain't earned a dollar, honest or otherwise," Billy admitted with a grin.

"Now, Bill, I want you to give up the desperado life," Sister Blandina insisted. "You can be decent if you try."

"At least I ain't shot that dentist yet," Billy said.

"No, and you mustn't, you've given me your word that you'd let him be."

I had heard Billy grumble more than once about the Santa Fe dentist, who had evidently done a poor job of extracting one of Billy's teeth and had only been spared a bullet because of Sister Blandina's intervention.

Billy even seemed to shine a little under her scolding —he had the manner of a nephew being called to order by his favorite aunt.

"And what is your profession, Mr. Sippy?" the little nun asked politely. Up to then I had been rather left out of the conversation.

"Ma'am, I write booklets," I said—I was never quite ready to call my dimers books.

"Goodness me, are you *that* Sippy?" she said, clapping a hand to her mouth. "But you're my favorite author."

She was up and off, returning a minute later with a copy of *Wedded but Not Won*—the first copy I had seen.

"A news agent in St. Louis sends them," she admitted —and then she blushed.

I may have blushed myself. I suppose I thought that nuns only read prayer books and catechisms; that this welcoming little nun, serving her order in that far, lonely place, should have passed her scanty leisure reading a thinly veiled account of my failure with Dora set me back on my heels for a moment.

"Except for *A Tryst at Twilight*, I believe I like this the best of your works," the Sister said. "The cowboy

195

yarns don't sway me—I suppose having real ones in and out all the time makes yours seem rather tame."

That very point had begun to trouble me, but before I could stammer my agreement Sister Blandina delivered some rather sharp criticisms of *Wedded but Not Won*.

"I'll speak plainly, I always do," Sister Blandina said. "I don't believe you were at all fair to the wife. Why, all she sought was a little kind attention, and perhaps a loving word now and then. If she'd got her due, she soon *would* have been won."

Kind attention. Loving words. Got her due?

"Why, the woman had her due!" I exclaimed, amazed that any reader would think she hadn't.

"Why, I'd like to see the man who could deny that woman her due, or anything else she might want!" I added. Memories of Dora's icy efficiency in such matters—indeed, in all matters—swirled like dust devils in my brain.

"Pooh, you men have such a limited comprehension," the Sister complained, though her eyes still snapped delightfully.

We burst into a debate and sustained it through most of the afternoon, as I followed the energetic Sister about the mission. She didn't skimp on her chores, but bookish people, encountering one another in a wilderness, *will* have their talk of books; after we'd finished disagreeing about *Wedded but Not Won*, we worked through Scott and Thackeray and Mrs. Humphry Ward; then we got onto the poets Mrs. Hemans and Byron. Sister Blandina even recited her favorite parts of *Lalla Rookh*.

Billy Bone was surprised, then bored, then disgusted. "Why, I've never heard such a fit of talking—you've both got book hydrophobia!" he said. He went outside and spent most of the afternoon throwing his knife at a horned toad, and was petulant and surly all the next day. By then we had left the mission and were back out on the plain.

I even felt a little guilty—I suppose, in hogging the

196

Sister's conversation, I had deprived the boy of his one source of motherly affection. He was plainly jealous, and whenever the Sister's name came up spoke bitterly about our book hydrophobia.

But the little nag of guilt didn't cancel my astonishment that the nun of La Glorieta, after a busy day of butchering, plastering, cooking, praying, and teaching the heathen, would take a candle to her cell at night and fix her interest on such a thing as *Wedded but Not Won* —a tale of domestic strife among the privileged of Philadelphia.

I suppose we all—even nuns—dream of a life other than the one we actually live on this indifferent earth.

Often in the hectic months that followed, when it seemed as if the whole Territory was chasing Billy, I thought of the small nun with the lively black eyes— wondering how near a thing her call to service had been. With her quick step and welcoming spirit, I have no doubt she could have had her due as regularly as Dora, had she chosen the domestic path.

I suppose I was half in love with her, inappropriate as that may seem. No doubt, had things stood differently, I would have failed in comprehension and brought woe to us both; but those eyes were so rewarding, and foolish dreams are much the sweetest.

The next time I saw her was the day she and Tully Roebuck walked Billy through the mob in Lincoln—it was lucky for Billy that Sister Blandina was in town that day, for he had shot down two citizens, and without her at their side neither he nor Tully would have made it to the middle of the street, much less to the safety of the jail.

15.

Puerta de Luna was much like other little Pecos settlements we visited during lulls in the Whiskey Glass war.
There were eight or ten adobe huts, all but two of them
inhabited by half-starved Mexicanos. One of the huts
was a combination cantina and bordello, and another
was a tiny store which dealt mostly in bullets.

The town could hardly have housed a flock of chickens comfortably, yet it was there that we found what was
left of the gunmen last seen in the Arroyo del Macho.
Moss Juykendall and Ike Pumpelly, both fallen to the
Texans' bullets, had been replaced by two colorful spec-
imens who had just drifted south from the Dakotas.

One of the newcomers, a boy no older than Billy, was
named Henry Knogle—the gunfighters cheerfully referred to him as the Tadpole.

The other *arriviste* was definitely no tadpole; he was
a giant of a fellow with a red beard whose name was
Barbecue Campbell.

Des Montaignes and La Tulipe were not in evidence;

they had refused to leave Greasy Corners, and no one could say absolutely whether they were alive or dead.

"Oh, I reckon the Tulip's alive," Billy said optimistically. "She told me that the day she died there'd be an earthquake, and the earth ain't quaked that I've noticed."

"It's apt to quake later in the day," Happy Jack Marco observed somberly. "It may just open up and swallow a certain person."

It seemed we had arrived at a moment of tension—the friendship of Happy Jack and Pleasant Burnell had evidently suffered a rupture. The two men sat across a table from one another, each with a gun in one hand and a fork in the other. They were attempting to eat lunch without once taking their eyes off one another, the result being that their vests were liberally splattered with frijoles that had failed to complete the journey to their mouths.

The sight was so comical that I wanted to laugh, but something told me that would be a wrong, perhaps even a fatal, response.

I didn't laugh, and Billy didn't either.

At the table beside them, Hill Coe, once the glory of Dodge City, was lying face down, dead drunk. Across from him, wearing a dark frock coat and sporting a mustache as thin as the lead in a pencil, was none other than Doc Holliday, the famous shooting dentist.

"Here's Billy," Viv Maldonado said when we walked in. His ear, though still showing a splotch or two, was no longer a fiery red.

"Why, is this the young terror? I've been anxious to meet him," Doc Holliday said, in a drawl that owed something to Alabama.

Billy nodded coolly to the older man; the remark had been slightly derisive and Billy knew it, but he pretended to be more concerned with the touchy situation that prevailed between Happy Jack and Pleasant Burnell.

199

"I wish you two would either eat or shoot," he said. "It's hard to get comfortable if you know you might have to be ducking lead spit at any minute."

"Mind your own affairs, little Bill, or take the consequences," Pleasant Burnell said, without even glancing at Billy.

Billy shrugged and made a move toward the bar, but he had his new 10-gauge shotgun in one hand, and the minute he got behind Pleasant Burnell he turned and walloped him in the head with it as hard as he could.

It was hard enough, too—Pleasant Burnell was out so cold it made the comatose Hill Coe look almost alert.

"That damn bastard has little Bill'd me once too often," Billy said.

"Yes, and he might try to do worse than that when he wakes up," Happy Jack observed. He was evidently somewhat perplexed by the new turn of events, and he kept his pistol trained on the prostrate man as if suspecting that he might only be playing possum in the hope of gaining an advantage.

"Why, the manners here on the Pecos are a shock to me," Doc Holliday said. "In Tombstone, cracking a man on the head with a goose gun would not be considered the correct etiquette at all."

"I could have cut him in two with it," Billy observed. "What's the Tombstone line on that?"

He faced the shooting dentist with a bit of bristle in his manner—like all the gunfighters, he was sensitive to even the slightest disparagement.

"It's a practical line," Doc Holliday said with a cold smile. "In Arizona, when somebody gets their gizzard shot out, we line up and draw cards—low card means you have to dig the grave, which can be a sweaty task in that rocky old state."

"That's one reason me and Henry tried Dakota," Barbecue Campbell observed. "Up there the ground's softer, at least in the summertime, and all the burying don't sweat you so. Of course, in winter, once the freeze

200

comes, all you can do is with kilt people is stack them in a shed and hope nothing don't drag them off."

It seemed the man had a keen interest in mortuary practices; he went on to discourse about them for some time, displaying an admirable power of observation.

I was so grateful for his discourse: not only was it interesting in itself but it prevented the wordplay between Billy and Doc Holliday from turning into gunplay, for before Barbecue Campbell was through describing the scores of burials he had had a hand in, Hill Coe had roused himself from his stupor and he and the shooting dentist were rolling dice.

Billy Bone, who loved beans, ate a pound or two of them, which relaxed him so much he took a nap in a corner. I secured a table with a healthy candle and scratched out a few pages of a half-dimer called *Sister of the Sangre; or, The Mission in the Mountains,* about a nun who robbed the rich.

Pleasant Burnell, when he finally awoke, seemed to be in a state of benign amnesia. He quite forgot that he had been mistrustful of Happy Jack and seemed unaware that the bromide that had put him to sleep had been the barrel of a 10-gauge.

"Dern, I never meant to nap so long," he said before he went off in search of a whore.

16.

Toward sundown of that day, as Billy was polishing his shotgun with a greasy rag, Joe Lovelady rode into town.

"Can't stay away from the fun, can you?" Billy said when Joe dismounted.

"I ain't had no fun since Nellie died," Joe said without rancor. "You ought to get saddled up. Old Whiskey's coming again, and this time he means to finish the job."

"Why, that old sock," Billy said pleasantly, peering through the barrel of his shotgun. "He does scamper around, don't he?"

"Jody Fay went to see him," Joe said. "The old man was rather fond of Elmer."

"Oh, I know I killed the most popular man in the country," Billy said, but he didn't seem regretful.

"He's coming with a pretty good crowd," Joe said.

"Why would you care? You ain't an outlaw," Billy said. "Isinglass likes you. He'll make you the boss of his ranch any day."

He spoke in his coldest tones. Joe hitched his horse

and went inside to inform the other men, who soon boiled out of the cantina. They were less nonchalant about the news than Billy way.

"I bet he's had trains running in gunfighters all this time," Happy Jack said. "And now the buffalo hunters are dead. It's just us."

"Why, Doc Holliday's here," Billy said. "If he's as good as his reputation, he can shoot down fifty Texans in an hour. I may just snooze on through this affair and leave it to Doc."

It was then discovered, to everyone's amazement, that Doc Holliday *wasn't* there. No one had seen him go, or heard him mention going; but a search party, after inspecting the crap-house and the two or three whore shacks, reported that the shooting dentist was distinctly absent.

"I expect that's why he's so famous—he leaves before the fight," Billy observed sarcastically.

"Yes, and we best do the same, if there's still time," Happy Jack said. "I wouldn't care to be wiped out in an ugly little place this this."

"Oh, you're so dern choosy," Billy said. But his good humor had returned. Probably he had been contemplating challenging Doc Holliday, and was relieved not to have to to it. The thought of a pitched battle with Isinglass and his forces didn't worry him in the least.

Fifteen minutes later we were all once again on the road—though of course it wasn't a road, or even a patch. We just loped off to the southwest, across the great carpet of grass.

Billy Bone, in high spirits, jumped two young wolves and chased them willy-nilly over the prairie for miles.

17.

We slept that night at a place called Skunkwater Flats—
in my view as good an example as one could find of the
whimsicality of Western nomenclature.

For one thing, there was *no* water, and the old cabin
where we all slept was in a gully, not on the flats. About
sundown the sand had begun to blow fiercely, so it was
nice to have the cabin, at least, though its door had
fallen off, but it was puzzling that a dry place in a gully
would be named Skunkwater Flats.

I asked Joe and Billy about it and they looked at me
as if I'd gone daft.

"That's just its name," Billy said.

"Oh, you mean God named it Skunkwater Flats?" I
asked with some irritation—my eyes were stinging and
my clothes were full of grit from the sandstorm.

"Go to sleep, Sippy. A place is just called what it's
called," Billy said.

Joe Lovelady seemed concerned, but not about nomenclature.

"We should have ridden all night," he said. "Old Whiskey will."

"It's too dern dark and blowy to be riding around in these gullies," Billy said with a yawn. "If that old man tries it he'll fall off in one and break his neck. Or else he'll get lost, and we'll be shut of him."

"Why, they say Old Whiskey has got a compass in his head," Happy Jack observed. "They say he's never been lost, night or day, rain or shine, in his whole life."

"If he gets in shotgun range I'll blow his dern compass out the other side of his skull," Billy said. Then he wrapped his black coat around him a little tighter, and was soon asleep.

Hill Coe had not been able to bring along enough whiskey to make him thoroughly drunk, so he and Happy Jack and Pleasant Burnell gambled most of the night. Viv Maldonado, who hated sandstorms as much as I did, made a kind of tent of his heavy serape and hid in it, muttering and grumbling in Italian. Simp Dixon said he didn't think he could sleep for fear of scorpions, which he claimed preferred sandy sites; but he lay down anyway and was soon snoring. His snore made the kind of sound a rasp makes against a horse's hoof. Henry Knogle, the Tadpole, whistled most of the night, while his large companion, Barbecue Campbell, slept sitting up, his head fallen forward. From time to time he sneezed, his nose tickled by his own fine beard.

Joe Lovelady went out and sniffed the wind; when he returned he carefully led his horse inside, to the surprise of the gamblers.

"Why, you're too cautious by far," Hill Coe said with a stern look. "Even if they find us I doubt they'd shoot the horses. It would be poor economy."

Joe didn't reply. His horse was a young sorrel gelding with a fine head. He stood where Joe placed him and didn't move during the night.

The wind howled and the sand blew through the open door; from time to time the wind blew out the candle, but the gamblers always relit it. Joe Lovelady tucked his blanket around him and slept with his back to the wall, his bridle rein knotted around one wrist.

"Joe might be right, Hill," Pleasant Burnell remarked. "They might shoot the horses, and if they do we're all fried fish."

"And I say none of them's Indian enough even to track us on a night like this," Hill Coe replied with a bit of asperity.

"The tall nigger's Indian enough," Happy Jack said. "He'll come on his camel, I guess—camels like sand-storms."

"I'll kill that tall nigger if he comes," Hill Coe said. He looked hopeful for a moment. I believe it had just dawned on him that if he killed Mesty-Woolah his fame would be so great that no one would dare recall his defeat at target shooting.

Soon the wind snatched the candle's flame again. The gamblers ceased to clink their gold; all were soon asleep.

I didn't sleep, though. I believed Joe Lovelady was right. Isinglass would ride all night and be on us in the morning. I didn't want to die, and I dreaded the thought of a battle; yet I felt curiously calm.

It was a calm I remembered from the War. I was a telegrapher; I never fired a gun at a Reb, or had one fired at me. But I worked the wire at Gettysburg, and many of the men in my camp seemed to feel the same helpless calm, before that battle—a resigned calm, for things had gone too far, and there was no stopping the roll of the earth that would bring first the light of morning and then the darkness of death to many thousands. The armies, those great geologic forces, would crash together like continents; we men could only await our fate.

The situations didn't compare, of course; now we were only a few men in a gully on the llano; at Gettysburg there had been more men in and out of my office

206

in an hour than would be in this whole fight, if there was a fight.

Yet, though the scale was different, the calm was the same; it made a kind of coat to my fear, and I passed the night tranquilly.

Toward morning the wind blew itself out and the stars shone brightly. The cabin was not roomy—Simp Dixon was stretched out practically underneath Joe Lovelady's horse.

I was nodding a little myself by then, but my most distinct and lingering memory of that night is seeing Simp Dixon sit up, strike a match, look briefly at a big pocket watch he pulled out of his vest, and then smile up at Joe Lovelady's horse before returning to his slumbers.

His smile was so wide and happy that I've remembered it always, and have often wondered if Simp could have been dreaming of home, or of a woman, and merely misdirected the smile at Joe Lovelady's horse.

Of course it may be that he just liked the horse—poor Simp was aptly named.

La Tulipe told me later that Simp had once kept a frog as a pet; it sat on a rock in an empty molasses bottle and lived on the moths and flies Simp caught for it.

A man who could befriend a frog might well smile at a nicely behaved horse; but it was to be Simp Dixon's last smile, and I've often wished I had inquired as to what pleased him so, before he went back to sleep.

18.

I finally slept for an hour, lying flat on the floor. I remember waking up in the gray morning just as Barbecue Campbell stepped over me to go to the door and relieve himself. One hand was at his pants button, and with the other he gave Joe Lovelady's horse a light shove, for the horse's rear end was partially blocking the door.

Barbecue had not even cleared the doorway before the fusillade met him: the Texas rifleman, hidden around the edge of the gully, could not have asked for a more imposing target; it may even be that his size saved some of us inside. The man was so tall and broad that he had to stoop and twist to get outside, and the first seven or eight bullets that slammed into him caused him to fall backward and wedge in the doorway.

He was dead instantly, of course, and his corpse functioned as a barricade long enough for the gunmen to roll against the walls and escape the bullets that would otherwise have poured through the open door.

The first fusillade continued for several minutes; bullets spit like sleet against the cabin walls from all sides, but fortunately the adobe walls were thick and none penetrated. The noise was deafening, though—Billy Bone pulled his old hat down over his ears and looked white, as if he might be getting one of his sick headaches.

The gunmen all showed a certain aplomb, considering the desperate nature of the situation. We soon heard squeals of anguish from the horses, all of which were being methodically shot.

"Why, them shit-asses!" Happy Jack exclaimed—one horse made a dying dash, fell down, and rolled over, kicking.

"Them damn terriers," Hill Coe said. He had two pistols loaded and sat with a rifle across his lap.

At that point it was not clear how many damn terriers there were—all that was obvious was that we were surrounded, and that all the horses except Joe's were dead. Joe kept the quivering gelding pressed against the wall, well out of the way of any bullets that might enter through the doorway above Barbecue Campbell's corpse.

The gunmen, far from panicking, seemed to be in a contemplative state, each sitting as snugly as possible against the wall, guns in hand, waiting for a moment when they might take the offensive.

Then the firing abruptly stopped. It was full light now —the sun was rising behind the riflemen to the east, making it impossible to see the massed assailants.

"We only want that damn little Bill!" a voice called out from the top of the gully.

"That's Jody Fay," Joe Lovelady said. "I was afraid he'd be coming."

Billy Bone said nothing; he sat clutching his new shotgun, and he still looked white.

19.

"Send out that damn little Bill, and you'll all be spared!" Jody Fay yelled again.

I was afraid the gunmen might be inclined to fall on Billy and hand him over—after all, none of them was especially fond of him; he was just a boy, not one of the compadres of the trail.

But no one seemed at all interested in complying with the Texan's request. Pleasant Burnell was happily picking his nose, and the others were just sitting around idly, waiting.

"Hand him over now!" Jody yelled. "Do it quick and we'll guarantee the rest of you safe passage."

"Safe passage to the nearest tree is what they'd guarantee us," Happy Jack remarked. "You should have killed that dern cowboy while you had the chance, Billy."

"I know it," Billy said. "Dern, I hate it that I missed."

I suppose what united Billy and the other gunmen

was their determination to defy any order, no matter who it came from, or what the consequences.

"What do you say we do, Joe?" Billy asked. He still had a pinched look.

"Nothing we *can* do but wait for night, if we can hold out," Joe said. "In the night a few of us might sneak by them."

That strategy didn't lift Billy's spirits; of course, it was scarcely dawn, and a long hot summer's day stretched ahead. We had no water, little food, and could not move more than an inch or two in any direction without running the risk of being shot through the doorway. A sizable pool of blood had already leaked out of poor Barbecue Campbell, and the flies were buzzing around it.

The situation called for patience. Joe Lovelady and most of the gunmen had it, but Billy Bone was not a patient boy.

"I'll be damned if I want to sit here all day," he said. "Let's charge them—at least we'd get a few."

"You are brash," Hill Coe said.

Joe Lovelady had been working with his pocketknife at a small chink in the west wall of the cabin. I saw that he had gouged a tiny opening. He put his eye to it, and then motioned for me to do the same. My first try was a failure—I merely got sand in my eye. But on the second try I got a clear look down the arroyo. Far to the west, well out of range of any gunfire, sat two riders: the old man on the black nag, and the tall Negro on the camel.

"I guess Old Whiskey's so rich now he just hires the killing done," Pleasant Burnell said after he had had a look.

The Texans, irritated at not getting prompt compliance with their request, began to shoot again. Once more a rain of bullets began to splatter against the walls of the cabin. After a furious twenty minutes of fire, they stopped.

211

"Ask for a parley," Hill Coe suggested when it was quiet enough that we could hear ourselves again.

"Why?" Happy Jack wondered. "They'll parley and then hang us just the same."

"I know, but it's boresome sitting here," Hill said. "A parley does pass the time."

"I'll talk," Vivian Maldonado said. "I know Mexican." The thought of being the besieged group's ambassador seemed to perk him up—although, of course, the Texans were speaking English.

"Parley!" Pleasant Burnell yelled. "We want to talk to Old Whiskey."

Billy Bone cocked his shotgun—I believe he thought a move to hand him over might be developing; but I was inclined to take Hill Coe at his word. He was bored, and a little talk was a relief from the bombardment.

"Mr. Isinglass can't come right now!" a voice yelled from the top of the gully.

"Okay, we'll listen to a deputy," Pleasant responded. "Send Tully, if Tully's around."

"Tully ain't around, I'll come myself!" Jody Fay yelled, "Flag of truce, now!"

"Flag of truce!" Happy Jack yelled.

A minute later Jody Fay began to walk down the gully, a white handkerchief tied to his rifle barrel.

"Old Barbecue's going to get fragrant before the day's over," Simp Dixon observed.

"You would too, if you were killed," Vivian Maldonado said. The men got to their feet and edged around the doorway, watching the Texan come.

Jody Fay was even skinnier than his brother had been, and he looked to be scarcely twenty. But he was unperturbed as he approached the cabin, the rifle with the flag of truce tied to it tipped casually over his shoulder. All circumstances considered, he seemed to be in a fairly pleasant temper.

"Okay, what's the parley?" he asked, stopping about fifteen feet from the door of the cabin.

"You're too quick to run, but I guess I won't miss you this time!" Billy Bone said, and before a man could move he fired both barrels of the 10-gauge into Jody Fay, who fell back as if a dray horse had kicked him.

Shock held the gully in silence for a moment—and those inside the cabin, myself included, were just as shocked as those on the ridge. But, looking back, I'm sure we should have foreseen it: the rules of civilized war meant nothing to Billy Bone.

"Goddamn, little Bill, why'd you kill him?" Happy Jack asked. "He came under a flag of truce, and now we're all fried."

Before Billy Bone could reply, the guns began to thunder again from the ridge. All we could do was scrunch down and take it. One of the spent shells stuck in Billy's shotgun; he had to pry it out with his pocket-knife.

Later, during the hot, still afternoon, when the Texans were cooling their rifle barrels in buckets of Pecos water and we were licking beads of sweat from our own upper lips, Happy Jack put the question again.

"Why'd you do it, Billy?" he asked. "Why'd you shoot him when we all agreed on the truce?"

"I don't recall voting for no truce," Billy said.

"But he carried the white flag!" Happy Jack said. "Why'd you shoot?"

Billy Bone smiled the pinched smile we had all come to dread.

"It just seemed like fun at the time," Billy said.

20.

It was a long, hot, sad, scorching day; nothing to do but listen to the flies buzz over Barbecue Campbell's blood. Billy Bone sat silently all day, now and then cocking the hammers of his shotgun. Despite the heat he looked cold and white. I believe he knew that day he was lost —we all knew it, for what he had done was terrible even under the harsh code of the West. One man killed for nothing; another shot down under a flag of truce—such marks could not be erased.

No one in the company chided him—it was pointless. He had become what he had long been supposed to be: a cold killer. Four days ago his reputation had only been built on gossip and exaggeration: but Jody Fay lay dead outside the cabin, and that was not gossip.

Now and then I saw Billy turn his eyes to Joe Love-lady, but Joe Lovelady wouldn't look at him, and Billy didn't speak. He just sat, wearing a sad expression.

Finally the burning sun completed its long summer's arch—it set behind the cabin. Through the little doorway, above the stiffened dead man, we watched the glow fade from the chalky ridge to the east, behind which the Texans waited.

The gunmen in the cabin turned their attention to their guns.

"It ain't gonna get very dark," Hill Coe observed. "Too much moon. We better try it in the gloaming."

"How many do you reckon's up there?" Happy Jack asked, studying the ridge. "I can't see none. Maybe they left."

"Plenty's up there, and they ain't left," Hill Coe said. He sounded quite cheerful. The prospect of action, even if it proved fatal, was a tonic to him—something to take his mind off the missed bottle, I suppose.

Joe Lovelady, who had scarcely moved all day, took off his hat and handed it to Billy, who took it but looked puzzled.

"Give me your hat and your coat," Joe said.

"Why?" Billy asked. "Neither one fits you."

"They might think I'm you," Joe said. "I'll go north— the rest of you go south. If I can get them in a chase it'll spread 'em, at least."

"It's a lot of trouble to go to," Billy said, but he took off his coat and hat and Joe Lovelady put them on.

"Give Billy all your weapons, Mr. Sippy," Joe said, turning to me. "Then once we're gone, surrender. If you've no weapons they might spare you."

"Why, that's a hanging crowd if I ever met one!" Billy said. "Texans are all rope crazy. Sippy might do better to keep his guns and shoot a few."

"I wouldn't want to shoot one," I said, and gave him my derringers. He stuffed one in each boot, shaking his head at my backwardness as he did it.

"There must not be many Yankees like you," he said, smiling at me with some fondness. "If there was many like you, they'd never have won the war."

Joe Lovelady was peering out the small hole he had made in the cabin. He evidently saw something that

215

interested him, because he motioned to Billy and Billy took a look. When Billy stepped back, he was grinning.

"It's your dern mule," he said. "She must have got loose last night."

I peeked, and sure enough there was Rosy, grazing on a sagebrush some half mile down the arroyo.

"If you can catch her, you might make it," Joe said to Billy.

"Why, it's Sippy's mule—I have no right to her," Billy said. "I may be low, but I ain't low enough to steal a friend's mule in a gunfight."

"Billy, she's yours," I said. "I don't mind walking a ways."

Billy peeked through the chink again at Rosy.

"Okay," he said. "Thank you, Mr. Sippy. If I make it through them, and they don't hang you right away, I'll come and slaughter the whole crowd and get you out."

Vivian Maldonado surprised everyone by handing his beautiful pearl-handled Colt to Billy Bone.

"You wanted it, take it, Beely," he said.

"But what'll you shoot, Viv?" Billy asked.

"I don't shoot," Vivian said.

"Dern, Viv, I never figured you for a suicide," Happy Jack said.

"You are the suicide, if you try to get out of this," Vivian said. "They will shoot you with ten bullets— twenty bullets.

"I will stay with Mr. Sippy," he added, with some dignity. "We will behave like gentlemen."

Joe Lovelady had been watching the fading light.

"It's time to run," he said, carefully turning his gelding around. "Could somebody just ease that corpse out of the door for me? I want to be racing when I leave the shelter."

Simp Dixon and Hill Coe positioned themselves by the corpse, prepared to yank it inside when Joe gave the signal.

Joe tightened his girth—then he handed Hill Coe his

pistol. "You might need this extra gun," he said. "I'll just keep my rifle."

Then he looked at Billy Bone, who had been watching his friend prepare to leave with a certain sadness in his face.

"Give 'em a race, Joe," Billy said. "I'm sorry I put you to the trouble."

Joe Lovelady thought the situation over for a moment. I don't know what he might have said to his friend had they been alone—perhaps he would have voiced a reproach, or perhaps left with a word of encouragement or kindness; he was of a kind nature, certainly.

But they weren't alone. I suppose Joe thought it best just to be practical.

"Bill, when you approach that mule, approach her soft," he said. "She's a skittish mule."

He reached across the horse and shook Billy's hand; then he gave his saddle a shake to see that it was set to his liking.

"Adiós, boys," he said—and he burst from that cabin like a wolf from its den, swinging into the saddle just as the horse cleared the doorway.

The gunfighters were right behind him, pouring fire up at the Texans as fast as they could shoot. The Texans, though they must have expected the move, were caught off balance—it was a few seconds before their rifles began to blaze.

"If they cut Joe down or hang him I'll kill them all," Billy said, in a shaky voice.

Then he dropped on his belly and wiggled out of the door like a snake. I doubt the Texans even saw him, for it was full dusk and they had their hands full trying to run down the scattered gunmen. Bursting cartridges flashed like fireflies up and down the darkening arroyo.

Vivian Maldonado and I sat until the firing stopped. To the south it continued for several minutes—it was Hill Coe, making his gallant stand.

But there was a final thundercrash—eight or ten rifles

217

fired almost at once; then, only the silence of the summer night.

"Let's leave this boy now," Vivian said, referring to the corpse of Barbecue Campbell.

It was so quiet on the prairie that I felt a stab of loneliness—what if all were dead, Texans and gunfighters alike? Viv and I climbed up out of the gully and looked around.

"I see their campfire," Vivian said. Sure enough there was a flicker, half a mile to the east.

To my surprise he started walking toward it.

"Aren't we going the wrong way?" I asked.

"I'm hungry," Vivian said. "I'm going to give up. They'll find us in the morning anyway. Or if they don't, we'll starve. At least if we give up they might feed us first and hang us some later time," he added.

I felt rather dubious about his reasoning, but I was hungry too and would have just wandered around getting hungrier if I'd left him, so I followed him toward the distant light.

When we got to the campfire only one Texan was there, a young wrangler not much older than Billy. They had left him to watch the spare horses.

"Dern, where'd you two possums come from?" he asked when we walked in with our hands up. He was so scared he could scarcely talk, but he officially took us prisoner. He shot off his rifle a few times to summon help, and then kept it pointed directly at us.

"Help yourself to the beans," he said.

Breast of pheasant could not have tasted better than those frijoles. While we were shoveling them in, Isinglass rode up with five or six Texans, all bristling with guns. I didn't feel too good about the situation, but the old man dismounted and looked us over placidly.

"Ain't you that circus monkey?" he asked Vivian Maldonado.

Vivian gave him a haughty look and kept on eating.

218

"He's a trapeze star," I explained quickly. "He's famous all over Europe."

"Oh," Isinglass said. "I wish my ranch was as big as Europe, but I've studied the map and it ain't."

Then he motioned for the boy to put down the rifle.

"Son, if you're planning to shoot them, shoot them," he said. "I've no doubt they deserve it. But don't just sit and hold a gun on the men while they're trying to eat— it'll just give them the rumbling stomach, and that'll keep them awake."

He untied his blanket from the saddle and bedded down practically in the ashes of the fire.

"I slept cold too often as a boy," he said, noticing my surprise. "Now I like to snuggle up to a nice blaze when I can."

The boy with the rifle fed the campfire all night, while the old man snored beside it and the Texans kept a vigilant watch.

"I guess they'll hang us in the morning, but I'm too tired to worry," Vivian said as he stretched out.

"Maybe Billy will save us," I said, though I knew if Billy Bone was still alive he probably assumed the two of us were already dead.

21.

The Old West is gone now, and yet, in another sense, it's the coming thing. I could make a profession just out of giving interviews about what they call the Battle of Skunkwater Flats, though none of the newspapermen or the historians really believe a word I say.

They've all made a study of it, you see, whereas I was just there. The very fact that I *was* there—it's about the only fact they can't dispute—just makes them edgy; in fact, it makes them jealous and produces much resentment. They'd all like me better if I were dead, like the other mighty men who fell that day.

I try to tell them it was just a long hot boring day, with a certain amount of fear mixed in—after all, I was squeezed into a sweltering cabin with a horse and a dead man and a bunch of moody gunfighters who made very little effort at conversation.

When the day finally ended, Joe Lovelady made his break and led off Mesty-Woolah and a few of the Texans, and Billy Bone crawled off unnoticed and caught my mule; the gunfighters fought until they were all shot dead, and then Vivian Maldonado and I walked over to the Isinglass camp and surrendered.

That's what occurred, but it's not good enough for History. The Battle of Skunkwater Flats has been studied as if it were Waterloo, or at least the Custer fight. They've measured it all with their calipers and are not happy to have an actual participant around to question the measurements.

For instance, there's the theory that Happy Jack Marco wasn't killed by the Texans at all—some believe Pleasant Burnell saw a chance to settle a score, and shot him in the back.

Now I dispute that. I know Pleasant Burnell wasn't really pleasant, and I doubt that he would scruple at back-shooting under normal circumstances, but when he dashed out of that cabin he knew he was outgunned twenty to one—it's unlikely he'd have chosen that unlucky moment to gun down one of his allies. If by some miracle he had managed to escape and still carried his grudge he could have shot down Happy Jack a little later on.

They quote me to that effect, but call me "unreliable." They don't believe me about Simp Dixon, either. The majority of the histories now claim he was shot within ten feet of the cabin. But there was still some light when Vivian and I came out, and neither of us saw the body. What probably happened was that he got wounded farther up the arroyo, tried to crawl back to the cabin, and died before he made it.

The one thing the authorities agree upon is that Hill Coe put up a splendid fight. When his corpse was displayed, alongside the others, in San Jon, New Mexico, two days later, a coroner counted eighteen bullet holes in it. I've seen the pictures, and it's plain to me that they tidied Hill up a bit. I observed, as I was driving the wagonful of corpses to San Jon, that Hill's right ear had been almost shot off, but somebody did a fine job of

221

sewing it back on, because it looks normal in the pictures.

No agreement will ever be reached as to how many Texans Hill killed before he fell. Some argue two, some argue six, and one radical fellow from Roswell argues none: he claims Billy Bone circled around and killed all seven of the Texans who fell, before he raced for the border: that theory is one reason you often see such a high count when people are reckoning up Billy's murders.

I tried to keep up with the literature and the theories for a while, but first it made me weary and then it made me sad: survival can be a rather deflating kind of thing.

They're all part of legend now, the sweethearts who died at Skunkwater Flats: they died and were raised to glory; I lived and became deflated and old. It's a melancholy thing because, hard though they were, I liked those gunmen who died in that windy gully. They only warred on one another, as near as I can see, and they brought some spirit to the ragged business of living, a spirit I confess I miss. Happy Jack Marco could tell a joke as brightly as any man I ever met; he had an uplifting laugh. Hill Coe rose from disgrace to die as gallantly as the hosts at the Alamo.

I guess I just don't care for the caliper approach. What matters it now if Simp Dixon died ten feet from the cabin, or a hundred? For they're all gone where Hickok is, and Custer, those sweethearts, and where Napoleon is and Hector and the other great fallen, and the soundest measurement in the world won't console me for their passing.

22.

I was sound asleep when I heard the splatter of bullets that killed Vivian Maldonado.

Shooting will bring you awake fast, but in this case it wasn't fast enough to allow me to say adieu to the brilliant pearl of Naples; he must have awakened full of vim and confidence because he simply jumped on the nearest horse and tried to run for it, with three or four Texans looking right at him. Perhaps Viv thought they'd be too surprised to shoot straight, but if so he miscalculated. Two or three of them shot sufficiently straight, and Vivian fell dead just across the campfire from Isinglass, who was sitting on his blanket drinking coffee at the time.

"Damn the man, why would he do that?" Isinglass asked. "Now we've lost our chance for entertainment."

He looked at me as if I alone could make sense of such an action.

"Perhaps he preferred the bullet to the noose," I said rather shakily—it's disturbing to see a comrade thud down dead before one is well awake.

"I had no mind to hang him for a while," Isinglass protested. "We could have strung up a trapeze in the big barn and let him put on shows. In his spare time he could have taught school. There's a terrible shortage of schoolteachers in this part of the country just now."

"I'm not sure he had the temperament," I said. Trying to conjure up an image of Vivian in the classroom was not easy.

"Well, he sure don't now," the old man said. Two of the Texans were even then dragging poor Vivian away.

"People from over in Europe have peculiar brains, don't you think?" Isinglass asked a little later. "Their brains just don't work practical, like American brains. My old partner, Lord Snow, seldom did the practical thing either."

"They've moved a bit past the practical in Europe," I said. "They've become civilized—some of them."

"Cecily says the same," Isinglass said. "Have you visited Europe?"

"Several times," I admitted.

"I've not had the advantage," Isinglass said. "I've been too busy buying up land."

I felt rather low. A small wagon stood nearby—the feet of two dead men stuck out of the end of it. I recognized the boots of Hill Coe and of the Tadpole, Henry Knogle. No doubt the others were a little farther forward. Billy Bone might be dead, and Joe Lovelady.

Still, I felt no particular fear for my life at that moment. Isinglass seemed to be enjoying our little conversation. Seeing that my hands were shaking, he even poured me a cup of the hot, bitter coffee.

"You should have slept closer to the fire," he said. "Maybe we can keep *you* for a schoolteacher. Had any experience in that line?"

Isinglass's sudden interest in procuring a pedagogue took one of the Texans aback. He was a short fellow with a drooping upper lip and a quarrelsome manner.

"Why, the man's a Yankee!" he declared. "He's a pal

of little Bill. It ain't safe to leave a man like him alive. He might escape and get the law on us if he's let to teach school."

Isinglass didn't welcome the interruption. He looked around at the man and his old eyes held a chill.

"When I require advice I'll write off for it," he said.

The quarrelsome Texan was too aroused to heed the warning in the old man's eyes.

"We kilt all the rest of them damn scoundrels," he argued. "I say kill this one too and leave no witnesses!"

"You can't even count," Isinglass informed him in a scornful tone. "That brash boy got away, and so did the cowboy who had sense enough to take his horse inside. I guess Mesty will catch the cowboy eventually, but it may take him a month. And who knows when we'll next hear from that boy?"

He stood up wearily, walked over to the Texan, and held out his hand.

"What do you want?" the Texan asked, surprised.

"Your rifle, I need it for a minute," Isinglass said.

The man handed over the Winchester, looking somewhat puzzled, and before he could move Isinglass clubbed him with it. He didn't seem to move fast or swing hard but the thud when the barrel hit the man's head is a sound I remember still.

"I despise loud talk this early," Isinglass said. "In fact, loud talk is never welcome, but I do expect to be spared it on a peaceful morning when the sun is barely up."

Another of the Texans knelt by the fallen man.

"My god, John's dead," he said. "He's not drawing his breath no more."

"Good," Isinglass said. "He's spoilt my morning once too often, and another benefit is this fellow here has a horse to sit on once we get around to hanging him."

"I thought you didn't want to hang him," the white-faced, puzzled Texan said. "That's just what Johnny wanted to do."

"Yes, but he was much too loud about it," Isinglass said. "I don't like to be told what to do with my prisoners by a man who can't even count."

"I guess I just lost the schoolteaching job," I said very quietly.

Isinglass smiled at me, whether in appreciation of the statement or the soft tones I don't know.

"As to that, I was merely thinking ahead to the time when we're civilized up, like the Europe folks," he said. "Right now there's no children to teach and no school to teach them in. But I've always been one to think ahead."

He sat back down by the fire and rummaged in his saddlebags. I thought he was probably looking for chewing tobacco, but to my astonishment he came out with a ragged and obviously much read copy of *Orson Oxx on the Pirate Isle; or, Captain Kidd's Defeat*.

"I have to do my reading in the morning," he said. "My eyes ain't good enough to read at night, unless I'm parked right under a lamp."

He must have noticed my astonishment at the sight of the book. The last thing I expected to see in the hands of the shifty old brute was one of my tales.

"Why, have you read it?" he asked. "It's a fine yarn."

"Mr. Isinglass, I wrote it," I said.

23.

My announcement startled the old man—a chill came into his eyes, just as it had a moment before he clubbed the Texan to death.

"You're nimble to make a claim like that," he said. "You're kind of a circus monkey yourself, I guess—and anxious to miss the hanging."

"It's true I'd rather not be hung," I admitted. "But it's also true that I wrote that book and the seventeen others in the same series. They're all listed on the back wrapper—if you'd like I'll recite them to you."

He turned the book over, keeping a skeptical eye on me. The one Texan who could read knelt behind him and looked over his shoulder. I recited the seventeen titles, beginning of course with *Orson Oxx, Man of Iron*. Then for good measure I recited the novel's stirring finale, a battle fought with rapiers on the yardarms high above Captain Kidd's burning ship, in which Orson Oxx runs the desperate pirate through the gullet before diving into shark-infested waters and swimming to Mobile,

Alabama. The Texans seemed to appreciate the recital a good deal; they ceased rattling their spurs or loading their guns, and when I went on to render word for word Orson's great battle with the giant crocodile he encountered in Mobile Bay, not a man moved until I finished describing how Orson whirled the giant reptile around his head and flung it to its death off a rocky cliff.

"Convinced?" I asked Isinglass when I stopped.

"Nope," the old man said, though I believe he had enjoyed the recital as much as the others.

"The name on the cover of that book is Benjamin J. Sippy," I said, pitching him my wallet. It had my name stamped on it in gold, and inside was my letter of credit and a little note I had been sent by the Chief of Police of Philadelphia telling me how much he had enjoyed my half-dimer *The Dying Policeman; or, the Strangler's Bet*. The chief even invited me to stop by the jail any time and said I could study the criminals to my heart's content.

All these, and a few other documents were studied in close detail by the criminals who held my life in their hands.

"Why, didn't you write *Sandycraw in Comanche Land*"? the one literate Texan asked. "I recall it was by the same fellow who wrote the Oxx stories."

"Yes, Sandycraw was my first creation," I said, and proceded to reel off the titles of the twenty-two Sandycraw adventures.

"Seventeen and twenty-two makes thirty-nine," Isinglass said. "That's a lot of books for one human being to write."

"Oh, that's not all," I said. "Those are just the series. I suppose I've written around sixty-five booklets in all."

"It's a hard thing to believe," Isinglass said. "There's a lot of words in this book. If you take these words and you multiply by sixty-five, which is the number of books you say you've written, it comes out to a terrible passel of words."

"Not as many words as you have acres," I pointed out. "My books are only about thirty thousand words long. Sixty-five of them would make about two million one hundred and fifty thousand words. If you have three million acres, then you own an acre for every word I've written, with about eight hundred and fifty thousand acres to spare. I'd have to write another several years to match you a word for an acre."

The old man seemed amused by my arithmetic.

"If I hang you today you'll never catch up, will you?" he said mischievously. I believed it pleased him to consider that he had accumulated more acres than I had written words.

"Not in this life," I said.

"No, and this rough old life is the only one we're sure of, ain't it?" he said, pitching my wallet back to me. Then he stuffed *Orson Oxx* back in his saddlebag and stood up.

"I best take you on home," he said. "Cecily might let me off for killing an acrobat, even if he was from Europe, but if she finds out I hung an author without even bringing him to tea there might be hell to pay. Cecily's an author too, you see. She writes books about the flowers out here on the prairie.

"Anyway, I'm out of good yarns myself," he added. "Can you still write them?"

"I suppose I can," I said. "I worked on one a bit just last week."

"Here's my offer," he said, picking up his saddle. "If you can write yarns that'll keep me awake long enough to digest my supper I'll contract not to stretch your neck."

"That's gracious of you," I said.

"No, it ain't, really," he said. "I've been bothered by severe indigestion lately. I've tried pills—now I'll try yarns. I hope they work."

"I hope so too," I said.

IV

Winds' Hill

1.

Isinglass insisted that I drive the wagonful of corpses from Skunkwater Flats to San Jon, a town he had established near the Texas line.

"You haul the bodies," he said. "That way you won't be tempted to do nothing impractical and spoil Cecily's tea."

The trip took a somber day and a half, the old man plodding ahead of me, sipping from his quart of whiskey, which he replenished about midafternoon from a barrel kept in the wagon.

The Texans, all trailing behind us, looked hopefully at the barrel, but were offered no whiskey.

"A man that allows his hired help to drink is looking for trouble and will soon find it," he remarked before plodding on across the grassland.

San Jon, when we finally reached it, consisted mostly of towering stacks of cedar posts and thousands of huge coils of wire—for it was Isinglass's aim to encircle the whole of the Whiskey Glass ranch with barbed wire, an aim defeated only by his own endless hunger for land. I recently saw an article in some Texas paper about old Leon, the Mexican leader of Isinglass's fencing crew, who spent his entire adult life in an attempt to complete the fence around the Whiskey Glass, toiling year after year on the long prairies with his mules, his men, his posthole diggers, and his wire, only to have Old Whiskey acquire, by purchase or fiat, another fifty square miles just as Leon thought his task was finally completed.

Except for the old man's fencing yard, San Jon consisted of only four buildings, but news of the battle at Skunkwater Flats had somehow spread and there was a crowd of some fifty people waiting to see the bodies of what was already being called the Greasy Corners Gang, although Barbecue Campbell and Henry Knogle had never even been to Greasy Corners, and the others had only stopped there for a few weeks because it seemed a convenient place to gamble and whore.

Soon the undertaker got started and a photographer was snapping away. I heard later that the undertaker had some trouble with Barbecue Campbell, rigor mortis having set in while the corpse was wedged sideways in the door of that hut; I believe they had to pile two anvils on him to get him straightened out, and even then it didn't really work. In all the pictures I've seen of the so-called Greasy Corners Gang, Barbecue looks as if he's about to pitch forward on his face.

"I wonder why people enjoy looking at dead bodies so much," Isinglass reflected. We simply left the bodies and continued on toward the headquarters of his ranch, still some sixty miles to the north. I was allowed to mount a horse for this part of the trip.

"I don't know that they enjoy it," I said, "but we'll all be dead someday. I suppose people have the notion that if they examine enough dead bodies they can figure out what death's like."

234

"There ought to be a way to beat it, that's what I think," Isinglass said.

Coming from such a monument to practicality, it was a surprising statement.

"If you mean death, I doubt there's a way to beat it," I said.

The old man looked distinctly gloomy. He had emptied the whiskey barrel in San Jon and was nearing the bottom of his last quart as we rode along.

"You'll do fine with Cecily," he said. "She's a damn pessimist too."

2.

"Do come in, Mr. Sippy—your room is upstairs, just to the left. Bertram will help you with your bath. Dinner is at seven-thirty; I do hope you'll dress. My father's clothes should *just* fit you."

Lady Cecily Snow spoke those surprising words to me as we entered the great hall of the huge granite pile, all turrets and towers, known as Winds' Hill. Lady Snow herself—her humor was in the main rather vinegary—scorned the name; she called the place Small Alp, in reference to the bare bump of earth thrust upward from the otherwise flat prairie on which the castle sat.

Isinglass clumped past her without a word, nor did she look at him. She was a beauty such as you'd expect to find in Scott or Bulwer: alabaster brow, dark ringlets in abundance, a complexion like rich cream, with a cinnamon freckle here and there, no doubt the work of the western sun. But Cecily Snow was in no one's pages; she stood in front of me in a hall as large as one you'd find at Blenheim, wearing a long white muslin frock. The fingers of the hand she offered me were long and thin.

"Ma'am, I'm too filthy," I said—it was no exaggeration, either; after all, I had just come from driving a wagonful of corpses.

But Lady Snow grasped my hand anyway, pressed it firmly, as we say in our books.

"Goodness, Mr. Sippy, I've seen dirt before," she said. "We're all very American here—no need for this formality.

"We're all regular cowboys," she added, though no one much less like a cowboy could be imagined. "How astonishing that you've come today, for I've just finished *Did She Sin?*."

Did She Sin?; or, The Desperate Game—it was another of my bitter domestic tales.

"Such a penetrating work," Cecily said. "I'm afraid I shall have to be rather cautious with you—it's plain you've a fine insight into the female heart."

Then I swear she blushed, still pressing my hand, before she turned and sailed off down that great hall with its stags' heads on the wall, its tiger skins on the floor, a warthog stuffed complete, and other trophies of empire and chase here and there. Why, there was even a hollowed-out elephant's foot for holding the guests' umbrellas, though I was the only guest and had no umbrella.

It was a moment I can never forget: standing filthy and covered with grit in that great hall, being told by a radiant young English beauty that I had a fine insight into the female heart.

The female heart? Benjamin J. Sippy? Did Benjamin J. Sippy know anything at all about the female heart? If so, which female heart? Did Dora have one?

Before I could assess these questions, an aged, leathery English manservant came out of a small closet where I suppose he must have been propped, mummy-like, for a decade or so. He began to inch his way up a long staircase.

It was hard to believe that a person so old could move, but I knew the man must be Bertram, and he was. It took him some twenty minutes to complete the ascension of the staircase, and another five or six to inch down the hall to my room, where, to my delight, a steaming bath was waiting.

For an hour I lay in it, soaking away the dust of New Mexico. From time to time a coolie almost as old as Bertram, who looked Egyptian, slipped in with fresh buckets of hot water.

Bertram, meanwhile, inched around the room performing an ancient ritual. He laid out Lord Snow's evening clothes.

The shoes gave Bertram a huge amount of trouble, I saw. He could scarcely bend to reach them, could scarcely lift them with the heavy shoe trees inside them; he finally did reach them, finally did lift them, but removing the shoe trees from the shoes seemed almost beyond his fading powers.

"Bertram, don't trouble yourself," I said. "I can easily do that."

"Well, I can't easily do it, sir," Bertram said. "But I *shall* do it. For if I don't, Lady Snow will sack me, and then where will I be?"

"I see your point," I conceded.

It was an easy point to grasp, for all around Winds' Hill—or Small Alp, if you will—for hundreds of miles lay the unbroken and, I had come to think, deadly, plain. It was a place where an English manservant who must have been in his nineties would be very unlikely to find a new situation.

"Thank you very much, Bertram," I said, having dried and dressed before he got the shoe trees out of the shoes.

"Not at all, sir," Bertram said, in a voice that seemed

to belong to the days of Prince Albert or some even earlier prince.

Then, at seven-thirty sharp, wearing the very well-made dress clothes of Lord Montstuart Snow, who had been dead for more than twenty years, I went down to dinner.

3.

Dinner was served by Mahmood, the old Egyptian coolie, in a great hall hung with smoky portraits of long-dead Montstuarts or lesser Cavendishes—for the first Lady Snow, Cecily's mother, was born a Cavendish, though, I believe, from one of the poorer tributaries of Cavendish blood.

We ate on a long cherrywood table from the time of Charles I: Isinglass at one end, Lady Snow at the other, myself more or less at midpoint between them. To my astonishment the first course was terrapin soup.

"Why, this is wonderful soup," I said, and I meant it. "But where did you get the terrapin?"

"From my father's aquarium," Cecily Snow said with a pleased smile. "It's quite a good one, though we've only a few terrapin left. I knew the dish must be a favorite of yours, since you mention it so often in your books."

"I mention it?" I said, as astonished by her statement as I had been by the soup. I had no memory of having

mentioned terrapin soup at all, in any of my writings—
though I supposed a chance reference might have crept
into one of the domestic tales.

But Cecily Snow was right. When later I had occasion
to check, I discovered that Orson Oxx had eaten terrapin
soup the very day he disposed of Captain Kidd, and that
Sandycraw, the Man of Grit, had even managed to par-
take of it while crossing the Tibetan plateau, on his way
to Lhasa.

Isinglass, though, was having no soup.

"I'll pass on the turtle squeezings," he said to Mahmood. "Just bring me my beefsteak and chili."

"You and I will be having mutton," Lady Snow informed me. "I'm sure you've had to saw your way
through enough tough beefsteak in your travels on
the prairies. Or 'chawed' your way, as they put it
here."

"Beefsteak and worse," I admitted. "Though Sister
Blandina did serve me some tasty mutton at her mission.
The Sister wouldn't agree with you, ma'am, on one sub-
ject, at least."

"Oh, what?" Cecily asked.

"That I understand the female heart," I said. "She
thinks I'm mainly off, in that department."

"Well, what would a nun know?" Cecily asked. "I
won't retreat, I'm afraid. I think you have a most uncommon understanding of the female heart."

"Not if he thinks females have hearts, he don't,"
Isinglass remarked.

"I have a heart, sir," Cecily said. "Surely you won't
be so bald as to deny me that."

"The she-bear has a heart, I reckon," Old Whiskey
said. "Comanche women have hearts, and what they do
to white men ain't much worse than what the ladies of
the world do, if you ask me."

"But there are no Comanche women now," Lady
Snow said evenly. "Nor Comanche men, either. You
killed them all. Do you regret it?"

241

Isinglass had his same quart jar of whiskey at the table. He took a long swallow before answering.

"I guess I did kill a lot of good Comanches," he said. "I kilt some decent Kiowa too, and all to make room for a lot of sorry white people who can't find their way from one water hole to the next. I suppose it was a poor job."

"That's a rather thin apology," Cecily said. "You eliminated an entire people—though I suppose you had help."

"Not much help," Isinglass said. He was mopping up the drippings of his beef with a hunk of bread. Besides the beefsteak he had consumed a huge bowl of fiery chili.

"Let's have the recital," he said. "This is about the time my indigestion hits."

"But there's dessert!" Lady Snow protested. "I know you won't eat it, but Mr. Sippy might enjoy some."

"No, I want the recital," Isinglass insisted. "I'm getting worried about Mesty. He ought to be back with that cowboy by now. If I worry too much, my indigestion is apt to flare up, and I might just hang this feller to settle my nerves."

"In that case we'll delay dessert," Cecily said, folding her napkin. "Shall we retire to the study?"

4.

We retired to the study and I read the first five chapters of my little novel *Black Beans*—it was all I had on hand except the rather scratchy beginnings of *Sister of the Sangre*. Isinglass put his feet on a huge leather footstool and sipped whiskey as I read, while Lady Snow merely folded her long hands and listened.

"How's your indigestion?" I inquired when I reached the end of chapter five—the straggling party of Texans, already lost on the llano, were just about to eat their last mule.

"It ain't showed up—I guess you've gained twenty-four hours," Isinglass said. He stood and started to trudge out of the room, then paused a moment at the door.

"It's just what I said tonight," he said. "Half the sorry white people who headed up that expedition couldn't find their way to the next water hole."

As we went back to have our dessert, a tasty pudding

made with wild plums, I saw the old man go out the front door.

"Where's he going?" I asked.

"He sleeps in the bunkhouse with the cowboys," Lady Snow said.

"But why?" I asked. We were at the foot of the great staircase; above us were rooms enough for a house party of sixty, at least.

"Surely in a house this size he could find a room to his liking," I ventured.

"Oh, the man is no fool," the lady said, taking my arm to lead me back to the dining room. "He knows he wouldn't survive a night in this house."

I thought it was a joke.

"But why, are the beds that hard?" I asked.

"As to that, you must judge for yourself—you'll soon be in one of them," Cecily said, amusement in her gray eyes.

"I don't quite understand, ma'am," I said. "Mr. Isinglass has survived the worst dangers of the West for eighty years. What could threaten him in a fine house such as this?"

"Me, merely me," the woman said, still with amusement, her hand still on my arm.

"Ma'am, I suppose my mind's going," I said, helping her into her seat at the long table. "I can't remember having mentioned terrapin soup in my books, and I'm afraid I can't grasp your meaning, either."

"It's really quite simple," Cecily Snow said in calm, unworried tones. "Mr. Isinglass robbed my father, destroyed my mother, exiled my brothers, and ruined me. If I catch him asleep I'll kill him. I do hope you like this pudding. I had to ride quite a way to find the plums."

244

5.

The stones of Winds' Hill were from Texas, but the shape and spirit of the great house were English: it was all turrets and towers, balconies, and bay windows; there were drafty halls where no one went, and half-rooms under the long stairwells for the servants, all of whom were as old as Bertram and the coolie. The kitchen would have provisioned an army; there was an Irish laundry, run by two old crones who spoke only Gaelic. The billiard tables were fine, but the majority of the cues had warped in the summer heat. The library held all the accepted authors in sets, row after row: the Greeks in Greek, the Romans in Latin, the French in French, and, of course, thousands and thousands of volumes of our good English authors, all in sound morocco with Lord Snow's arms on the covers. There was even a glassed-in arboretum with an artist's studio behind it; Cecily grew strawberries in the arboretum and used the studio to make the fine drawings of prairie grasses, weeds, and flowers for her botanical masterpiece, *The*

Flora of the Llano Estacado, not published until more than a decade after her disappearance.

I treasure her book now more than any other—certainly more than those trifles of my own. My eyesight's going, but by squinting through my specs I can still see how fine the drawings are—what a quality of attention, even passion, that gifted woman bestowed upon the sage and buffalo grass and even the rough prairie weeds.

Many a day now I do little more than turn the pages of Cecily's great book—it's become quite a collector's item, I understand. The drawings bring back to my mind's eye the woman herself: her clarity of eye, the graceful gesturings of her long hands when she talked, her low laugh and high understanding.

That night, standing on the balcony outside my bedroom, watching the white moon float above the prairies, I realized why Lord Snow had named the place Winds' Hill; in all my weeks in it there was scarcely an hour when the wind was not keening its disquieting symphony, using the eaves and the turrets and the very windows of the house as instruments. The symphony of the winds had several movements, many tones, many tempos, timbres loud and timbres soft; some days the wind sped down from Canada, gathering depth and tone as it screamed over the thousands of empty miles; other days it would turn and float softly up from the south, bringing the warmth of Mexico, of even a hint of salt from the distant Gulf.

But, constant as the wind was, it was no less constant than the war of wills between the old plainsman and the English lady beauty, a contest fully as intense and just as mortal as anything that occurred at Skunkwater Flats or Greasy Corners.

I was not sleepy that night, though you would think that with all my travels and my worries I would have sunk straight to bed—particularly since my bed was a commodious four-poster with the first really clean sheets I had encountered since leaving Philadelphia. One of the Irish crones had even turned them down.

But of course my worries were far from over. I knew nothing of what might have happened to Billy and Joe; both might already be dead, in which case my chances of leaving Winds' Hill alive were very slim, for it was plain the old man would hang me at his caprice, however lively the yarns I beguiled him with.

I am no chess player, but I came to realize that night that I had become a living pawn—though *whose* pawn had yet to be decided. That I was still alive was probably because Old Whiskey, on one side of the board, hoped to use me to capture the beautiful but elusive queen.

As to the queen's strategy, well, I had not long to wait to discover *that*. There was a little balcony off my bedroom—I stood on it for an hour, smoking one of Lord Snow's fine cigars and watching the moon light the grasslands. I sensed a presence behind me and turned to see Lady Snow, in a long gown, her hair flowing almost to her waist, standing by the commodious four-poster.

"Would you care to couple with me, Mr. Sippy?" she asked, as directly as could be.

"What?" I asked doltishly—of course I was very much taken by surprise. Sandycraw eating terrapin soup in Tibet could have seemed no more improbable than Cecily Snow's appearance, much less her words.

"I should like it so," she said, unembarrassed. She had brought her hairbrush and was still brushing her long hair.

I had supposed for some time that that had ended for me—the element of life that Cecily simply called coupling. I supposed I had lost it for good when I left Kate Molloy unkissed. During my weeks in the New Mexico Territory it had seemed far more likely that I would meet a noose or a bullet than a woman interested in carnal love.

247

But there one stood—not in Scott and not in Bulwer, either—in my bedroom, slowly brushing her hair.

"You see, the cowboys will no longer oblige me," she said. "They're afraid he'll kill them."

"Well, won't he kill me?" I asked, putting down the cigar.

"Of course, but he means to kill you anyway," Cecily said. "I doubt you've much to gain by restraint."

"Ma'am, *carpe diem,* then," I said, taking the hair-brush from her and putting it on the table by the commodious bed.

6.

The next morning not long after sunup I stood on my airy balcony and watched Cecily ride off on her bay thoroughbred to search for wildflowers, weeds, or obscure prairie grasses that she wished to paint. She was accompanied by seven greyhounds and numerous whippets, and she led a black donkey which carried her easel and various scientific supplies.

Isinglass and some twenty cowboys were mounted too, but they did not accompany Lady Snow. In fact, they left Winds' Hill in the opposite direction. Before they were out of sight, old Mahmood crept in with my breakfast—kidney, as I might have predicted, and some excellent scones.

Well, I didn't waste the day, I can tell you. I doubt that Scheherazade spent all day combing her hair, either. I ate my kidney and repaired to the study; the fact that I had a good pen and smooth English paper to write on, after weeks of making do with the poorest tablets, seemed to lend wings to my imagination. Before

Cecily Snow swept in many hours later, beautiful and dusty, to order tea, I had completed ten new chapters of *Black Beans;* my bedraggled Texans were than almost at the end of their harrowing march to the city of Mexico.

The conspicuous pile of pages seemed to amuse Cecily no end.

"Why, you're quite productive," she said,

"I'd like to get a day or two ahead," I explained. "There might come a morning when my brain doesn't function, and it doesn't seem wise to have nothing on hand to read. Mr. Isinglass's indigestion might flare up."

"It's very likely to flare up no matter what you read, Mr. Sippy," she said as she started up the stairs. "I'll explain once I've washed my face."

She soon reappeared, all fresh and lovely, just as the old coolie brought in the tea.

"Mahmood, explain to Mr. Sippy why the master has had so much trouble with his digestion lately," she said.

"Vineglass," the old Egyptian said, a twinkle suddenly lighting his eye. "I grind very fine, put in chili."

"Vineglass?" I asked, as the man tottered out.

"Wineglass, he means," Cecily said, buttering herself a bun. "Mahmood hates him, Bertram hates him, we all hate him. It gives us a great deal of pleasure to grind up the wineglasses and put them in his chili, but the fact is we're almost out of wineglasses, and except for mild dyspepsia, Mr. Isinglass is as fit as he ever was.

"I'd marry anyone who could kill him," she said, looking pointedly at me. Then she ate her buttered bun with relish.

I was still trying to picture the wineglasses—the two aged servants, or more probably four; I expect the crones got in on it too—and the beautiful young woman grinding one up each day. Did they have a special grindstone, such as the Indians use for grinding corn? Macabre though it was, I wanted to know the mechanics.

So I ignored the part about marrying and killing and asked for details.

"No, we use a chemist's pestle," Cecily said, spreading strawberry jam on a second bun. "It used to be such fun, but the results have been so disappointing that we've all grown rather tired of it—you could do the one for tonight, if you'd care to, Ben."

It was the first time coming West that anyone had called me by my given name.

7.

"My father was quite a good friend of Mr. Darwin's," Cecily told me a night or two later, sitting on my bed. "Mr. Darwin took a great interest in mollusks, as you probably know—barnacles particularly. But he was never quite satisfied with his work on their reproductive systems, which are rather complicated. He wanted my father to carry on with it, but my father liked mammals better. Mr. Darwin quite fancied me when I was a young child—he perceived that I had a brain—so he tried to get me to go on with the barnacles, and I *did* for a while, to please him. But it then turned out that I was far more gifted as a botanist. At first it seemed I was better at the botany than at the drawing, but now quite the reverse is the case. I'm a competent botanist, but it's the drawing I really care about."

Then she got off the bed and walked out on my balcony, readjusting her gown as she went. The wind was low, for once, the prairie almost silent. There was no light in the long bunkhouse where Isinglass and the cowboys slept.

"I expect he knows we're coupling," Cecily said. "He's a quick old brute."

At that point I had no idea what Isinglass knew, or what he thought. He tramped in each day at dusk, ate a beefsteak and a large bowl of chili with a powdered wineglass in it, washed that down with about a quart of whiskey, heard my colorful chapters, and tramped off without comment to bed. Or, if he did comment, it was only to make brief criticisms of my hero's ineptitudes.

Then, at dawn, he rode off with his cowboys as Cecily left with her greyhounds and her easel.

Once or twice, on days when I was several chapters ahead, I was invited to accompany Cecily on her botanical expeditions, but my total ignorance of botany, coupled with a feeble interest in weeds or grasses which she found passionately absorbing, soon proved an irritant to her.

"I supposed I hoped you weren't frivolous," she said tartly, as we were riding home the second day.

Her tartness had not diminished much when she came to my bed that night. Conscious of being somewhat in disfavor, I became rather nervous and faltered a bit at the outset; though the event was soon rescued, at least to some extent, Lady Snow was conspicuously bored.

"I call that meager coupling," she said. "Not only are you frivolous, you're quick."

"I warned you I was a faltering old party," I reminded her.

She usually left bed rather briskly, but this time, though somewhat disdainful and with a bit of a pout in her expression, she stayed, her long hair spread across my pillows.

"The old brute wants to breed me, you know," she said. "*Has* in fact, twice."

"Isinglass?" I asked, much surprised.

"I'm not a botanist for nothing, though," Cecily said. "I've sworn never to bear his child. There was an old Comanche woman here when we came. She showed me quite a useful plant. It's sick-making, but one loses the fetus very quickly.

"My father's great passion was genetics," she went on. "It's what brought him to Texas in the first place. He and the old brute thought they could breed buffalo with cattle—in fact old Willie is still doing it. They thought they'd produce the perfect animal for this new country. My father was a sound biologist in some ways, but he had no depth in genetics—there he was rather an amateur. My own studies with the mollusks went farther than his."

"So it didn't work out with the buffalo?" I asked.

"You can see for yourself," she said. "We've got a little museum of failures here—someday, if you have the curiosity, I'll take you. The only things not in it which ought to be are my half-brothers—the results of the old brute's efforts with my mother."

Then she laughed, a lilting laugh.

"The old brute is a worse geneticist than my father was," she said. "He supposed my mother would give him the perfect child, but he failed to consider that my mother had more than a dollop of rather weary Spanish blood. If my brothers had been born in Spain they would simply have been shut up in some dim room in the Escorial and never seen again, except by servants."

"Where are they?" I asked. No doubt there were plenty of dim rooms in Winds' Hill.

"Cabins here and there, in remote places," Cecily said. "Unless the poor goggle-eyed little creatures have died already, which would probably be a blessing."

"You're not much of a sentimentalist, are you, Cecily?" I said. She spoke with more feeling for the plants she studied than for her parents or her brothers.

"I ain't, for a fact," she said. "Am I to understand that to be a complaint?"

"Oh, I don't suppose it's a complaint," I said. "Merely an observation."

"Before I was ten I knew almost as much about the reproductive systems of mollusks as Mr. Darwin," she said. "My father bred everything from gamecocks to buffalo. He saw nothing wrong with my becoming a scientist, and he let me watch and learn. I suppose my studies have rather robbed me of sentiment where coupling is concerned. I'm more interested in energy than sentiment, if you please—though I do try to be cordial about things.

"Haven't you found me to be cordial, Ben?" she asked, a little later.

"Oh, quite cordial," I said—for even in her moments of disdain she had very winning eyes, and such beauty as to make you tolerant of the nettles in her words, even as you were being stung by them.

"You're an irritating Yankee," she said. "Are you going to be rude just because I don't pretend I've fallen in love with you?"

"Cecily, I just wish you'd stay the night," I said. "You never do. Don't be so heartless. I know I was rather nervous earlier but I suspect a nap would repair that."

She immediately got off the bed and took her hairbrush from my table, where she always put it.

"I certainly shan't stay the night," she said. "You're an anatomical moron if you think my heart is the organ you've been invited to apply your attentions to."

Fool that I am, I did like the way she put things—not another woman of my acquaintance could have put the matter so crisply, not even my crisp wife.

Cecily started for the door and then turned and gave me one of those perplexing smiles that haunt me still.

"Visit our aquarium, Ben," she said. "Consider the mollusks. See if you can tell the difference between the male and the female. You'll have to look closer than you've looked at me, I'll assure you."

"You come in the dark and you leave in the dark," I pointed out.

"My room is next to yours," she said. "I don't recall that you've made the slightest effort to detain me in the daytime."

"You seem so bent on study," I said, feeling doltish again. "But perhaps I will visit the aquarium. What if I do?"

Cecily smiled again.

"Oh, we'll have a little tutorial some evening," she said. "Perhaps you'll have to pass a little examination to see if you're capable of summoning the powers of observation that a prominent author ought to have."

"Now you're mocking me," I said.

"Lightly," she admitted. "You know, Ben, it isn't your pen that's been keeping you alive. It isn't all those pages you pile up every day. *I've* been keeping you alive. The old brute would dispose of you at once if I complained, and I'm very tempted to complain."

"Where's the aquarium?" I asked, amused by her threat—a novel one, in my experience.

"That's better, we'll go tomorrow," she said. "It can be our little outing."

She smiled again, and left.

8.

I had not been asleep an hour before I heard a terrible howling sound from Cecily's room. When I first awoke it was only an angry murmur, but before I could even swing my feet out of the bed it had risen to a bloodcurdling scream.

I leaped up and rushed to her door, regretting that I had no firearm. The screaming was terrible—I could only think of scalpings and savage torture. Perhaps a lone Comanche had found his way into the house and was scalping Cecily, as revenge for the war Isinglass had made on his people.

I rushed to the door, thinking it would be locked, but it wasn't, and before I could get my balance I had very nearly tumbled into Cecily Snow's bed. She was propped up on a pile of pillows, calmly reading a large book called *Plant Geography*. The howling came from one of her closets.

"Why, Ben," she said, amused. She marked her place in her book. "Perhaps I've done you an injustice. I confess I never expected you to show quite this degree of initiative."

"But who's screaming?" I asked, completely confused. My mind still held a picture of a Comanche with a bloodstained knife gloating over Cecily's rich tresses —yet there the woman sat, coolly pursuing her scholarship.

"Oh, that's only Van Leeuwenhoek, my little hyrax," she said. "He does scream quite remarkably, doesn't he? It means the nigger's coming. Van Leeuwenhoek hates the nigger."

She got out of bed and went to her closet, emerging a moment later with a small odd-looking furry creature not much bigger than a rabbit. It had ceased screaming, but continued to emit an angry murmur.

"Van Leeuwenhoek is from the Congo," she said. "He's a tree hyrax, nocturnal, but that's not the unusual thing about him. Observe his footpads."

She held the trembling little creature up so that I could see. His footpads *were* rather curious, though I found it hard to care. Many animals must have curious feet.

"What do you make of those footpads, Ben?" Cecily asked. "Now look closely. It's part of your examination."

"Cecily, I thought you were being scalped!" I said. "I don't care about the animal's footpads. I admit it's curious that he can scream like a woman who's being scalped."

"Mr. Balzac would care about his footpads," Cecily said, with some temper. "It's why you're only a dime novelist, Ben. You've no ability to look closely at anything."

"I thought you said I had an uncommon understanding of the female heart?" I said, rather stung.

"Pooh, that was only to irritate the old brute," she said. Then she thrust one of the little creature's feet practically into my eye.

"His footpads resemble an elephant's," she said.

"There's an elephant's foot standing in the great hall— do observe it the next time you pass by. In fact, Van Leeuwenhoek's closest relative is the elephant. I find that fact entrancing, don't you?"

She crawled back into her bed, cuddling the little furry creature against her bosom as if it had been her child. It hid its odd little face amid her tresses.

"Cecily, can't I stay the night?" I asked. "I'm a bit wrought up. I had it in my mind that you were being scalped."

"Oh, I don't know, Ben," she said. "My hyrax would be terribly jealous if you stayed the night. We've a sort of *tendresse*, you see, and you might spoil it."

"But it's just an animal!" I said, growing rather vexed.

"Yes, an animal," Cecily said. "And what are you, if not an animal? Mr. Darwin said the only animal most humans ever really notice is the one they see in the mirror, and it's a damning truth."

Before I could answer, the hyrax let out another of its terrible screams. It hopped around on the bed, scream- ing, and then clutched Cecily's neck as if it were her baby.

"The nigger's close," she said. "Van Leeuwenhoek always screams when the nigger's close."

I decided there was no point in arguing and started to leave the room, but before I could, Cecily turned back the covers a bit and patted the sheets with one hand.

"I don't like the nigger," she said. "I suppose I might be cordial, since this could be your last night. I expect the old brute will have him kill you in the morning."

The hyrax darted back into the closet, and I climbed wearily into her bed.

259

"Why, it's that aloof cowboy," Cecily Snow said the next morning.

I had been sleeping soundly despite the fact that she had predicted that this would be the day of my death. I was still a bit groggy with sleep when I stumbled out on the balcony to see what she was talking about. Joe Lovelady and Mesty-Woolah stood in front of the bunk-house, in conversation with Isinglass.

"That's Joe Lovelady," I said. "I didn't know you knew him."

Lady Snow looked at me with a touch of hauteur.

"He worked here once," she said. "I don't suppose I would want to know him, but I would have liked to couple with him a little. He refused me on the grounds that he was married, as if that had any bearing on the matter."

"Well, it would to some people," I said.

"Only to you dull Americans," Cecily said. "Is the man a friend of yours?"

"Why, yes, Joe's a friend," I said.

"I suppose the old brute plans to execute you together," Cecily said. She might have been saying he planned to buy us both a first-class ticket on a train.

Then, serene as a queen, she crossed the hall to her bath, leaving me to assess the situation as best I could. I looked again. The old man and Joe seemed to be having an amiable conversation from what I could see—very likely Cecily was exaggerating the menace to suit her own ends.

I dressed and hurried out.

The three men were moseying along together toward the cookshack where the cowhands took their meals. When I came out they stopped in front of what was called the chicken house—it was where Lord Snow had once kept his gamecocks. Cecily claimed he had once had some distinguished fighting fowl, but skunks and other predators had gradually reduced them until only one violent old rooster remained, an ill-tempered bird who flung himself at the netting of chicken wire if a person approached too closely to suit him.

Mesty-Woolah stopped when he saw me approaching. Isinglass and Joe Lovelady took another step or two, still chatting. From their manner you would have supposed they were just discussing the weather, or the price of beef on the hoof, or brands or calving or the roundup or some other easy staple of rangeland conversation—and for all I know, they were.

Joe Lovelady smiled when he looked up and saw me. I thought he looked weary and supposed he had ridden hard, though at that point I had no inkling how hard, much less how far.

I was about to offer him a warm greeting—I liked Joe immensely, and was eager to know where he had been for three weeks—when something happened that to this day I can neither forget nor clearly remember. It happened in a second, so fast that I wonder if even the retina of genius—of Mr. Dickens or Mr. Darwin—could have caught it; when I try to recover a memory of it now I only get confusing particles.

Mesty-Woolah moved; perhaps he whirled: I remember the briefest flash, though I saw no sword; in none of my memories of the three men walking that morning do I remember Mesty-Woolah having a sword—not, that is, until he had used it.

There was just the briefest movement, a swish of sound: Joe Lovelady was still smiling at me, but there was something wrong with his head. The smile seemed suddenly to be coming from above his right shoulder. Then his body tilted slightly, swayed a little, and toppled toward the chicken house. A great fan of blood spread across the chicken-house wall; my clearest memory is of that perfect fan of blood, and then Joe's head was rolling past Isinglass, who put out a foot and stopped it.

The old man looked at me, perplexed.

"The head jumps to the right," he said. "You'd think as clean as Mesty cuts, it would just stay on the neck until the body falls down dead. But it don't—it jumps to the right."

The sound of his words became faint, as if he had receded to the heavens. It seemed I was being swallowed by a pool of warm black ink. I sank into it calmly, hearing sounds like the voices of giant frogs, before the black sleep came.

10.

"It's foolish to try and tolerate a feller with that kind of ability if he's on the wrong side," Isinglass commented that evening at dinner.

I was still feeling rather peaked; the cowboys had revived me from my faint with a hatful of water from the horse trough, and I came to in time to hear Cecily Snow, mounted on her thoroughbred, castigate Isinglass for having allowed the African to besplotch her father's chicken house with Joe Lovelady's blood. "It will have to be repainted, and the sooner the better," she said before riding off.

The day had passed somehow; I hadn't fainted again, but I was still so weak I could scarcely lift my soup-spoon. Cecily, seeing the condition I was in, had nobly sacrificed another terrapin, but my mind was not on the soup.

"Joe Lovelady wasn't your enemy," I told the old man. "He always spoke of you with respect."

"Well, his mistake was to save that brash little Bill,"

Isinglass said. "If he'd let me have that boy he'd have been welcome to his head."

I believe he was saddened by the day's events, though —his bowl of chili remained as untouched as my soup.

"I'd have made that man my foreman," Old Whiskey said. "I offered him the job once. It ain't my fault he chose to save a killer. In fact, it's my regret. A cowhand like him don't come along but once in a lifetime."

"Couldn't we change the subject?" Cecily asked. "I found the man aloof to the point of rudeness, myself."

But neither Isinglass nor I wanted to change the subject: Joe Lovelady was who we wanted to talk about, and we talked on and on, not merely about his death but about the great ride that led to his death: for the cowboy and the African had raced one another halfway across the West—up the Pecos, across the Jicarilla country, around the great Shiprock butte, north of the Navaho canyon, south from the desert of monuments: days of hiding, nights of racing, until the cowhorse at last drew up lame and the camel was shot with Joe Lovelady's last bullet as the race finally ended, somewhere on the Mogollon Rim. Then the two men rode back on Navaho ponies, Mesty-Woolah's feet trailing the ground, both men too exhausted to fight or even talk.

We had no idea then, Isinglass and I, how far the two riders had gone; but we knew that it must have been far, and that a song would soon arise about it from the prairies and the rimrocks that both of us would hear for the rest of our lives.

"It was his bad luck that he drew Mesty," Isinglass said, "for Mesty was the one man in the West who could have kept up with him."

"You mean you couldn't have caught him yourself, Willie?" Cecily inquired in her tart tone.

"I'm shocked," she went on. "Around here we've all become accustomed to the notion that you can do anything you set your mind to. *Couldn't* you have caught that impertinent cowboy, really?"

"Nope," Isinglass said simply. "I couldn't have tracked him—I ain't got the eyesight no more. Besides, I don't own a horse that could have matched that sorrel of his. Now I don't own a camel that could match it, either."

"I won't miss the camel," Cecily said. "Nasty beast."

"I don't know but what that run finished Mesty," Isinglass said. "He looks finished to me. He's done nothing all day but sit on the porch singing those wild nigger songs that I ain't heard him sing in fifteen years.

"He's taken to the shade," he added somberly. "And Mesty was never one to seek shade."

"So you think he'll just die, the nigger?" Cecily asked coolly.

"He might just die," Isinglass said.

"Delightful prospect," Cecily said. "If he dies I'll plant a rose on that cowpoke's grave."

Both Isinglass and I looked at her with distaste but Cecily kept on eating.

A great thing had happened; also a tragic thing. Isinglass had ordered the tragedy, and yet he seemed as saddened by it as I was—perhaps more saddened, even. I believe he felt he had come to a moment of turning that day, and that the turn he made had not been upward. He ate only two bites of his beefsteak and never touched his chili.

"I don't know who I'll get to catch that killing little Bill if Mesty's done for," he said. "I guess I'll get Tully Roebuck."

"But Tully's a friend of Billy's," I reminded him.

"Well, I imagine the man needs money," he said. "That blind child will be a passel of expense."

"I think I'll sack this slattern of a cook," Cecily said. "She's overcooked the mutton again."

One hardly ever got to sleep much past dawn at Winds' Hill. Something unusual seemed always to be occurring, and whatever it was, it occurred early.

The next morning I was awakened by a sound I had not heard since Dora and I were in Cairo, after having done the Nile: the sound of a Mohammedan praying.

In this case, it was Mesty-Woolah, who slept in a room high up in one of the castle's several towers. He came out of the tower onto a tiny balcony and prayed in a loud voice, prostrating himself toward Mecca.

He could have sung the bass line in an opera—his deep voice carried far out over the prairies. The cowboys, most of whom had already sadddled up, stopped to listen. Isinglass was repairing a shoe on his old black nag's hind foot; he did not look up.

Cecily Snow walked into my room, already in her riding habit.

"Noisy nigger," she said. "Since you're up I thought

you might ride over with me and inspect the museum of failures. Allow yourself a little edification today, Ben."

"I feel like I belong in just such a museum," I said.

"I don't want any moping, let's go," Cecily said.

Riding north from the corrals, we happened to pass the narrow grave where Joe Lovelady's body had been put. It was the freshest of perhaps a dozen graves, the others belonging to Whiskey Glass cowboys who had fallen to the normal perils of range life: snakebite, gunshot, wild horse, high water, lightning, or stampede.

The previous day I had tried to help a little with the burying; I had felt mostly numb and dull. But as we rode by and I saw the poor grave, a flood of tears suddenly poured out of me. My bridle reins grew as slippery as if we were riding in a downpour.

Cecily, perched on her sidesaddle and surrounded by her dogs, found my display of grief rather trying.

"That man was exceedingly kind to me," I said when I had control of myself again.

"I'm sure," Cecily said. "Perhaps you'll live to immortalize him in one of your popular novelettes."

We rode north over the plain for several miles, coming finally to a large barn built down in a grassy arroyo. A portion of the arroyo had been fenced, and within the fence were some of the most discouraged-looking animals I had ever seen: they looked vaguely like cattle, and even more vaguely like buffalo; they were dull-colored, with spindly legs, swollen midsections, and heads no larger than a calf's. Most of them were dreadfully pigeon-toed and walked as if they might pitch over at any moment.

"These are our cattalo," Cecily said. "I'm only glad Mr. Darwin isn't here to see them. I'm afraid they represent rather a downward step on the ladder of evolution."

Inside the great airy barn, admirably lit by a number of ingenious skylights, other downward steps were preserved in huge glass vats of formaldehyde—embryos of such complex deformity it was hard to tell in some cases what species had been crossed.

On a platform at one end of the barn were fourteen stuffed ponies, each with a brass nameplate in front of it and a small saddle on it. All the ponies were black.

"The Cavendish ponies," Cecily informed me. "My mother was sentimental about her childhood and insisted on bringing them."

Except for the embryos and a few bins of miscellaneous skulls, the barn was rather a pleasant place, and the aquarium, which was the size of a small cottage, quite remarkable indeed; it had both fresh- and salt-water compartments and contained an octopus, many great goggle-eyed fish, turtles and terrapins in abundance, and hundreds of Cecily's beloved mollusks.

"Of course, it's a great expense, hauling salt water this far inland, but I do believe I'd go daft without my mollusks," Cecily said.

A little stone building behind the barn housed a well-equipped laboratory. Cecily put on a scientist's smock, pried a couple of barnacles loose from a rock in the aquarium, and proceeded to give me an extensive lecture on their reproductive systems, most of which passed well over my head. All I saw was a squirmy mass; but I was grateful that the fires of science had rendered Cecily a good deal less chilly.

In another mood I might have taken a keen interest in the museum of failures, but my mind kept slipping back to Joe Lovelady. There was so much I wanted to ask him, now that I couldn't. I couldn't fathom why he had returned so meekly to his death—unless his fatigue itself was so deep as to be a kind of death.

"Oh, we might as well go, you're very dull today, Ben," Cecily said. "I'll say one thing for old Willie, he's very rarely dull. *He* can look at an animal—they interest him as much as they interest me."

We were trotting back along the bed of a small creek,

on our way to Winds' Hill, when Cecily suddenly stopped her horse. She had spotted something in the dirt of the low creek bed.

"Fossils," she said. "That's why I always ride in the creek, if there is a creek. Once I finish with the flora, I intend to go into the matter of fossils a good deal more thoroughly than I have so far."

She dismounted and took a little pickax from her saddlebag; soon she was pecking at the bank of the little creek as happily as if she'd just found gold. My offer to help was crisply declined.

"Amateurs like you have ruined far too many fossil beds already."

I was feeling rather tired. I thought I'd just take a nap while Cecily was at her work, so I stretched out on the warm prairie, hat over my eyes, and fell asleep almost at once.

I don't know how long I slept—an hour, or perhaps two—but a puzzling strain of music brought me awake. It seemed to be harmonica music. Then the harmonica broke off and I heard Cecily's lilting laugh. I opened my eyes and felt at once that my time sense must have become confused, for I thought I saw Rosy, my long-lost mule, grazing near Cecily's thoroughbred.

Can't be, I concluded, about to go back to sleep. But then the harmonica started again; I blinked a few times and looked again at the horses, and it *was* Rosy. She still even wore my saddle.

I sprang up and looked down the creek bed, only to see a sight that quite stunned me. A familiar 10-gauge shotgun was propped against the creek bank, and Lady Snow, looking very fair and fetching indeed, was tootling on a harmonica, now and then stopping to laugh lightly as she cast her reckless glances at the outlaw boy, Billy Bone.

12.

"Hello, Sippy," Billy said. "Had your nap out?"

He looked as dirty and scrappy as ever, and his tone was a little cool. It was clear he would have been better pleased if I'd slept for a week while Cecily Snow gave him harmonica lessons.

The cool tone stung me a little, for I was as glad to see him as I had been to see Joe, but I soon saw it would be foolish to blame the boy. He had just been taken in hand by the most polished seductress in the West, and had already fallen in love. The appearance of an old fogey from Philadelphia could only detract from his bliss.

"Billy, it's wonderful to see you," I said, but he was looking with such awe at Cecily that I doubt he heard.

"It's such a splendid day, I thought we'd have a little music," Cecily said, and then she began to play that old, sad air "Barbara Allen."

The woman had gifts, one had to admit—she played "Barbara Allen" so sweetly that to my embarrassment I was soon in tears again. First I thought of Joe in his shallow grave, and then of Simp and Happy Jack and the other sweethearts, all dead; next, the memory of my nine daughters plucked hard at my heartstrings; then I thought of Kate Molloy, whom I had lost for no reason at all, and of hopes and yearnings without end. I cried so hard that I couldn't see, and came near to falling off the creek bank, blubbering shamelessly.

Billy was embarrassed by such a display, but once I got my sight back, I noticed that Cecily was merely looking at me over the harmonica out of cool gray eyes, pleased, I'm sure, that her music had had such an effect.

"Don't mind him, he's a Yankee," Billy said. I suppose he was afraid my blubbering would drive Cecily away—which only shows how little he knew about women, this one in particular.

"Oh, Billy, we've lost Joe," I mumbled finally. "It was a terrible, terrible thing."

"Did the nigger really cut his head off?" Billy asked.

I merely nodded.

"Well, that's the talk in San Jon, but I didn't know whether to credit it," Billy said.

"It's true," I said. "I was less than twenty feet away at the time, but I had no inkling it was about to happen."

"Dern it, I'll never know what was wrong with Joe to let it happen," Billy said with some annoyance.

"But he was unarmed, Billy," I said.

"Not when the race ended," Billy said. "That's not what the Indians say."

Of course, I didn't know then that many Navaho and even a few Apache had been spectators to the race.

"They went through the Indian lands," Billy said. "Some of the Indians followed them. They say at the end the tall nigger was too tired even to lift his big knife. Joe could have shot him easy, but he shot the camel instead, and then, instead of grabbing a horse from the Indians and running away, he borrowed two horses and rode back with the nigger. Now why would he do that?"

To me, it sounded as if Joe had saved Mesty-Woolah,

271

who then killed him. I didn't know what to make of it, nor did Billy, but we were soon set right by the crisp insight of Lady Snow.

"It takes a talent to kill," Cecily said. "That cowpoke didn't have it."

Billy looked at her as raptly as if she were the Oracle of Heaven, though she had only made a rather brutal point.

"That's right," Billy said. "Joe couldn't even shoot that nigger with the man standing there helpless."

"Do you think you'd make a better job of it, Billy?" Cecily asked.

I felt a little throb of annoyance that she already chose to use his first name. The ways of women never cease to startle, I guess. There Billy Bone sat: young, short, dirty, ugly, and violent—and American—a boy with no grace and no learning, and yet the tall, brilliant, beautiful daughter of the Cavendishes and the Montstuarts had chosen to make him her paramour—I could see that plainly.

I don't think Billy heard the question the first time. He was so entranced with Cecily Snow that if he could have forgotten to breathe I've no doubt he would have suffocated then and there.

"Do you think you could kill that nigger, Billy?" Cecily asked again, and this time Billy heard. Cecily had an avid gleam in her eye.

"Sure I can kill him," Billy said. "They say he sits around praying every morning when the sun comes up. If I'd known about that I could have killed him long ago. The thing to do is wait until the sun's right in his eyes and then shoot him while he's praying."

"Brilliant!" Cecily said. "It's the perfect plan. Shoot him tomorrow—oh, do!"

"Tomorrow—I sure will," Billy said, though I believe he was a little surprised by her eagerness.

"Do you have a good rifle?" Cecily asked.

"Uh, no," Billy said. He looked embarrassed at having overlooked such an elementary thing.

"I guess I'll just have to get close enough to shoot him with my shotgun," he said.

"I don't think much of that plan," Cecily said bluntly. "The nigger has an extraordinary nose. He might sniff you out. Mr. Isinglass claims he can tell just by smelling whether a gun is loaded or unloaded."

"But Isinglass says the man's finished," I said. "He says the chase wore him out. Why not just let him die? It'd be much safer."

"Nonsense, the nigger might recover," Cecily said emphatically. "We mustn't underestimate the nigger. It would be hard to get close enough to finish him with a shotgun—my greyhounds might raise a howl."

"I guess I can ride back to San Jon and buy a Winchester," Billy said. "If I leave now I might get back by morning, if Sippy's dern mule don't balk."

"Oh, no, I wouldn't hear of you going to that kind of trouble just to indulge me," Cecily said, knowing full well he would have walked to China to indulge her.

"I have an excellent rifle," Cecily said. "I often used it in Africa on some rather large antelope and found it quite reliable. I'm sure it would riddle that nigger."

"How'd I get it?" Billy asked.

"I'll bring it to you tonight—to this very spot," Cecily said. "That is, if you'd care to wait."

"I'll wait, you bet," Billy said.

"Come along, Mr. Sippy," she said, standing up. "It's almost teatime, we must get home."

Then, as if it were an afterthought, she handed Billy her harmonica.

"Keep it," she said. "Keep it, to remind you of me."

13.

"*Mister* Sippy?" I asked, as Cecily and I were riding back to Winds' Hill. I didn't wish her to think I was unaware of the little subtleties she practiced with given names.

She ignored me in her amiable, cool way.

"I did take some comfort from the fact that we were on a first-name basis, Cecily," I said. "Why must I be called *Mister* Sippy again?"

"Why, I've a new beau now, haven't you noticed?" she said with a smile. "You and I have to be a little more guarded in our intimacies. My new beau's talent for killing might get out of hand if he heard us billing and cooing, don't you suppose?"

"I have no intention of billing *or* cooing!" I informed her staunchly.

"Nevertheless, you shall when I require it, which will be very seldom if you keep on in that tone," she said before cantering ahead.

I became increasingly nervous as we approached the

castle. It was obvious that I was expected to be an accomplice to the murder of Mesty-Woolah. Of course, Mesty-Woolah was no angel—he had killed Joe Lovelady right before my eyes; probably there was no counting the innocents he had slaughtered at Isinglass's behest over the years. He was a professional warrior—it seemed rather finicky of me to scruple about such a man.

On the other hand, Joe Lovelady had apparently chosen to spare him, and Joe Lovelady had as fine a moral barometer as anyone. It's not likely he would have approved of having the man shot down while at his prayers. I didn't approve of it either, though neither Billy nor Cecily gave that aspect of the matter the slightest thought.

And yet, I couldn't speak to Isinglass or warn the man directly without endangering Billy—and despite his deadly ways I could not help but be fond of Billy, a boy with such lonely eyes.

I fretted all the way home, wondering what to do. As Cecily had frequently reminded me, Old Whiskey was no fool—he might ferret it out, and if there was blood spilled in the dawning it might be Billy's blood, or mine, or even Cecily's.

But you forget luck in such frets, I guess—and much turns on luck.

We had no sooner arrived home than it became apparent that Cecily and Billy had drawn the lucky card.

"Mr. Isinglass wished me to inform you that he has departed for the Quitaque," Bertram declaimed in his ancient voice when we arrived for tea.

"Oh, good, how delightful, where's the nigger, then?" Cecily asked at once.

"He's been left at home," Bertram said. "The master thought he needed a rest. I need one myself, but there's no rest in sight for the butler," he added.

"Oh, go sit in your closet, Bertram," Cecily said. "You *are* such a gloomy sort."

14.

"I don't understand why you women like outlaws so," I remarked during tea.

"Why aren't you eating your muffin?" Cecily asked. Her humor had improved considerably since discovering that Isinglass had left.

"It's not much of a muffin," I said, although I suppose there was nothing wrong with it.

"Well, you're not much of a writer," Cecily said merrily. "Judge not that ye be not judged."

"You ignored my question," I told her. "Why *do* women like outlaws so much?"

"Can't speak for my sex," Cecily said, her mouth full. She took my uneaten muffin and buttered it.

"Then why do *you* like them?" I persisted.

"Not boring, that's why," she said, pausing from her steady intake for a moment.

"Not boring like you," she amended.

"I didn't bore you at first, did I?" I asked.

"Only from the moment I laid eyes on you," Cecily

said, pouring herself more tea. "You *are* the most boring man I've ever met, Ben, except for my cousin Elphinstone. I will admit that my cousin Elphinstone runs you a close second."

At that point I abandoned the notion of talk and just sat there and watched her eat.

15.

That night, shortly after dinner, Cecily went for a moon-light ride, carrying with her the fine sporting rifle which she had used to such deadly effect on the antelope of Kenya.

I sat in the study until quite late, trying to read a Wilkie Collins novel—*Poor Miss Finch*, it was called. My efforts with it were completely unsuccessful; it may be a very fine novel indeed, but if so I can't say, for I could not manage to forget Cecily Snow long enough to raise an interest in Miss Finch, poor or otherwise.

When midnight came and Cecily hadn't returned, I went up to bed, feeling almost as old as Bertram. Where *was* Cecily? And *what* were they doing? Though I knew perfectly well that it would be a little short of insane to allow myself to care one way or the other what the woman did—she made Dora seem almost human—un-fortunately I *did* care. I tried to refuse to allow myself to, but it didn't work: my affections had slipped their brake.

It seemed a long night as I alternated between the Pillow of Jealousy and the Pillow of Guilt—the latter because I had not been able to summon up the moral courage to go tell Mesty-Woolah that perhaps he ought to skip his prayers, for once. I reminded myself over and over again that he was a deadly killer: I myself had seen him kill two men, one of them a friend—but that didn't soften the Pillow of Guilt.

Cecily Snow did not return that night. Once it was light enough to see, I got up and looked, and the corral where her thoroughbred was kept was empty.

Then I got back in bed—it was not yet sunup.

It occurred to me that perhaps the two of them had simply eloped: romance might have triumphed over murder.

That theory was soon disproved. The sun rose; Mesty-Woolah came out and sang a few syllables of his prayer, and two shots rang out from the vicinity of the barn.

That there were only two struck me as odd—Billy would never stop with two if he could shoot five or six times. But of course it was an English sporting weapon; it would only hold two shots.

After a time I got out of bed and went out on my balcony. I could see across the east wing of the house to Mesty-Woolah's prayer platform, on which he was stretched out face down, apparently dead.

Most of the cowboys had left with Isinglass; only three wranglers were there. Later, all three of them climbed up in the tower and confirmed that Mesty-Woolah was dead. Being lazy, they simply rolled his body off the porch and let it fall. Shortly after that, two of the wranglers fired several shots at one another in a dispute over who would dig the grave—of course, it would have to be a long grave, and none of them was eager to undertake it. Despite emptying at least two guns in the dispute, no one was hurt, and a skinny wrangler named Pedro spent the rest of the morning with shovel and pickax, digging the grave.

279

I was beginning to feel very depressed. Mahmood crept in with my breakfast. I dabbled at the porridge and left the rest. I could think of no reason to live, although I had no immediate or firms plans to die.

At eleven Bertram wobbled in, carrying a small silver tray as if it were an anvil. Though it was only a silver tray, it seemed almost more than he could manage— though in fairness I should admit that the note which lay on the tray was written on *very* heavy paper. Lady Snow skimped on nothing.

The note itself was characteristically crisp:

DEAR MR. SIPPY:

Do join Billy and me at the museum for a picnic lunch at one thirty P.M.

Cook will pack the hamper—remind her there *must* be horseradish! Please carry it carefully, the teapot is rather precious.

LADY (C.) SNOW

P.S. You might wish to bring your kit—you're leaving.

16.

My kit, as Cecily called it, consisted of nothing more than the clothes I had been wearing the day I arrived at Winds' Hill—now laundered and mended by the old Irish crones. I had been wearing Lord Snow's clothes during my stay, but before noon I surrendered these to Bertram, reminded cook about the horseradish, saw that the teapot was well padded, and set off, carrying the picnic.

Of course, I had to pass the graveyard where Pedro was still trying to excavate a grave long enough to hold the Negro of the Nile, who lay on the hot ground, dead and unturbaned, beside the fresh grave of Joe Lovelady.

I had never had a really good look at Mesty-Woolah— a look not clouded by fear, I suppose I mean—so I stopped and took one. His turban had been dislodged in the fall from the porch, and I saw that his hair was white. Dead, he looked like an old man—not so old as his master, Isinglass, but older, certainly, than myself. Perhaps that was why Joe hadn't killed him when the two of them finally stood exhausted on the Mogollon Rim. Perhaps he had seen that the man was old.

There were two bloodstains on Mesty-Woolah's tunic, near the heart. I knew the minute I saw them that Cecily Snow had killed the African warrior, as neatly as she had once killed the antelope of Kenya.

The historians and the legend-makers still dispute this point, imputing to Billy Bone powers of marksmanship that he never remotely possessed. It was more than one hundred yards from the corner of the barn where the shots were fired to Mesty-Woolah's tower—and Billy Bone in all his life never killed a man who stood more than twenty feet from him. Billy was a blaster, not a marksman. It may even be that he was myopic, though the truth of that will never be known. He seldom fired a rifle, and Cecily's gun was unfamiliar to him: I doubt he could have hit the tower itself twice in a row, much less Mesty-Woolah's heart.

"Just in time, we *are* famished!" Cecily said when I arrived with the picnic. The two of them were lounging in the shade of the big barn, Cecily looking lovely and frisky; she had grass stems in her hair, and was so impatient for the lunch that she ate half the cold mutton before Billy and I could even get a tablecloth spread.

"We're eloping, Mr. Sippy, ain't that grand news?" she said, in high good humor—she might have been a parlormaid announcing that she was running off with the scion of the Sackvilles or the Cecils.

To say that Billy was smitten is not to put the matter strongly enough: he looked at Cecily with wonder, as awed as a child might be on seeing the full moon for the first time.

"Leaving today?" I inquired. It would have been sensible. News travels fast on the prairies; it would not be long before Isinglass, in Texas, heard that Mesty-Woolah was dead.

"Goodness, not today—we needn't flee like servants,"

Cecily said. "Billy has a few chores to do, and I *would* just like to finish my work on the thistles and cockleburs —this *is* the perfect season to do them. I expect we'll set out on our travels in about a month."

"I hope it ain't longer," Billy said. "I'll barely be able to wait as it is."

Beside a blooming beauty such as Cecily Snow, any man is apt to seem a pallid organism, but few faded as completely as Billy seemed to as he sat with her that afternoon. He reminded me of one of the nearly transparent fish Cecily had shown me in her father's aquarium. An outline was visible, but the fish—as you ordinarily think of it, with guts and fins and scales— didn't seem to be there.

Neither did Billy, that day. He was the boy Cecily Snow had chosen to cast her womanly light on, and in this case the light was so strong that the boy all but disappeared. He said little and never took his eyes off Cecily unless she happened to throw him a direct glance—in which case he quickly found a stem of grass to look at.

Cecily's appetite was such that Billy and I were lucky to get a few bites of mutton and a biscuit apiece, and a few swallows of tea.

"I'll take that hamper back, you go with Billy—and if you don't look after him perfectly I shall be very vexed with you, Ben!" she said to me firmly after we'd packed up the scraps.

I had ridden out on an old plug one of the wranglers assigned me, but I noticed, when I arrived, that one of Isinglass's better cow horses was saddled and ready for Billy—his shotgun was in the saddle scabbard. They must have chosen the horse while the wranglers were in the tower inspecting Mesty-Woolah's body.

When it was time to go, Cecily stood not five feet from me and gave Billy a kiss as passionate as if he were a very Byron—it embarrassed him deeply and discomfited me—before mounting her thoroughbred. I, of course, was to be reunited with Rosy, whose behavior was as equivocal as ever.

"We'll meet here in one month, now don't forget me, Billy," Cecily said as she rode away.

"I won't forget you, Snow," Billy promised.

"Snow?" I asked, when the woman was out of hearing.

"She said to call her that—it's like a pet name," Billy said.

V

Let Me Fall

1.

We had scarcely ridden a mile before Billy Bone began to seem like himself again. Cecily's blushing light faded, and the boy who had seemed to be only a contour became solid again.

"Billy, are we going any place in particular?" I asked. We were riding northwest.

"Just to the north pole," he said, laughing his familiar childish laugh.

"Oh, is that all?" I said, going along with the joke.

"I'm going to kill Isinglass's whelps," he said a moment later. "Snow told me where to find them."

"Billy, they had nothing to do with Joe's death," I said, assuming—incorrectly—that he was determined to enact a terrible revenge for Joe Lovelady's murder.

He looked at me as if I had gone completely daft.

"Who said anything about Joe?" he asked.

"But if it's not revenge, why kill them?" I asked. "From what I hear, they lead miserable lives as it is."

287

"Then maybe they'll like dying," he said, turning a stony face to me.

I shut up, and we rode many miles without a word being exchanged. Of course, Billy always turned sulky at the merest hint that something as impractical as morality applied to anything he did or might do—particularly killing.

At that point, though, it was not the fact that he contemplated killing Isinglass's half-English children that shocked me most: it was the realization that he was not thinking of his dead friend. Revenge I can understand —it was the custom of the country, perhaps the custom of the race.

But Billy was shedding no tears for Joe Lovelady, perhaps the truest friend he ever had. The murders he contemplated sprang from quite a different motive, and I found out what that motive was that night, as we sat around a campfire eating the three or four biscuits Cecily had generously left us as provisions for our trip.

Billy could never hold any mood long—he seemed to be in the grip of one of his terrible headaches, and he just looked forlorn and depressed.

"I wish Snow could have come," he said. "A whole month is a long time. She might forget me completely in a whole month."

"Doubtful," I said. "If ever there was a woman of firm purpose, she's it."

"I got a headache," he admitted. "Do you have any more of those general pills?"

I did have a few, pilfered from the well-stocked medicine cabinet at Winds' Hill.

"It feels like a big hand is trying to squeeze my brains out through my ears," he said when I handed him the pills. "Do you think the Devil does it?"

"I don't believe in the Devil, Billy," I said.

"The Tulip does, though," he said.

"Oh, is the Tulip alive?" I asked.

"Sure she's alive," he said. "So's Dezzy. They're still in Greasy Corners."

"How's Katie Garza?" I asked.

"Fine as ever," he said quickly, in a tone meant to close comment on that subject.

"She's going to be a little jealous when you elope, I expect," I remarked, ignoring his tone. "If I were you I'd ride fast and I'd ride far."

Billy did not answer for several minutes. Then he said a curious thing—to this day I remember the sad look in his young eyes when he said it.

"I'm getting too big a reputation, Sippy," he said. "Sometimes I wish they'd just let me fall."

2.

A little later, when the pills worked and his headache subsided, his mood improved substantially and he revealed the true motive for our expedition.

"Snow says I've got to kill those little bug-eyed whelps now," he said.

"But why, Billy?" I asked. "They're her own half-brothers."

"She says they hate her because she's beautiful," he said. "She says when Old Whiskey dies they'll catch her and kill her."

"Oh, I doubt they'll catch Cecily," I said. "My opinion is she'll not likely be caught except when it pleases her to be."

"She said you'd be jealous," Billy remarked, with no rancor. "But there's a plot. That's why she killed the tall nigger. He was supposed to do it for them."

"Cecily's been reading too many penny dreadfuls," I remarked. "Anyway, Mesty-Woolah's dead and Cecily's quite safe. Who would dare try to kill her?"

290

"Tully or somebody," he said. "Some gunman."

"Billy, that's nonsense," I said. "Nobody's plotting to kill Lady Snow."

"If Snow said it, it's true, and you better not call her a liar just because you're jealous," he said. He looked at me coldly.

"Billy, would you kill *me?*" I asked. "Do you think it's just your right to kill anybody, even a friend? I am your friend, you know."

He looked at me again and finally managed a sheepish grin.

"I guess you are a friend," he said. "It's just that sometimes I wish you didn't talk so dern much."

3.

The next morning we crossed the North Canadian, at that season just a dry crack in the plains, with some muddy ground in the center of the crack.

"Isn't this another of those rivers you're not supposed to cross?" I asked, hoping to dissuade him from his mission.

Billy had risen in a sparkling mood. He spat defiantly into the mud.

"Yep, now I'll have to be careful that this nag don't fall on me," he said. "That's what the Tulip predicted."

It was a beautiful breezy morning, marred only by the behavior of Rosy, who kept reaching her head around to nip at my toes. One nip almost removed a couple of them, irritating me so that I whacked her several times with my saddlebag.

"You should have stolen a horse," Billy said. "Then you wouldn't have to put up with such an ugly mule."

"I don't think I want to give Mr. Isinglass any more excuses to hang me than he already has," I said.

"I hope we run into the old cud," Billy said. "He's another one Snow thinks ought to be killed."

"I'm sure she does think so," I said. "If you kill Isinglass and her half-brothers, she'll be about the richest woman in the world. The whole Whiskey Glass ranch will belong to her."

I just said it casually, not laboring the point. Of course it was obvious to me that that was why Cecily wanted the half-brothers eliminated. Bug-eyed or not, they were Isinglass's sons and would stand to inherit a portion of the ranch. And Isinglass was eighty-five. With him dead, and his boys, too, Cecily would be an heiress to rank with any Vanderbilt or Astor.

I didn't really expect Billy to flinch at that consideration, or even to recognize it, and of course he didn't.

"She already owns a bunch of houses over in England," he said. "I guess she's plenty rich already. She said she might take me to India and buy me an elephant. What do you think them shit-asses in Tularosa would think if I came riding in on an elephant?"

"I think a good many of them would leave town immediately," I said.

Billy's spirits continued to rise as we loped across the prairies; and as his rose, mine sank. I could not think of what to do—I didn't want to continue meekly along on a mission of death. Cecily had made her half-brothers sound like helpless morons. I didn't want Billy to shoot four morons.

For an hour or two I contemplated turning right the next time Billy turned left. Kansas was not so far away. I could probably strike a wagon trail and make it to some settlement before I starved.

But the hours passed and the miles slipped by, and still I rode along. The plain was immense and empty, and this time we had no Joe Lovelady to guide us. Billy was no plainsman, nor was I—there was a good chance we'd miss the boys entirely and end up in Denver or somewhere. Billy Bone was impatient, and not particularly firm of purpose—if we missed the cabins on the first pass, he might give up. Also, there was the possibility I could spot the cabins first and steer him around them. It seemed the likeliest way of thwarting the murders.

We camped that night on the Cimarron River, this time with no biscuits to eat. We had not seen so much as a rabbit all day—only a few hawks and buzzards, soaring high. Both of us were very hungry.

"Let's eat the rest of the pills," Billy said.

"I don't know if it's wise," I said. "Some of these pills have been in Cecily's father's medicine chest for over twenty years. They're pretty old pills."

"I'd rather eat an old pill than nothing," Billy said.

I gave him a handful and he munched them slowly, looking increasingly unhappy.

"It's times like this that I miss Joe," he said. "You're no better than I am at rustling grub, Sippy."

I decided to hold off on the pills myself, but after about an hour my resolve weakened and I poured myself a handful. For the second time on our travels together I joined Billy Bone in making a meal of pills.

4.

That night I heard a strange sound, persistent enough to wake me. I raised up on an elbow to see what it was. A heavy drizzle was falling. The campfire had begun to sputter, and Billy Bone sat beside it, sobbing like a beaten child.

"What is it, Billy?" I asked.

"I hate it when it rains," he said. "Next it'll start lightning and I'll see the Death Dog out there."

"This is just a sprinkle," I said. "It's not really a storm."

He looked at me miserably.

"Nobody likes a person like me, Sippy," he said. "I'm just alone. I was always alone. There ain't really no place for me. I wish they'd just let me fall. Joe fell, and I bet he's peaceful."

"Joe liked you," I reminded him. "Katie likes you. I like you."

"I think she liked Joe better," Billy said, after a minute.

"No, Katie loves you," I said. "I know she was fond of Joe, but she loves you."

"It don't matter, I'm still alone," Billy said hopelessly.

"What about Cecily Snow?" I asked. When Billy's spirits sank to a certain depth, one would say anything to try and elevate them even an inch.

"Oh, Snow's probably forgotten all about me by now," he said, moving closer to the fire.

He pulled out his pistol and handed it to me.

"Shoot at the Death Dog if you see him," he said. "You're a better pistol shot than me."

He pulled his shotgun out of its scabbard and cocked both barrels. Then he lay down and rolled up in his blanket, gripping the shotgun tightly.

"Billy, don't go to sleep with it cocked," I said. "You might jerk or something and shoot yourself."

He didn't answer.

I stayed awake as long as I could, hoping he would go soundly to sleep so I could lower the hammers on the shotgun.

But he didn't go to sleep. After a while he put the shotgun aside and began to blow into the harmonica Cecily had given him. He couldn't really make music, but he could make sounds, and he was still making them —soft, tentative sounds—when I went to sleep.

5.

The next morning mist and drizzle cloaked the great plain. Billy slept late, as usual, while I stared at the muddy trickle of water that constituted the Cimarron in late summer. I was wondering if there were any fish in it, and if so, whether I could catch any of them in the only net I had—my hat.

"All you'll get if you try it is a wet hat," Billy said when I informed him of my speculations. "I thought I heard sheep," he added.

"That was my belly growling," I said. I was feeling very hungry and gloomy.

"No, it was sheep," Billy said. "Build up the fire. I'm gonna go kill one."

He was gone all day, by the end of which I had burned every stick within a five-mile radius. I had also tried to catch a fish in my hat, and ended up with no fish and the wet hat Billy had predicted.

That night it occurred to me that Billy must have had an accident. Perhaps La Tulipe's prediction had come true—perhaps his horse had fallen on him. I felt nervous and guilty for letting a whole day pass without having considered that possibility. To the north, the Mesa de Maya was already growing dark and I knew there was little chance of finding him until morning.

I ate the last of the pills and spent the night belching and worrying.

The next morning I set out north over the great misty mesa, wondering how I would ever find Billy. At tracking I was hopeless—I might have tracked a streetcar, but anything else would have had an easy escape. If I could manage to ride in a straight line I knew I would eventually come to the Purgatory River, a stream in whose existence I only dimly believed—it sounded like Dante to me, although I confess I never got that far in the great man's book. If Billy was down, hurt, dead, it would only be by the purest chance that I found him. The clouds seemed to sink lower and lower; thanks to the mist I could scarcely see a quarter of a mile.

I squished all day across the Mesa de Maya, feeling quite hopeless, but calm and rather detached. From time to time I said a few words to Rosy, who was not exactly in a skipping mood herself. Some idiot had once told me that reciting several stanzas of poetry in times of distress would have a cheering effect. I decided to try that and found that my dull brain had sprung a leak, allowing all the reams of poetry once stored there to trickle out. I, who had faithfully read my Tennyson and my Browning, who once could recite stanza after stanza of *Lalla Rookh* or Mrs. Hemans, seemed to have retained only one stanza of poetry, and that from the melancholy ballad Cecily Snow had played for Billy:

> *I was taken sick, so very very sick,*
> *Death on my brow was dwelling,*
> *And none the better will I ever be*
> *Till I get Barbara Allen . . .*

It was hardly a stanza to cheer a starving traveler lost on the Mesa de Maya on a rainy day with only a rude mule for company.

The day seemed to last a week; I suppose I must have nodded in my saddle for a few minutes, when my wet nap was rudely interrupted by Rosy, who abruptly broke into a dead run, almost spilling me from the saddle. I lost my stirrups but managed to grab the saddle horn and hang on. We seemed to be racing through some ground-hugging clouds, which, once I got the sleep out of my eyes, proved to be nothing more than a herd of sheep. Then I heard a loud barking and discovered that the reason Rosy was running was because we were being chased by two dogs the size of buffalo yearlings. Indeed, they looked as shaggy as buffalo—Rosy was leaping over whole clusters of sheep in her efforts to escape them.

"Call off the hounds, it's Sippy," I heard Billy shout; then somebody yelled a command in Spanish which in the heat of the chase I didn't attempt to translate. Fortunately the command worked. The dogs immediately stopped chasing us. Rosy continued to run in circles for a few minutes, in a perfect panic—I don't think she realized the dogs had given up. The sheep did their best to get out of her way, and I did my best to stay on. When she finally exhausted herself we were on the banks of a foggy river. The drizzle had slackened during our chase; the mist lifted enough that I could spot a low cabin on the riverbank to the south.

I rode to it, keeping a tight rein on Rosy, who was well aware that the dogs were still in the vicinity. Even before I got to the cabin I smelled the mutton cooking, and my mouth began to water. Billy Bone stood in front of the cabin. Beside him, turning a lamb on a spit, was a tiny little old man in the cloak of an Andalusian peasant.

"I might have known it would take you all day to get here," Billy said.

6.

I was so hungry I ate practically the whole lamb, as old
Estevan—who *was* an Andalusian peasant—watched
me stoically. Billy Bone, who contented himself with a
rib or two of my lamb, had eaten a whole one himself
earlier in the day.

"Two dead lambs and two dead people in one day,"
Estevan said, in perfectly good English. "If you come to
visit very often, Señor Billy, there won't be no sheep
left, or no people either."

"You'll be left, Estevan," Billy said. "I ain't fool
enough to shoot a good cook."

Estevan had snow-white hair and very bright black
eyes. He was smaller than either of his dogs, two speci-
mens of a giant sheepherding breed unfamiliar to me.

"They come from over the mountains," Estevan said,
when I asked about the dogs. I suppose he meant the
Pyrenees. I was pretty sure they didn't grow dogs that
big over the Rockies, which were visible to the west
once the rain finally stopped.

Billy's relaxed manner, my hunger, and Estevän's ex-cellent lamb had distracted me for a while from the deadly nature of the mission Billy had undertaken.

"I don't see any dead people," I remarked.

"They're in the cabin," Billy said.

"They were my little ones," Estevän said. "When Señora Snow brought them to me they were no taller than my sheep. Even though they never spoke one word in their lives, I could understand them."

"What do you mean, never spoke a word?" I asked. Cecily had never told me they were mutes.

"No, señor," Estevän said. "They lived in silence, but they were good with the sheep. I don't know why Señor Billy shot them, but then I have lived all my life with these sheep. Many things puzzle me that people do."

I didn't ask for details, but later Estevän lit a candle and urged me to enter the cabin.

"Come, see my little ones," he said. "Maybe they are talking to the angels right now. Maybe they were only meant to speak in the great heaven."

The cabin contained three small bunks, two of which had bodies in them. The corpses wore the same rough cloaks that Estevän wore. He had put a kind of cheese-cloth over their faces, but pulled it back to show me the "little ones." Neither boy was as old as Billy; their chins were not distinguished and their eyes did bulge a bit, but they were not the horrors Cecily had described.

I put the cheesecloth back over their faces.

"How did he kill them?" I asked, wondering at the irony, for two sons of the West's greatest cattleman had died dressed as sheepherders in a lonely cabin on the Purgatory.

"Señor Bill?" Estevän said. "He just shot them at the campfire, when the dogs stopped barking. Nobody was asking him any questions. I thought he would shoot me, too, but he just killed my little ones."

"I think it was a mighty bad thing to do, Estevän," I said.

The old man looked sadly at the shrouded corpses of the boys for whom he had cared, for so long.

"I think so, too, señor," he said. "It seemed like a bad thing. I cried all day. But I guess someone will kill Señor Billy pretty soon too—he is not going to last long. And if my little ones are speaking their first words to the beautiful angels in heaven, it is not too sad. They never got to speak down here on earth."

7.

The next morning the sun shone bright and hot again. The only clouds in the whole sky hung over the tops of the mountains, far to the west.

Estéván was up before me, digging the graves.

"I didn't want to do the burying yesterday," he said. "I like a good warm day if I have to bury someone. This sunshine is good, and it's going to be warm in the earth after a while. The little ones will have a good dry grave."

Billy was in excellent spirits when he finally got up. He even helped with the grave-digging. A bad conscience would never be one of Billy's problems; I've often wondered how such a likable boy could be such a blank domino when it came to conscience. I've never come up with a respectable theory about it, though. In general Billy tended to do all his thinking when he was miserable, and then all this thinking centered on his own misery. He may have given some thought to Katie and Cecily occasionally; he may have spared a little for Joe Lovelady at some point; but Billy Bone didn't spend many hours of his life thinking about his fellow human beings. The notion that they had some sort of a right to life probably never entered his head, and might have struck him as comical if it had.

The long and short of it was, killing people just didn't bother him. It didn't excite him, as it does some killers, but I don't believe any of his killings caused him a moment's depression.

As soon as we had buried Esteván's little ones, and heaped the warm dirt over them, Billy saddled up and got ready for the long ride to the Rio Animas, where the two remaining children of Will Isinglass and the first Lady Snow lived with Esteván's brother. They too herded sheep, and they too were mutes.

"You better hurry and saddle your mule or you'll get left again, Sippy," Billy said. Esteván had quite a bit of jerked mutton hanging on a little line behind his cabin, and Billy was stuffing his saddlebag with it.

"I don't think I'll be going, Billy," I said.

He seemed startled, but after a moment went on packing his jerky.

"Well, this *is* a free country," he said. "What do you plan to do, help Esteván herd these dern woolly sheep?"

"I hope he does, Señor Billy, you killed my helpers," Esteván pointed out in a practical tone.

"I don't really have any plans," I said. "I just don't want to tag along while you do Cecily Snow's killing for her. All these boys do is herd sheep. How can they possibly be a threat to Cecily?"

"You don't know everything, Sippy, just because you're a Yankee," he said. He was really just brushing my question off.

"You don't even believe they're a threat yourself," I said.

He mounted his horse, still perfectly amiable.

"Dern, you'd argue with a stump, Sippy," he said.

"You know I ain't gonna change my mind now. I hardly ever change my mind."

"This time you should try it, Billy," I said. "Otherwise you'll be riding a long ride just to do a dirty deed."

He looked at me quizzically for a moment—the mention of a dirty deed at least seemed to give him pause.

"Billy, please don't do the dirty deed," I said.

But Billy Bone just grinned.

"Save one or two of those tasty lambs, in case I pass back through," he said before riding away to the west.

8.

"I've still got my mule," I told Estevàn. "Maybe I could beat him to the Rio Animas and warn your brother and the boys."

Estevàn looked skeptical—he was slipping rapidly into a mood of fatalism.

"You don't even have a gun, Señor Ben," he said. "I don't think you should go. Somebody else will shoot Señor Billy pretty soon. You don't need to take the trouble."

"But taking the trouble might save the other two boys," I pointed out.

Estevàn, though, had been carried away by his own vision of the poor mute boys babbling to one another in heaven.

"They all could speak together at last," he said. "It's good to think about."

I saddled up Rosy and left him to think about it, though it saddened me to leave the old man, smaller than his giant dogs and with no "little ones" to care for.

He offered to kill another lamb if I'd stay—he himself lived mostly on jerky—but I had some gallant notion of outflanking Billy at that point, and set out in a high lope for the west.

Much of my gallantry had rubbed off by the time I reached the town of Trinidad that evening. The discovery that there was actually a hotel there that provided hot baths took care of the rest of it. I stayed in the hotel more than a week, wrestling with my conscience between frequent soaks. I also recaptured a certain measure of literary inspiration and ripped off a double-dimer called *Mutes of the Mesa; or, The Sheepherder's Remorse*—easily the best thing I had written since *The Butler's Sorrow*.

In my strolls about the town I did make a few inquiries about the best route to the Rio Animas. Billy was an erratic traveler; I might waste a week and still beat him there, or so I told myself. But the mule skinners and tradesman I inquired of merely looked at me askance and drew a finger slowly across their foreheads—a gesture meant to indicate that I could expect to be scalped if I insisted on traveling in that direction.

"You might run into Bloody Feathers," one mule skinner said.

"I have run into him," I said. "He didn't seem so hostile."

"Well, his friends are rough," the man said, making it clear he considered my judgment to be amateurish.

I bought myself another full complement of weaponry —pistols, rifles, derringers—but the prospect of overtaking Billy seemed more and more fanciful, and eventually, sunk in moral paralysis, I abandoned the notion and fell in with a small wagon train to Sante Fe.

9.

At that point I never expected to see Billy Bone again—
it seemed likely that our destinies had diverged forever.
And yet, not a week later, I ran into him on the Rio de
las Vacas on the very day that he killed the Apache boy,
the most debated and inexplicable of all his murders.

The wagoneers I traveled south from Trinidad with
were a rough crew, prone to loud cursing and ear-biting,
eye-gouging fights while in their cups. By the time we
reached Taos Pueblo I had concluded that it was only a
matter of time before my own ears became eligible for
biting, or my eyes for gouging. I lingered in Taos for a
day, pretending illness but really only intending to let a
certain space grow between me and the wagon train; I
even contemplated a visit with Sister Blandina at the
Glorieta mission.

But before I could make up my mind, a young Indian
came in from the west who reported having seen a fabulous beast: a white mountain lion. The creature had
been sighted several times, north of Jemez Pueblo. This

excited so much talk that I thought I'd just drift over that way and have a look for myself. I had begun to consider leaving the West—a white mountain lion would be a remarkable thing to see before I did.

Of course, I should have known better than to credit such hunters' reports. When I reached Jemez Pueblo I found a village of singularly uncommunicative people. Only the old woman could speak any English, and she disclaimed all knowledge of any white mountain lion. There had once been an old white wolf in the vicinity, but that was years ago, she said.

I was greatly disappointed. A book had already begun to take shape in my mind which would involve Orson Oxx and Sitting Bull, both of whom would be in pursuit of the fabulous white cat. I could call it *The White Cougar; or, Death in the Rockies.*

But the people of Jemez Pueblo sullenly denied the existence of such a beast. Their skepticism caused my confidence to slip, but I set out up the Rio de las Vacas anyway, hoping to catch a glimpse of *something* white; even a wolf would do.

I rode north up the river for two days and saw nothing but a few brown deer, and one skinny antelope who seemed to be lost. No white mountain lion appeared. I knew I was getting closer and closer to the Jicarilla country; I knew too that I wasn't going to see any white mountain lion; but I couldn't make myself turn back. I wanted to will the fabulous white cat into existence even if I willed it into existence and it ate me.

At night, by the huge campfires I built, I saw the white lion in my dreams. But by day, as I wandered into increasingly barren, wind-eroded country, the thin buttes splotchy with black ore, I saw few beasts at all— though some of the wind-sculpted hills themselves were most exotic formations, follies cut by the unending wind, castellated and Gothic. Seeing their shapes in the long dusk was as spooky as anything in Beckford or Mrs. Radcliffe.

I woke on the third morning feeling sobered, even rational. The quest for the fabulous white lion suddenly seemed quixotic. Did I think I was the Ahab of dime novelists?

I knew perfectly well that I wasn't, though I still liked the notion of putting Sitting Bull in the same book with Orson Oxx. While waiting for the coffee to boil, I scratched a few notes to that effect, and, while scratching, heard someone playing the harmonica and playing it very badly.

Billy Bone trotted over a ridge. He had the grace to look abashed when he realized I had heard his awkward music. He stuffed the harmonica in his shirt pocket and loped right up to the campfire, evidently in a perfectly fine humor.

"Billy, you haven't seen any white mountain lions, have you?" I asked.

"Nary a one. I hope you'll share the coffee," Billy said.

Then, two hours later, only a few miles down the Rio de las Vacas, he shot and killed the young Apache boy.

10.

Cecily Snow knew horses. The gray she had selected for
Billy was a fine animal. His gait was quite a bit longer
and swifter than Rosy's, which is why I was fifty yards
or so behind when Billy shot the Apache boy.

I heard a shot but saw nothing when I looked up. I
assumed Billy had just shot at a snake or something,
though it was unusual that he had used his pistol—for
he would have been all day hitting a snake with his
pistol.

Still, one makes lucky shots. I saw him looking down
at something and still assumed it was a dead snake. A
large sprig of sage obscured whatever it was he had shot
at until I was almost on it: there lay the boy, who looked
to be ten at most. He was already dead.

"Oh, Billy!" I said, jumping down. In a moment I saw
quite well that there was nothing to be done.

Billy wore his stony look. For a second I thought he
might as well go on and kill me.

"He jumped out at me," he said. "Any Indian fighter

will tell you the kids and the women are the most dangerous."

"But he has no weapon," I said. I felt myself grow weak. I may have fainted on my feet for a few seconds. When I came to my senses, Billy had already ridden on. There was nothing he hated more than criticism of his killing.

Then I saw a little Apache girl standing silently on a ridge, perhaps fifty yards away. Not knowing what else to do, I picked up the dead boy and carried him toward her. The little girl vanished, but when I walked over the ridge I saw a small hogan another hundred yards or so west. I carried the dead boy to it, feeling that very shortly I would be dead myself. But there were only an old woman and two girls at the hut. The old woman began a high tragic wailing when I lay the little body down. The girls looked on, silent and tearless.

There was no sign of menfolks. The old woman knelt in front of the hogan, wailing, and the two silent girls looked on.

"I'm sorry for this, very sorry," I said, feeling so weak I could hardly stand. I stumbled back to Rosy and rode south as fast as I could. In about an hour I caught up with Billy, who seemed to be in no great hurry.

"I'd ride a little faster, if I were you," I said. "This is Bloody Feathers's country. When he finds out you shot that boy he may want to do worse than pick you up by the ear."

It startled Billy a little—he rarely dwelt on the past, but one thing he did remember was watching Bloody Feathers hold Vivian Maldonado up by his ear. He looked around as if expecting to see Bloody Feathers right behind us.

"Do you think he's around?" Billy asked.

"It's his country," I said. "Of course he's around, somewhere."

At least he had the sense to be scared. The cockiness immediately left his face.

312

"We better go find Tully," he said. "He's a good Indian fighter."

"Tully's in Lincoln," I said. "And Lincoln's a long way away."

"We won't get there talking," he said, spurring his long-gaited horse.

11.

There's a school of writers who now mainly want to whittle down the count of Billy's killings, and the Apache boy is the first one they try to drop off the list.

Why? Because it's the one that makes him look the most cold-blooded, of course. You could argue that he killed the four Isinglass mutes because Cecily Snow bewitched him—it's probably true. You could argue that some of his other victims were shot because he expected that sooner or later they would try to kill him: self-defense in advance is what that claim amounts to. Billy probably looked at it that way himself on the rare occasions when he gave his killings any thought at all.

But the Indian boy poses a hard problem for those who want to claim Billy as a misunderstood hero. None of the great heroes of old went around shooting unarmed ten-year-olds.

Some go as far as to deny that there ever was an Indian boy at all, which means attacking me, the only living eyewitness. So they do attack me, fiddling with maps and time schedules in order to prove that I couldn't possibly have seen what I claimed I saw. The radical fellow from Roswell won't even allow that I was *with* Billy on that part of the trip—he claims there are people who saw me in Taos that day; his theory is that I made up the story of the Indian boy because I was jealous of the fact that Tully Roebuck's little book about Billy sold more copies than mine, and this despite the fact that Bloody Feathers himself confirmed the killing in more than one interview.

Of course, Billy didn't help matters. He told three or four different stories about the Indian boy himself. Katie Garza said he told her that the Indian boy threw a knife at him, and that he ducked the knife and shot on the reflex; but while he was in jail in Lincoln he told Tully that he just shot to scare the boy, who happened to jump the wrong way at the wrong time and was unlucky enough to get killed. Then, just before he escaped, he told a newspaperman from Las Cruces that the Indian boy was an eighteen-year-old brave, fully armed—so that nonsense was soon in print.

I suppose they'll argue it forever—or until all the black dirt of life finally washes off Billy and leaves him a pure, clean legend.

As for me, I withdrew from the controversy long ago. I know the truth all too well, but I try not to think about it now because it makes me too sad. I'll never forget riding up to that sprig of sage and seeing a dead child lying beside it, shot down by someone hardly less a child, who would himself soon be dead. It floods my heart with sorrow to think of that day at all—of the dead child and the living, the silent girls, the poor hogan, the old woman wailing as the Trojan women wailed for the dead boys of Troy.

Billy and I spoke of the Apache boy only once, that same afternoon: we had stopped to water our horses in the Rio Salado. I was heavyhearted, and I suppose I looked it. He looked at me with a certain sympathy, though I know it seems odd to say it: shoot a mere boy in the morning and yet show sympathy for a tired old writer in the afternoon.

But life's that way.

"Don't look so blue, Sippy," he said. "They'll gun me down pretty soon, and then you'll be spared days like this."

"Billy, I don't want them to gun you down," I said. "I'd like to be spared *that,* if I'm spared anything."

"Know what I dreamed the other night?" he asked rather cheerfully.

"I couldn't guess."

"I dreamed I was dead and the Death Dog was licking my skull," he said. "I didn't have a body but I still had my eyes, and that old dog was licking my skull. I can't wait to tell that one to the Tulip. She'll enjoy that one."

"I bet she will," I said.

12.

We pressed on south as hard as we could, looking over our shoulders for Bloody Feathers every minute or so—both of us got cricks in our necks from looking back so often. I heard later that Bloody Feathers was far to the north, on an elk hunt, the day Billy killed the boy; but in our imagination he was right behind us.

Billy was firmly convinced that Tully Roebuck was the man most likely to save him from the Jicarilla chief. Apart from napping a little at night and resting the mounts when we had to, we raced on to Lincoln.

I know Billy was really scared, and I suppose I let that lull me into thinking he would take a conservative line with the public, at least for a week or two—in which way of thinking I could not have been more wrong. Before we had been in Lincoln for an hour he had shot down two perfect strangers, a banker and a cattleman, had been arrested by Tully and both his deputies, and was being held for the time being in a hardware store—

317

the howling mob in the street being so violent that there was no immediate way to get him safely to jail.

I didn't see the killings. I was in a saloon, refreshing myself with a glass of whiskey and a very tasty beefsteak; but when I heard the report of a 10-gauge shotgun I knew that my hopes for an armistice had been shattered.

Both Tully's deputies were in sight of Billy when the killings occurred, but one was helping an old lady into her buggy at the time and the other was sitting on the steps of the saloon where I was having my beefsteak, engaged in trying to pull a horseshoe nail out of his boot. Neither of them were any use at all as witnesses, so, as usual, there's a muddle of theories about what really happened. Some claim the banker and the cattleman were leaders of the Sante Fe ring, a group that held a lucrative contract to supply cattle to the Mescalero Apaches, and that Isinglass had actually hired Billy to assassinate them so he could get the contract. Of course that's rubbish, in my view.

The simpler theory is that the banker, whose nickname was Bucketmouth, spat a huge spew of tobacco juice, but aimed it poorly, so that a pint or so splattered on Billy's leg, whereupon Billy promptly turned his shotgun on the banker and his companion.

By then I was a little numb; it had become irrelevant why Billy killed people. The occasions which might prompt him to murder were so numerous that it wasn't useful to think about them.

"Why, that little varmint, he's killed Sam Bradley," the barkeep said, peeking cautiously out the door. "I think he got Bucketmouth too."

"I doubt he'll stop there," I said, and I did doubt it.

But Billy was at his cockiest just after he'd killed someone. He neglected to reload the shotgun, and before he knew it both deputies had piled on him. I looked out the door and saw Tully come running across the street.

"That little varmint picked a bad day to do this—I guess he don't keep up with the news," the barkeep said. His complexion was the color of a radish, leading me to believe he had been imbibing his own stock from time to time.

"What is the news?" I inquired. I saw that Tully and the two deputies had Billy handcuffed, but that a crowd was gathering surprisingly fast.

"The judge is coming this week," the man said. "They're going to try two train robbers and a Mexican horse thief on Thursday. They can stick the little varmint right in court and hang him with the rest of the rough old crew."

13.

It was evident to me from a cautious peek out the door that hardly anyone in the rapidly growing crowd was inclined to wait until Thursday to enjoy a hanging. Several cowboys who happened to be in town were soon dispossessed of their ropes, and loud demands were made of Tully Roebuck to yield up the prisoner. Two particularly inspired citizens borrowed axes from a Mexican woodcutter and began to whack at a nearby tree—I suppose they meant to use the trunk to batter in the door of the hardware store.

As the man who had ridden into town with Billy only that morning—a fact observed by quite a few of the rioters—my own position was far from secure. The crowd meant to hang *somebody,* and promptly; if Tully and the deputies stood firm, the men with the ropes might decide I was a less expensive alternative, in which case Orson Oxx and all my other heroes would very likely fling no more giant crocodiles off the cliffs of Mobile Bay.

Then into that maelstrom of incipient riot, Sister Blandina came riding on a poky little donkey. I rushed out of the saloon the minute I saw her, and all but embraced her on the street.

"Sister, I'm extremely glad to see you!" I said, though at that point I had no conviction she could really save Billy. I suppose I just hoped she could save me.

Sister Blandina did not seem particularly surprised to find a mob in the streets of Lincoln, waving lariat ropes and trying to cut down trees.

"Hello, Mr. Sippy," she said, stepping off her donkey. "What a ruckus you're having to put up with."

"Yes, and it may get worse," I said.

Sister Blandina looked angry. She was as light of foot as ever, and clearly not pleased by the spectacle of public disorder.

"I do think these weeks when the court's in session have a bad effect on people," she said. "Don't you agree, Mr. Sippy?"

"It's not having a good effect on *these* people," I agreed.

"Well, it never does, Ben—it never does," Sister Blandina said. "I'll be glad when we get some theaters here in the Territory. I believe if the citizens had more access to plays they might not carry on this way. But in far too many cases I guess courtroom theater is the only kind they ever see."

"This play may not even make it to the courtroom," I said.

"What happened?" she asked.

"Billy Bone shot two men—I don't know why," I said. "He's barricaded in the hardware store—Tully and the deputies have him safe for now."

"Why, they'll kick that hardware store to kindling in no time!" Sister Blandina said. "I'd better just help them get him to the jail."

She started across the street briskly, then turned to look at me.

"Did he just shoot them down?" she asked.

"More or less," I said. "I was inside eating and didn't see it. They may have offered him some insult, but it couldn't have amounted to much."

"Poor violent soul," she said. "Will you come with me, Ben?"

I was so scared I could barely scarcely put one foot in front of the other, but I came with her. She was so small no one noticed her at first, and she walked right into that crowd, brushing this sleeve and that; and, as they did notice her, the rioters jerked back, abashed. Several quickly removed their hats. I kept close at her elbow and we plowed through the crowd. Sister Blandina never slowed. She marched right through that crowd and rapped on the door of the hardware store. Tully Roebuck, who took such events as calmly as any man I've ever known except Joe Lovelady, opened the door and let us in.

"Sister, you're a welcome sight, and you too, Mr. Sippy," Tully said.

Billy and the two deputies were crouched behind a barricade of nail kegs. The deputies were too scared to speak, and Billy looked white and small, as young-looking, almost, as the Apache boy he had killed such a short time before. He managed a wan smile at the sight of Sister Blandina.

"Billy, I'm sorry for you, but I can't save you long," the Sister said. "Come along now, while I've got them embarrassed, and let me walk you to jail."

"I doubt you should trouble about me, Sister," Billy said. "I expect I deserve the worst."

"What you deserve is not for this mob to decide," Sister Blandina said. "Don't try my temper, Billy! Come."

She took one of Billy's arms; Tully took the other. The two deputies and I kept as close behind as we could, well aware that Sister Blandina's power of sanctuary might not extend to us.

322

Then we walked out into the blinding sun, and through that hoarse mob, which had grown suddenly dead silent. Sister Blandina looked at each man as she passed. For myself, I expected to be snatched at any second; I'm sure the trembling deputies expected the same.

But the power of the woman was enough; soon Billy was chained to a bench on the upper story of the old stone jail. Sister Blandina stood outside the bars looking at him sadly. Her victory, as she well knew, had been a very limited one; I believe the little nun was on the verge of tears.

"Sister, I'm sure glad I didn't try your temper," Billy said, attempting to joke.

"Where's the good in you, Billy?" Sister Blandina asked. "I seemed to see it once. I wish I could see it now."

Billy just shook his head. He didn't expect to answer the question, and in a moment, Sister Blandina turned, tears on her cheeks, and left.

14.

They say that when Custer fell that June morning, General Crook's Crow scouts knew of the defeat within an hour, though they were then in Wyoming, one hundred miles to the south. No one knows how they knew, unless there's some telegraphy of the wind that the native people hear.

The news of Billy Bone's arrest in Lincoln spread almost as fast—fast enough, at least, that by sunset of that day Katerina Garza and *los Guajolotes* were on their way north from San Isidro—I didn't know that at the time, but read it years later in a feature article about Katie written after she had blown up the banana boat—and, some claim, herself, too—in Nicaragua. The writer claimed that the gang arrived the next morning, and that one caballero snuck into town disguised as a woodchopper, prepared to give the alarm if any sudden attempt was made to hang Billy. At that point I believe Katie meant to charge the crowd at the head of her men and either rescue Billy or die in the attempt.

Nothing quite so dramatic occurred, of course. News came in the morning that the circuit judge had been delayed indefinitely; he had put on his pants with a red centipede in them and had almost died from the sting.

This put a heavy burden on Tully Roebuck, who had a full jail at the time and a bitterly disappointed crowd outside it, every member of which thirsted for a few quick hangings. Tully was so short-handed that he even deputized me, but all I did during my stint as a lawman was play dominoes with Billy, and that was no fun. Billy didn't like being chained to his bunk and was rude and quarrelsome to an unusual degree. He cheated flagrantly and asked me at least a hundred times to steal him a pistol.

Tully had left another deputy with me, a skinny fellow named Snookie Brown, and when Billy got tired of nagging me to find him a gun he set to work on Snookie.

"I'll take my chances with nothing but a derringer," he said several times. "Just slip me a derringer, Snook —I'll leave for Mexico and never be seen in Lincoln County again."

I think Snookie Brown rather liked Billy, but he was not about to be cajoled into arming him or otherwise assisting an escape.

"Can't help you today, Bill," Snookie said. He was laconic to a fault.

"Well, you would if you were my friend," Billy said. He had come out of his first depression and was very far from resigned to being hanged.

"Deputy Sippy's been your friend longer than I have," Snookie observed truthfully.

"He's a dern Yankee—they're too law-abiding," Billy remarked with a contemptuous glance at me.

"Now, Bill, Tully said not to let you charm me into supplying you no gun," Snookie said. "There's no harm in your trying to charm Tully, though—he'll be back directly."

Tully Roebuck did spend a good deal of time in the

cell, chatting with Billy and even taking a hand at dominoes once in a while. Little reference was made to the killing of Bucketmouth, the banker, and the cattleman, Sam Bradley. Few locals had liked either one of them, it appeared, and no one at the jail exhibited the slightest rancor at Billy for having gunned them down.

Indeed, after twenty-four hours of high tension, the mood in Lincoln relaxed to such a point that it was difficult to remember the fatal violence that had recently occurred.

Things became so relaxed that it was hard even to stay awake through the hot days. The morning Tully deputized me he warned me against even sticking my head outside the jail unless I wanted it shot off; but by the third day, most of the folks who had drifted into town hoping for cheap entertainment had been forced to go back to earning a living. The time soon came when I could have taken a nap in the middle of the street and been in no great danger.

The situation looked so placid that Tully decided he could afford to take off for a day or two. He ran some cattle up near Encinoso and wanted to go check on them.

"Heard the judge might have to have his leg sawn off yet," he informed Billy, Snookie, and me the morning he was ready to leave.

"I would rather take bitter poison than have a dern red centipede bite me," Snookie said. "I don't step into my britches without shaking them out good first."

Billy snorted with disgust at the report of this cautious behavior. "Dern, you're so careful I expect you'll live to be two hundred years old, Snookie," he said.

Then, the next morning, he killed Snookie Brown himself.

15.

Had it not been that I had developed a taste for chilies and eggs, I suppose it's possible that Billy would have shot me, too, that blazing morning. To this day I don't believe Billy would have killed me—but then I don't imagine Snookie thought he would kill him either, and Snookie was wrong.

The escape itself was a matter of near-perfect planning on the part of Katie Garza. Instead of leading a cavalry charge through town, she bided her time in the hills until she judged that the hanging frenzy had subsided and that the town of Lincoln had sunk back into its normal stultified state.

Then she slipped in herself, in the hour before dawn, and left a Colt wrapped in an old piece of sacking in the little outhouse behind the jail. When Billy was led down for his morning visit he found the gun, and as soon as he had his pants buckled again he stepped out and threw down on Snookie Brown, who misjudged his man and tried to run, rather than merely handing Billy the keys to the handcuffs and leg irons.

Of course, Billy shot him and took the keys, unburdened himself of the irons, and ran back into the jail to get his 10-gauge—he *did* like that shotgun.

I was across the street, downing my chilies and eggs; I heard the shot and then the thunder of hooves. By the time I got to the door, Katie and her caballeros were there; they had Billy's horse, and he was soon mounted. As he swung into the saddle, Billy saw me and waved.

"You better grab your mule and come with us, Sippy," he yelled. "When they find out I'm gone they'll hang you for spite."

Thing were happening very fast—just seeing the *Guajolotes* was a shock—but I knew that what Billy said was true, and I was not long in deciding to run.

It was then that the accident happened. Billy's horse —the one Cecily Snow had chosen for him from the Whiskey Glass *remuda*—suddenly reared and fell backward, all so quickly no one could move. The horse had been perfectly reliable until that moment. I was close enough to see the look of shock on Billy's face as he realized the horse was going over.

Billy almost jerked free—he twisted sideways and the horse didn't crush him in the crash itself, but Billy lay stunned for a second longer than the horse, and as the horse fought to scramble up it pawed Billy once or twice and rolled across Billy's right leg. The horse regained its feet and stood there calmly, but Billy Bone was not so lucky: he didn't move.

Katie Garza recovered quickest. She yelled at the *Guajolotes* and they hastily lifted Billy and put him in the saddle of her white mare. Katie got up behind him, supporting Billy with her arms, and prepared to ride.

"Bring Billy's horse!" she yelled at me as she turned the mare. "He might need it before we get to Mexico."

16.

Billy Bone's right leg was badly broken, and he had a deep gash across his back where the horse had pawed him. He recovered consciousness before we were a mile out of Lincoln, but soon fainted and proved too weak to ride by himself. Katie Garza held him in the saddle all afternoon.

One of the oldest of the caballeros knew something of bone-setting, and was able to set the leg when he stopped on the Pecos to water the horses. Billy yelled and screeched but didn't faint. When he recovered, Katie tried to persaude him to ride his own horse, but nothing she could say would induce him to mount it.

"No," he said, white-faced and grim. "That's the horse the Tulip was talking about. She said one would fall on me if I crossed the North Canadian, and one did. I'd rather be hung right here than risk him falling backwards on me again."

Katie made one of the caballeros switch mounts with Billy, and we were on our way.

329

"We need to hurry on over to Mexico," Katie said. "Tully and half the territory will be after you this time."

She didn't know, at that point, about the Apache boy, or about the four mutes, her own half-brothers. It was my view that Isinglass would soon be coming, and Bloody Feathers as well.

But Katie knew enough to hurry. A terrible sandstorm blew in as we were near the Hueco Mountains; the sand felt as sharp as particles of glass, but Katie would hear nothing of seeking shelter. She put one of her men on each side of Billy to hold him on his horse during his faint periods—and on into the sand and the wind and the bitter night we went.

Long before we reached San Isidro the next day, I was only semiconscious myself—not since my stage ride across some of the same harsh country had I felt such paralyzing fatigue. I didn't know we were descending into the Rio Grande until I felt the cold water rise above my thighs. I remember some confusion during the crossing—Billy fell off, but Katie somehow found him and towed him across the river, herself clinging with one hand to her horse's tail.

I was so tired when we arrived in the village that I collapsed on my saddle the minute I pulled it off Rosy —I just dragged the saddle to the nearest tree and stretched out with my head on it, not even bothering to untie my blanket, which in any case was wet.

I must have slept through much of the afternoon, and then a night; it was the tinkling of the bells on the village goats that woke me in the clear dawn.

To my surprise, Katie Garza was sitting beside me, fully dressed, a rifle in her lap. She looked worried and was sipping now and then from a brown bottle of tequila.

"I'm too old for this chasing around," I said. "No energy anymore."

"They don't care about you, Ben—you can nap for as long as you want to," Katie said. "It's Billy they want."

330

"We're in Mexico," I reminded her. "Tully can't come here."

"I'm not worried about Tully," she said, handing me the bottle.

The liquor was so strong I felt I had swallowed a flame. It did wake me, at least. Katie Garza kept looking toward the river.

"Billy's got a fever," she said. "He's babbling about all the people he's killed lately. Is any of it true?"

"Well, some of it, at least," I said.

"How many has he killed?" she asked bluntly.

"I'd have to clear my head in order to be sure," I said. "In the last few days I've lost count."

"Did he kill all the mutes?" she asked.

"I saw two of them dead," I said. "Then we parted company. I assume he killed the other two."

"He's talking about an Indian boy," Katie said. "Did he kill an Indian boy?"

I just nodded.

Katie sighed. "We better go south as soon as his fever breaks," she said. "Maybe we can hide in the mountains."

"Who do you think will come?" I asked.

"My father and my Apache brother," she said. "They won't be stopped by this little river. They don't care if they kill Billy in Mexico or Texas."

"It all seems so pointless," I said. "When I met Billy he had only killed one man, and that was mostly an accident. Now he shoots down half the people he meets. I wish he'd stayed with you the first time we came."

"I do, too, but it's just wishful thinking," she said, worry in her face. "I just hope he'll go south. I don't want to fight my pa and my brother, but I don't want them to kill Billy, either."

I accepted the bottle and took another sip of the flame.

17.

Billy's fever raged for two days. Katie attended him the whole time, keeping him wrapped up and getting enough water down him to keep him from becoming dehydrated.

The nervous caballeros were made to keep watch along the river, waiting for Isinglass or Bloody Feathers.

The third night the fever broke; the next day Billy was able to sit by a table in the sun, eat *pozole,* and sip a little beer. But his grip was so weak he had to hold his beer bottle with both hands. He looked small, pallid, and depressed; sitting with him, it was hard to believe such a pinched and weary boy had killed nine men in a little over a month.

"Read to me, Sippy," he said. "I got a headache—it might go away if I listen."

I didn't think *Mutes of the Mesa* would be quite the thing, so I read him *Sister of the Sangre,* and most of *Black Beans.* Generally after five or ten pages Billy's head would slump on the table—he'd be sound asleep.

Even when awake, he had little energy, little desire. His eyes were lifeless, and he met all Katie's entreaties about the south with a listless shake of his head.

"This is as much of Mexico as I ever intend to see," he said one day when she had pressed him.

"Okay, if you don't want to live," Katie said. "It just looks like you'd want to live."

Billy had no color in his face at all, not even when he sat in the sun several hours a day, and he had no force in his voice either.

"I should have listened to the Tulip in the first place," he said. "But I didn't, and now it don't matter. I can't uncross that dern deadly river."

"That's just an old drunk woman talking," Katie said. "What does she know?"

"She said a horse would fall on me, and one did," Billy replied.

"That horse was girthed too tight, that's the only reason it reared," Katie said. "Are you going to quit trying to live because a horse was saddled in too much of a hurry?"

"Talk all you want, I ain't going south," Billy said. "If your pa comes I'll kill him."

"What if the Indian comes?" Katie asked.

Billy smiled a weak smile. "Why, if the Indian comes, I expect he'll kill me," he said.

18.

The Indian didn't come, and neither did Isinglass. The mood in San Isidro slowly relaxed a little. Katie Garza devoted herself to trying to build Billy up, both in body and spirit. She fed him the tastiest food she could concoct and kept him out in the warm sun most of the day. An old wood-carver in the village made him a little crutch. He would hobble down to the river with Katie each day and they'd drink beer and shoot. I judge Billy's marksmanship never improved.

"I can't understand how a man who can't hit the side of a hill from fifty feet could get himself in so much trouble," Katie told him one day when we were enjoying a light lunch of tortillas and beans.

"I guess I need specs," Billy said. "My eyes start to water when I squint at a target too long."

The days were beautiful and clear. I resumed my morning walks by the placid river and scratched away in the afternoon on a little half-dimer called *Lynched in Lincoln; or, the One-Legged Judge.*

Katie and Billy spent the evenings in her room—occasionally, from my seat under the tree, I would hear him trying to toot on his harmonica. Sometimes I would hear Katie laugh—a sound with even a note of girlish joy in it, a sound such as one of my own happy daughters might make.

I hope it was joy: Katie Garza had a true heart, and I hope she and Billy sang a few more bars of the sweet melody of love in that time of waiting.

But it was a short time, and a sad time, a chill cast into its warmth by the fact of Billy's murders. Some days it would make me sad to see how hard Katie tried, for she threw all her young energy and great spirit into the effort to make Billy Bone want to live again, to get the spunk back into his grin and that old lively glint back into his eyes.

The truth is, Katie failed. Billy hobbled around, he shot his gun, he spluttered into his harmonica, and he lolled with Katie in their little bed in the room behind the cantina. Perhaps, in private moments that I didn't see, he was the old Billy for an hour, but even that I doubt.

Something had left him—call it hope or energy or confidence or what you will: one didn't need to name it in order to feel its absence. His laugh had no ring, his fun no strength and no surprise. Katie kept smiling, but it was clear her heart was heavy: she must have felt as if she were trying to stuff a ghost back into its body—she might get a leg in, or an arm in, but then the ghost of Billy would float away, secure in its absence.

The caballeros got tired of guarding the river. They went back to horse racing, gambling, fistfights, and tequila. A few left San Isidro to pursue light banditry on the stagecoach routes to the north; they came back not much richer, but with splendid new Yankee hats.

Often, at night, Katie would leave their room and come and sit with me under my tree. Sometimes I scribbled by lantern light—the long afternoon siestas

I had begun to take left me wakeful until midnight or after.

"I can't do nothing with him, Ben," she said one night, clearly miserable. She drank a whole bottle of tequila, but said no more the whole evening.

I was glad she had stopped calling me Mr. Sippy. I had fallen a little in love with Katie myself, though I don't believe she ever noticed.

Three days later, though his leg was far from healed, Billy Bone saddled up the cow horse that had fallen on him and prepared to ride away to keep his rendezvous with Cecily Snow, whose name had not been mentioned during our stay in San Isidro. Billy, I suppose, had only been counting days, waiting for the month to be up.

Few men have ever mastered the skill of leaving a woman. Billy Bone, who lacked all polish, did it very poorly. When I walked up, he and Katie were standing by the horse, and Billy looked every bit as nervous as he had the first time he left San Isidro.

I suppose, at bottom, he was as much afraid of women as the rest of us; certainly he didn't enjoy upsetting one, and that's an almost invariable consequence of the moment of leave-taking, if the woman's in love with you at all.

Katie Garza wasn't weeping and sobbing this time, though.

"This is the third time you've left me for no reason," she pointed out in a low, cold tone. They stood in front of the poor cantina. Billy, still quite crippled, struggled with the saddle, and then struggled to mount. Katie, three feet away, made no move to help him. Her eyes were dark black, and there was no smile of love on her face.

"You know you won't last a month across that river," she said. "You know that, don't you?"

Billy was pallid—his color had never really come back. I had learned to identify a certain pallor as his headache look. He didn't look either happy or well, but he was stubbornly going.

"Aw, Katie, I'll be fine," he said, avoiding her cold, steady eye.

"I'll look you up in a month," he added. "I'll be hunting someplace warm when the northers start."

Katie said nothing at all. She looked at him, silent as a stone.

Billy started to turn his horse but stopped. I suppose he felt too remiss.

"Thanks for saving me from that necktie party," he said. Then he looked at me.

"I wish you'd come with me, Sippy," he said.

"Why?" I asked. I was taken quite by surprise.

"Hell, I don't know why," he said with a trace of his old crooked grin. "I guess I've just got used to having an old Yankee writer along."

I think now he must just have been seized by a moment of fear.

"Go with him, Ben—he'll need someone along who can think," Katie said in a low tone.

Then, as Billy started again to turn his horse, she walked over and caught his bridle rein.

"If you betray me for a white woman, you won't be alive when the northers come," she said. "My pa won't have to kill you, or my brother, either. I'll find you and I'll kill you myself, no matter where you go."

She turned loose of the horse and started back to her room.

Billy Bone looked stunned. That Katie knew what he was about to do must have struck him as more incredible than any prophecy of La Tulipe's. He had not learned Lesson One about women—I tried to take him through it later in the day, but he was still too shocked to listen.

He could only sit on his horse and look at Katie, astonished and dismayed.

Katie kept walking toward her room. Then the sobs

337

rose in her—I saw them rising. She walked faster, then she ran. She disappeared into the darkness of the tiny room, one hand to her mouth to check her sobs; she never looked back at Billy.

I had little to pack except my scribblings. Rosy tried to bite me as I was saddling her, but I at least knew Lesson One about mules.

As we were about to cross the river, Billy stopped and looked at me angrily.

"Did you tell her about Snow?" he asked.

"Of course not," I said.

"I can't think who told her then," he said.

"Oh, I expect you told her," I said.

"I did not!" he replied, indignant that I would suggest it.

"Billy, you were out of your head and babbling for two days," I said. "You told her about killing the mutes —and the Indian boy. Maybe you mentioned Cecily Snow."

The indignation immediately left his face; he looked aghast at the thought that he might have mentioned his new love to his old. Many a more experienced man might have been given pause by such a realization.

"I wish I'd never come here!" he said.

"But if you hadn't, you'd have missed knowing Katie," I pointed out. "Not only did she save you—she loves you."

"I ain't worth loving!" he said, almost in tears. "Do you really think I talked about Snow when I was sick?"

"Billy, it doesn't matter," I said. "Women always figure these things out. Katie would have known about Cecily if you'd never said a word—and maybe you didn't say a word."

"But how do they do it, Sippy?" he asked.

"I don't know, but they do it," I said.

He sighed and nudged his horse into the Rio Grande. A few minutes later we were in the Texas desert once again.

338

VI

I looked to the East, I looked to the West;
I saw his Coffin coming. . . .

1.

By midafternoon another sandstorm began to beat at our backs. Glassy dust swirled around us, driven by a keening, howling wind. Soon the landscape we rode through, featureless enough at best, was hidden by surging billows of grit. Even the moutains that had loomed before us were soon obscured.

We made a cold camp that night. Neither of us was hungry, and we were both too tired to struggle around in the wind trying to find enough wood for a fire. I felt very low, and, from the few glimpses I had of Billy, he felt just as low. We turned our backs to the wind, wrapped in our blankets, and got what sleep we could.

At dawn the sand was still blowing fiercely. We rode silently, the wind at our backs all day—the sun was only a dim ring in the dust. I was not certain where we were, and I'm sure Billy had no idea himself, but before evening we struck a river that could only be the Pecos and followed it north. I was in such a melancholic state that it was almost a comfort to consider that we would probably starve before reaching any settlement; it would no doubt be painful, but at least Billy Bone could claim no more victims, and Cecily Snow would be denied her elopement with a famous outlaw.

Thwarting Cecily, if only in some small particular, seemed, in the mood I was in, reason enough to die of starvation on the banks of a forlorn river.

Billy Bone was bitterly depressed, too.

"I wish Katie had just shot me," he said at one point. "It would be easier than having your lungs sandpapered for two days."

But we stumbled on, through weather that turned day into dusk, expecting to have to endure another fireless, foodless night—then Rosy suddenly stuck her head up and brayed loudly, only to draw an answering bray from a donkey.

A minute or two later we spotted the donkey, and Billy recognized it.

"Dern, that's the Tulip's donkey," he said. "The one with the funny name."

Sure enough, it was Bonaparte; and the dim shapes, which we had been about to pass without interest, thinking them to be small sand dunes, turned out to be the hovels of Greasy Corners. Two horses were hitched outside the China Pond.

"Now this is luck!" Billy Bone said, his spirits immediately improved.

Mine remained rather at the low end of the thermometer, but I admit I was glad enough to follow him into the saloon, out of the sand.

2.

Nowadays you'll hear it said that certain things have a timeless quality—but it was more distinctly a *placeless* quality that struck me when we pushed into the China Pond. La Tulipe, the old yellow woman, sat on her stool, smoking her pipe; two dusty, drifting cowboys were bargaining with a sad young whore, while Des Montaignes stood behind the bar, chewing tobacco and spitting frequently. The place might have been a hut on the old Silk Road; it might have been in Persia, in Turkey, in Egypt, in old Babylon—any place where sands blow and caravans pass.

The sight of Billy Bone startled the cowboys greatly, though Des Montaignes and La Tulipe didn't bat an eye.

"Dern, it's you," the skinnier of the two cowboys said. He looked distinctly frightened, and I believe all thought of the dispirited whore was immediately driven from his mind. He and his companion both looked somewhat familiar; it turned out they had been in San

Jon the day Isinglass and I came in with the wagonload of bodies.

"Why wouldn't it be me?" Billy asked pleasantly.

I must say the skinny cowboy—his name was Dewey Sharp—proved forthright almost to a fault.

"Why, Bill, you've been here about a minute and you ain't shot us down," Dewey said with a likable grin. "From what I hear, a minute's about as long as anyone lasts in your company these days."

"Dewey, you know I wouldn't shoot you unless I really needed to," Billy said, grinning at him. "Who's your handsome friend?"

"Why, Waco Charlie, ain't you two met?" Dewey said.

"No, but I'm glad he's here—we'll make four at cards," Billy said.

"You was right, I shouldn't have crossed the North Canadian," he said to La Tulipe. "A dern horse nearly killed me."

"No horse is going to kill you," La Tulipe said. She seemed glad to see him, although her husband wasn't.

"You leave, I don't want you here, Beely!" Des Montaignes said with some vehemence. "You leave or Big Whiskey will come."

"I didn't know you were scared of that old cud, Dez," Billy said, leaning on the bar and staring at Des Montaignes from point-blank range. "A big whiskey is what I'd like to drink," he added.

Des Montaignes took a couple of dirty glasses from under the bar and poured us both drinks—Billy seldom drank much alcohol, but he gulped this down in a few hasty swallows. For all his boldness, he looked shaky and pale. His leg was a long way from healed, but he had already grown impatient with the crutch and hobbled around without it as much as he could. He didn't look like a formidable killer—but then, he never had.

He demanded another glass of whiskey from Des Montaignes and took it over to the table where the cowboys and the poor whore sat.

"What's the game?" he asked, sinking into a seat.

"Come with me, I have a good bed," the young whore said. She had stringy brown hair and broken teeth. I believe she had given up on Dewey Sharp and Waco Charlie.

"Dot's my name," she added.

Billy didn't know how to respond to her bold invitation. Despite his recent experiences, he remained painfully shy with women. "Ask Sippy, he's older than me, and richer, too," he said.

"You mean you really want to sit around and play cards in the trouble you're in?" Dewey Sharp asked.

"I ain't in trouble, Dewey," Billy said. "I just stopped through for a nap on my way to Chicago."

That was the first mention he had made of his place of elopement.

"They say Old Whiskey hired Long Dog Hawkins to kill you," Dewey said. "Besides that, Tully's vowed to bring you in, dead or alive."

Billy perked up at the mention of Long Dog Hawkins, a formidable assassin who had made his name killing settlers during the range wars in Wyoming. With the deaths of Hickok and Hill Coe, he was—except for Billy —the most feared killer in the West.

"Long Dog Hawkins!" he said. "Dern, I didn't know I was *that* dangerous."

"If I had more time I'd wait around and turn Long Dog into a dead dog," he said, and laughed his boyish laugh for the first time in weeks. Then he finished his second whiskey and demanded that Waco Charlie cut the cards.

3.

It was Des Montaignes who eventually went off with the whore named Dot. La Tulipe stirred up a bowl or two of prairie-dog stew, so greasy it would have been inedible if Billy and I hadn't been starving. Waco Charlie, who as almost as mute as the mutes of the Mesa, nonetheless proved to be by far the best cardplayer on hand; after an hour of play none of us had a handy cent left to wager, so I rolled up in a corner by La Tulipe's little stove. Billy Bone and Dewey Sharp were still exchanging gossip about Long Dog Hawkins, whose nickname derived from the long-barreled Colt he favored for his assassin work.

"It's good to be back in New Mexico," I heard Billy say before I fell asleep.

The next morning, when I wandered out to relieve myself, the wind had died, but some of yesterday's fine dust still hung in the air; the rising sun was coppery and muted.

To my surprise, Billy Bone had already saddled his horse.

"Hurry up, Sippy—today's the day we have to meet Snow," he said.

"Billy, she's eloping with you." I said. "She's not going to want me along. I think I better just stay here."

Billy looked completely surprised.

"Don't you want to go?" he asked. "Snow won't care, as long as you don't act too jealous."

"I think she might," I said. "I certainly wouldn't want to anger her, either."

Billy looked genuninely confused. I think he had taken it for granted that I would be part of his honeymoon entourage.

"But I've forgotten how to talk to her," he said. "What if she's changed her mind and don't want to go? Then what'll I do?"

"What any man has to do when a woman changes her mind," I said. "Either accept it or see if you can change it back."

Billy seemed almost panicked by the thought that I wouldn't be along to ease his way with Cecily.

"We're going to Chicago," he said. "She says we'll stay in grand hotels. Don't you even want to see Chicago and stay in them grand hotels?"

"I've been to Chicago several times," I said. "It's a fine city. The two of you will do nicely there without me."

Billy seemed stumped, but not angry. He struggled onto his horse and sat looking at me, a sad look on his bumpy young face.

"I sure never thought you'd end up in Greasy Corners, Sippy," he said. "Snow will get a laugh out of that. She thinks you're too fancy as it is, but this sure ain't as fancy a place as Chicago, from all I hear."

347

"No, it doesn't approach Chicago," I admitted, looking at the miserable hovels that made up the town.

"I guess I'll just tell her you were too jealous," he said. Then he turned and loped out of town.

Travel with Billy was interesting, but no one would claim it was relaxing. When he rode away that morning I discovered I was far too tired to contemplate immediate travel. I found a spade and spent an hour shoveling out one of the abandoned huts; I knocked down a wasp's nest or two and displaced a great many scorpions and spiders, but when I finished, the hut was a fair place to nap, and I napped—much of that day, as well as healthy portions of the next three.

I bathed frequently in the cool Pecos, and in the evening wandered over to the cantina to play cards with Dewey Sharp and Waco Charlie; the latter extended generous credit. Des Montaignes had fallen in love with Dot the whore, and the two seldom appeared, but La Tulipe dispensed his whiskey liberally and often took a hand at cards.

Dewey and Waco Charlie were experiencing a lull in their careers as cowboys. They had recently worked for Isinglass, but when he ordered them to move to one of his Texas divisions they concluded they didn't care to travel in that direction and had quit and drawn their pay, planning to go to California, where they heard there were fine opportunities for experienced hands. Then, upon reaching Greasy Corners, they had quickly succumbed to the idle life.

"It's a long way to California," Dewey observed one evening. "We may just wait till next year to try her."

Waco Charlie, once he got used to me, had become almost loquacious. "Might try her next year," he said.

The third day, two more disenchanted Whiskey Glass cowboys drifted into town. Isinglass had ordered them to help the fencing crew for a day or so; this affront to their positions as sovereign horsemen was too much, and they had decided to head for Powder River.

"Old Whiskey don't own that state yet," Grady Lee, the older of the two, said.

Apart from a few speculations about the topography of Wyoming, their talk was all of Billy Bone, the most hunted killer in the West. The three appeared shocked when informed that Billy had been in that very saloon only a few days previously.

"Well, he better skedaddle, that little varmint," Bob Blocker, the other cowboy, said. "Tully's getting up a posse, and Long Dog's around somewhere."

"If that's all, it won't be enough. Billy's swift and well armed," Dewey Sharp volunteered.

"But it ain't all, them's just the small fry," the cowboy said. "Bloody Feathers has vowed to kill him for murdering that little Indian, and Old Whiskey's thinking of going after him himself."

Waco Charlie turned white at the mention of Bloody Feathers—he was sensitive to the mention of blood, even in a name, it appeared.

"If Bloody Feathers was ever to get after me, I'd cut my own throat, just to save time and worry," Dewey Sharp said.

350

"I guess they'll catch little Bill somewhere then," Bob Blocker allowed.

"They'll catch him here," La Tulipe said. Then she went back to popping at her pipe.

The cowboys looked startled, and I was also a trifle surprised—I supposed Billy and Cecily were on their way to Chicago already.

"But he ain't here, is he?" Grady Lee asked, peering nervously into the corners of the bar.

"He's on his way back now," La Tulipe said, a gleam in her old eyes.

Dewey Sharp certainly didn't welcome that news.

"Dern, Powder River let her buck!" he said, coining a phrase that was to echo through the West for decades. "When do we start?"

"But why would little Bill be coming back here?" Bob Blocker asked La Tulipe.

"Because we've saved him a grave," the old woman said.

I supposed the Tulip was just having her little joke. Perhaps she was tired of the cowboys and wanted to scare them off. From every point of view it seemed unlikely that Billy would return to Greasy Corners—it was hardly the resort that would do for a honeymoon with a great English lady. The heiress to the Cavendishes and the Montstuarts would not be likely to flourish in the China Pond. Even Dot seemed a shade too fine for the China Pond.

In a way, I regretted it, too, for the fact was, I missed Billy. It seemed likely that my travels with him were ended, the book of our adventures closed. That night in my poor hut I did a little wistful dreaming: I imagined a better Billy, shed of all his violence, his habit of casual murder, his headaches, and his fear of the Death Dog.

Despite all that he had done, I guess I just liked Billy, and now that he was gone and it was unlikely I would ever have to watch him kill another man, my mind got

351

busy and created a happy little life for him. I couldn't quite get Cecily Snow into the picture, but I did give Billy my old skill, telegraphy. Before I went to sleep, I imagined him running a busy little telegraph office somewhere—in Illinois perhaps.

But the next morning the double blast of a 10-gauge shotgun woke me, and when I rushed outside I saw that the real Billy Bone had come back, as La Tulipe predicted; and not only that, he had promptly shot the liver out of her husband, Des Montaignes.

5.

Des Montaignes's error was simple. Unimpressed with lineage or much of anything else, the old mountain man had simply walked up to Cecily Snow and made a rude suggestion almost the minute he saw her.

He did have at least the discretion to make the suggestion in French—Cecily told me this later—but for all his traveling he had had too few opportunities to observe aristocratic behavior. Dewey Sharp, who saw it all, said Des Montaignes was quite taken aback when Cecily turned to her young killer and said, "Billy, this filthy old beast wants to couple with me."

Whereupon—according to Dewey—Billy turned red in the face, shoved his shotgun into Des Montaignes's stomach, and emptied the gun—emptied the stomach too, I suspect.

Billy was still shaking with anger when I got there— he was attempting to reload so he could blast Des Montaignes again, though the man was as dead as a rag. Both empties had stuck in the barrel, and Billy was too enraged to pop them out.

"Billy, he's as dead as he can possibly get," I pointed out.

Billy reluctantly gave up the effort to remove the swollen shells from the bloody shotgun.

"Well, I wish the stinking fool were still alive so I could kill him again," he said.

Cecily Snow dismounted from her thoroughbred, nodded coolly to me, and promptly engaged the four Whiskey Glass cowboys to help set up her tent—or, to be accurate, her father's tent; I noted a number of mentions of it when I finally read Lord Snow's engaging book, *Shooting in Simla,* some years later.

It was, of course, a magnificent tent. Billy and Cecily had ridden in accompanied by four pack mules, one of which carried only the tent; another was loaded with foodstuffs; a third with Cecily's clothes; and the last with her easel, paints, and botanical books. The eloping couple obviously did not intend to travel particularly fast.

"I'm surprised you didn't bring Mahmood," I said to Cecily when I saw the tent—it was the sort of tent that usually comes with a full complement of coolies.

"Couldn't—the old brute hung him. He finally figured out about the wineglasses," she said cheerfully.

La Tulipe hobbled out of the China Pond and muttered a few French I-told-you-sos over the carcass of her old mate; then she motioned for me to take a leg, she took the other, and the two of us dragged the man away with the same lack of ceremony that had characterized his own treatment of the suddenly dead. La Tulipe did indicate that she might offer the cowboys a few free drinks if they'd dig the grave.

I felt a little queasy and a good deal in need of a wash, so I headed for the Pecos. By the time I was clean, and reasonably settled in my stomach, the tent had been set up not far from the river, and Cecily had arranged her easel and was sketching a small yucca plant.

"I've never satisfied myself about these yucca, Ben," she said when I strolled up. "They *are* remarkably subtle."

"Where's Billy?" I asked.

"Oh, he's taken one of his headaches—I've made him go to sleep on a cot," Cecily said. "Imagine that squalid creature upsetting Billy like that. He's rather a delicate boy, really. Don't you agree?"

"Yes, his health varies," I said. "But that won't be the case much longer if the two of you plan to stay here."

"Oh?" Cecily said, with a hint of *froideur* in her voice. "I suppose you consider that you're the very one to stabilize him."

"Hardly," I replied. "What I meant was his health won't vary much once he's dead. And Billy will soon be dead if you stay here. Several of the most accomplished killers in the West are looking for him now, and two horses and four mules leave a rather obvious track."

"Phoo, I've mussed up this drawing hopelessly," Cecily said, ripping it off her easel. "It's your fault, Ben. Shall we take off our clothes and go swimming?"

"I just *was* swimming," I said, not sure that I'd heard her right.

"Not with me though," Cecily said. "I've indulged in quite a few fond memories of you recently, Ben. Except that you're quick when you're nervous, we enjoyed some tolerable coupling, didn't we?"

She was briskly folding her easel and putting away her paints.

"I'm such a poor artist when I'm feeling like coupling," she said. "What's the water like?"

"Very wet," I said. I had just begun to realize that the woman was perfectly serious.

"I'll just go back to the tent and get a blanket and something we can dry off with," she said, picking up her easel.

"Cecily, Billy just blew a man in two for suggesting what you're suggesting," I told her. "What do you think he'll do if he wakes from his nap and finds us? Besides, aren't you eloping with him?"

"Yes, but we aren't making much progress this afternoon. What's the harm in a little coupling?" she asked.

"Cecily, he'll kill us," I said.

"Quite incorrect, he'll only kill you," she said, with a look that I knew meant she was growing impatient. "I'll convince him you debauched me with some Yankee trick. But what a lot of fidgeting you're doing, Ben—I assure you he's quite sound asleep. And after all, coupling is greatly improved by a bit of danger."

"No, thanks, it's too big a bit, this time," I informed her. "Besides, you've been mighty rude to me, you know."

"I hope so. You're most unaccommodating; now I'll have to locate one of those hairy cowboys," she said hotly before picking up her easel and marching back to the tent.

6.

Cecily found no willing cowboy that day—in fact, she found no cowboy at all, for Dewey Sharp and Waco Charlie and the others were not foolish men. They put up Cecily's tent, dug Des Montaignes a hasty grave, and left. Dot, seeing that the prospects were bleak in Greasy Corners for the moment, asked the boys to take her with them, and they did.

When Billy came out of the tent about sundown, he was still pale and a little shaky, but the fact that much of the town's population had deserted didn't seem to surprise him.

"They don't want to be around when the bullets go to whistling, do they, Sippy?" he said to me, sitting in one of Lord Snow's camp chairs.

Cecily was inside dressing for dinner, which would consist of three cold guinea hens from Winds' Hill.

"Billy, if you know they're going to whistle, why stay?" I asked. "Sooner or later one could whistle right into you."

"I know, but Snow don't like to rush her travel," he said.

"I thought you were bound for Chicago," I reminded him. "Unless I'm very turned around, this isn't the way to Chicago."

"No, we're bound for Galveston now," Billy said. "There's weeds and things down that way that Snow wants to paint."

I was about to make one or two stern points, but before I could, Cecily Snow came out, as beautiful as Helen, and we ate the delicious guinea hens by candlelight under a high moon. I played the part of Mahmood —set up the table, smoothed the linen, carved the hens.

Nothing was said by anyone about the happy couple moving on, and afterward I took a plate to La Tulipe, who sat on her stool outside the deserted cantina, crooning a low song. When I offered her the food, La Tulipe just smiled.

7.

That night I slept poorly. In one of my wakeful moments I realized I had forgotten to inquire about Bertram, of whom I had grown rather fond. Had he been hung with Mahmood, or was he still propped in his closet at Winds' Hill?

When Cecily had loaned me one of her father's camp chairs, finally I got up and went outside and sat in it for the rest of the night, leaning back against the wall of my hut, watching the white moon and wondering when the killers would begin arriving.

I felt restless, uneasy, puzzled, leaning there against my hut; but then, in a flash, I grasped Cecily's reasoning —saw it with the unhappy clarity that comes a tic too late in a chess game, after the fatal move has been made: she wanted Billy to kill Isinglass. That was the reason for the tent and the lingering. In all likelihood Cecily didn't mean to go to Chicago, or Galveston either; if she had considered that she was departing Winds' Hill for good, four mules would not have been enough to carry her clothes.

Undoubtedly Isinglass had been gone on one of his restless tours when the elopement began—otherwise Cecily and Billy would not have had the leisure to pack the four mules.

Just as certainly, the old man would soon return and follow them—and he was known for his capacity to cover the miles. If Isinglass arrived first, and Billy did kill him, Cecily would be sole heir to the greatest ranch in the world; then no doubt Bloody Feathers or Tully Roebuck or Long Dog Hawkins would remove Billy, an unpredictable young killer who might at some point become an encumbrance to a great lady.

It was cynical reasoning, I know—perhaps I wronged Cecily Snow. She may have nursed a genuine fondness for the boy, as she did for her hyrax. But I couldn't rid myself of the feeling that the trap was closing on Billy Bone, and that Cecily Snow had baited it with scientific care.

Convincing Billy that he should be worried did not prove easy, though. The next day he was in perfect spirits—it was a day of fine clear sunlight, and we spent most of it lounging on the banks of the Pecos, watching Cecily work at her easel, a little distance away. She worked with severe concentration, only now and then pausing long enough to flash Billy one of her winning smiles.

"I never thought I'd be lucky enough to know no one like Snow—much less run off with her," Billy said. He responded to Cecily's smiles with a shy, boyish look.

"Billy, the trouble is you haven't really run off with her," I said. "You're only a day's ride from Winds' Hill. Do you think Isinglass will just sit down and let her go?"

"No, the old cud will be coming, I know that," Billy said. "I'll just have to kill him. Snow says he wants to marry her and make her have a baby."

"You might kill Isinglass, but what about the others?"
I asked.

Billy didn't answer—I don't think he really heard me.
He was lying flat on his back, looking up at the deep,
clear sky—not a worry in his head that one could detect.
He might have been a farm boy or a cowboy, resting
from some pastoral labor; and yet the flecks of Des Montaignes's blood still stuck to the barrel of his shotgun.

Twice more that day I tried to warn Billy, to make him
realize that killers as able as himself were on the move.
I didn't attempt to describe to him what I assumed was
Cecily's plan: to convince him that his grand elopement
had something to do with property. He wouldn't have
grasped it, and if he had, he wouldn't have believed me.
Every time I tried to suggest that he and Cecily ought to
be moving on, he just looked bored.

"Sippy, ain't you ever going home?" he asked in the
late afternoon as Cecily was folding her easel.

"I may, Billy—I don't know," I said.

I felt a drooping sadness at that moment, hard to explain. He merely wanted me to shut up; he could not be
made to consider the future at all.

Later I concluded that was one reason Billy killed so
easily, in such a conscienceless way: he apprehended
no future, neither his own nor his victims'. The present
swallowed Billy as the whale swallowed Jonah.

We dined outside Lord Snow's fine tent, this time on
some jugged hare Cecily's cook had packed. I doubt
Billy had ever tasted jugged hare before.

He seemed to find it exceptionally tasty. "Why, this is
a lot better than them jackrabbits Joe used to cook," he
said.

Cecily smiled at him indulgently before favoring me
with a cool, regal look.

"Our Philadelphia gentleman doesn't seem to think
so," she said. "Was yours not jugged to your taste, Ben?"

"It was fine," I said. "It's just that I've a poor appetite
when I'm nervous."

"Sippy doesn't like all this bloodshed—he just come out here to rob trains," Billy said, in my defense.

"Yes, I've noticed he's a fastidious man," Cecily said. "Not brute enough for these circumstances, I'm afraid."

"But I'm brute enough, ain't I?" Billy asked. The cutting way she spoke to me seemed to give him a moment of doubt.

"You certainly are," Cecily said. "I expect I'd have to roam this world far and wide to find a more perfect little brute than you, Bill. How glad I am you're mine."

I didn't say another word, but Billy Bone was still basking in the glow of that strange compliment when Cecily led him to the tent and drew the flaps.

8.

I was too nervous to sleep—too heavy with foreboding, too depressed. The Tulip sat on her stool outside the China Pond. Except for the lovers in the tent, she and I were the last citizens of Greasy Corners. When I walked up, she was tapping tobacco into her long pipe.

"I can't get Billy to examine the situation," I said, ignoring formality. "You talk to him. Persuade him to go."

La Tulipe seemed half asleep, even as her old fingers moved on the pipe. She didn't say a word.

"He's only a boy yet," I said. "He might change."

"Let the worms change him," La Tulipe said. "He killed my old man."

It surprised me—she had shown no trace of sentiment as we dragged Des Montaignes away. And yet she had followed the old trader across the West, from the Columbia River Gorge to the Rio Rojo. I had come to think of her as a kind of oracle, I suppose—I had forgotten that she, too, had a woman's heart.

"The Indian's coming tonight," she said. "Old Whiskey's coming too. They're all coming."

I went back to my chair, my forebodings in no way lightened. I wondered if I dared wake Billy and tell him what the Tulip had said.

In Bulwer such a night would be dark and gloomy; lightning would flash and the Death Dog might appear. But this night was as beautiful as any I spent on the plains. The moon was an ivory slice, the stars intense, the breeze soft. Once I heard Cecily sigh from within the tent.

At midnight Billy came out, his shirt hanging loose. He walked over near my hut to relieve himself, and saw me sitting there. I believe he even realized how tense I was—it may have been one of the few times Billy Bone really noticed me.

"Can't sleep?" he asked.

"No, I can't, Billy," I said. "I'm too worried—I think you're in a lot of danger."

For a moment he seemed concerned. "Dang, Sippy, you lead too hard a life," he said. "Maybe you oughta go home and just let the dang Territory take care of itself."

"I wish you'd run, Billy," I said. "I wish you'd catch a horse right now. Go east or north, and don't stop. I'm rich. I can wire you some money once you get to Kansas City or Fort Worth."

My plan seemed to amaze him.

"Why, I wouldn't leave Snow just to miss a few killers," he said. "I'm a first-rate killer myself—they'll just have to watch out."

He started to go back to the tent and then stopped.

"Have you got any of them general pills?" he asked.

"Yes, a few," I said. "Do you have a headache?"

"Oh, not me, I'm fine," Billy said. "I thought you ought to eat a few yourself. They might help you sleep."

Then he slipped back into Lord Snow's tent and left me to stare at the starlit plain.

9.

There's a popular book called *The Wind's Four Quarters,* written by a newspaperman who spends all his holidays researching Billy's life. He's made it his hobby to ride all the trails that led to Greasy Corners. Of course there's nothing left of the place now—even the last adobe wall has been broken up and the chunks sold for souvenirs, no different except in color from what they try to sell you in Greece or Rome, if you try to have a picnic on the Acropolis or in the Colosseum.

This newspaperman has written the longest book yet about what happened the next morning: he's taken Isinglass and Tully Roebuck, Katie and Bloody Feathers and the killer Long Dog Hawkins, and followed them practically from birth to their arrival at that clump of hovels on the Rio Pecos. He's mapped each arrival, marked where each one stood, developed very reasonable theories about how each meant to kill Billy that morning.

Of course, like all the rest, the historians and outlaw

collectors, he came up against the awkward fact that I was sitting there in Lord Snow's camp chair, not thirty feet from where Billy fell. He was polite, though—he came to see me and told me what happened that day, and when I demurred and explained how it really happened, he smiled and did his best to overlook my bad manners.

I don't guess I blame those people much—the scholars and the believers. Billy's death was simple, and yet even the simplest events grow mossy with the passage of years. If the students accepted the simple view of events in past times, how would their stiff brains ever get any exercise?

After Billy went in at midnight, I relaxed a little. His calm had an effect on me. Perhaps I was just doing too much speculating. Isinglass sometimes went as far afield as New Orleans—he might not return for weeks. Tully Roebuck hated to leave his blind daughter—perhaps he wasn't coming at all. The talk of Long Dog Hawkins could have been pure rumor—and no one knew for sure that the Indian boy Billy killed had even been one of Bloody Feathers's people.

Katie Garza I gave no thought to—of all of us, Katie loved Billy best; I assumed she was merely nursing her bruised heart in San Isidro.

Perhaps it was all worry for nothing; perhaps no one was coming. Billy and Cecily might have a slow trip to Galveston and sail away to live happily ever after in some great Cavendish pile in the gray North. Billy might dispense with his shabby saddle and learn to canter and jump in the English style—though I admit *that* was hard to imagine.

I suppose I dozed, as the night waned, but it was not a deep sleep, and the sound of a racing horse brought me wide awake. Billy Bone must have heard it too, for he hobbled out of the tent, grimacing at the soreness of his leg. He was using the stock of his shotgun as a crutch.

It was full dawn; I saw it all quite clearly. Billy's old shirt hung open, as it had during the night. We had not cleared the table after dinner—I was not as well trained a servant as Mahmood. The plates were still on the table, and Cecily had forgotten one of her fine ivory combs. Billy picked up a scrap—a bite of cheese, I think —and awaited the approaching rider with half-awake curiosity; he seemed anything but scared.

Then I saw the white mare come racing out of the long shadow to the south—Katie Garza almost ran past me before she checked her horse. The mare was flecked with sweat. I remember clearly how anxious Katie looked, as if fearful of having arrived too late. She had her gun in her hand.

"Oh, dern!" Billy said, with a horrified glance at Katie. "This is gonna give me a headache."

Katie swung off the mare, dropped the rein, and shot Billy before he could move. He didn't fall flat; he gripped the shotgun and slid into a seated position. Katie walked closer to him, her gun cocked; I saw her glance at the ivory comb on the camp table.

There was a spot of blood on Billy's breast—not much.

"I guess it's one cure for a headache," he said, still clinging to the shotgun.

Then, from the wind's four quarters, the losers in the race to kill him moved out of their hiding places. Isinglass stepped in view from behind the tent, Winchester in the crook of his arm. Tully Roebuck emerged from the China Pond, a pistol in each hand. Bloody Feathers stood atop the old, rotting pile of buffalo hides where Jim Saul and his crew had made their last stand. And a small weasel in a dark coat—it was Long Dog Hawkins—appeared practically at my elbow, carrying a huge Colt: he had been hiding behind my own hut.

"Now here, goddammit, it ain't fair!" Long Dog complained, addressing himself to Old Whiskey. "I've rode all the way from the Wind River and this Mexican whore has cheated me of my bounty."

Katie raised her gun and shot him, as coolly as she had broken the beer bottles that morning on the plain nearby. Long Dog fell backward, almost beside me, slumped down, and didn't move. The spot of blood, in his case, was in the middle of his forehead.

"Well, Long Dog's a dead dog, like I predicted," Billy said, and he too slumped flat. Tully Roebuck came walking over, his guns still cocked. Bloody Feathers jumped off the hides and joined his father.

Katie knelt down by Billy and shielded his eyes with her hat, for the sun had broken the horizon and was shooting its strong rays into his face.

I joined the group around the fallen boy.

"Hi, Tully," Billy said in a weaker tone.

He looked at Katie with a crook of a smile.

"You ought to let on that Tully got me," he said. "Tully's got politics to think of."

"Hurry up and die, *chapito*," Katie said softly. "I've ridden a long way and I need to water this horse."

The remark scored big with Billy Bone.

"That's spunk, ain't it, Sippy?" he said.

"That's spunk," I agreed, but before my words were out Billy Bone had obeyed her request.

Katie Garza laid her hat over Billy's face. Then she stood up, broke into sobs, and flung herself into her father's arms. Tully Roebuck—he really liked Billy—was crying too, and my own eyes were not dry.

Bloody Feathers had a long knife in his hand. While Katie sobbed on Isinglass's breast, he stepped over to the corpse of Long Dog Hawkins and took his scalp— the last scalp taken on the southern plains, some say.

"I promised old Grandmother a scalp for that boy she lost," he said. "I guess this dirty hank of hair will do as good as any."

"Brash boys always come to bad ends," Isinglass said, looking down at Billy.

Cecily Snow stepped out of the tent then, wearing a long white gown. She noticed her comb, picked it up, and fixed it in her tumbled tresses. Then she smiled at Isinglass. Though her scheme had failed—if it *was* her scheme—she showed no trace of disappointment.

"Well, Willie, you took your good time coming," she said. "I suppose it's no longer of much moment to you what sort of brute kidnaps me."

Then Cecily walked over and knelt by Billy. The harmonica she had given him was still in his shirt pocket; she lifted it out. Then she raised Katie's hat briefly, and placed it back over his eyes.

"Why, my little beast is dead," Cecily remarked, looking at me. "Things do catch up with one, don't they, Ben?"

I didn't answer—I was too shocked by the realization that the enmity she had always claimed she felt for Will Isinglass was clearly very much less than absolute.

Cecily raised the harmonica and began to play "Barbara Allen"—the air she had tried to teach Billy. Then a low voice began to sing to the tune—it was La Tulipe, standing by her donkey. Somewhere the old yellow woman had learned the English air. I broke down completely, as I had the first time Cecily played the song. It was such a sad thing to hear, on the cusp of the great American plain, with Billy Bone dead in the dust.

Katie Garza jerked away from her father, flinging Cecily a look of disgust. I expected Katie to shoot her, but instead she caught her tired mare and led her down to the Rio Pecos to water. Bloody Feathers wiped off his knife and followed her to the river.

10.

Isinglass whistled up some cowboys, who soon disman-
tled Lord Snow's tent and packed it back on the mule.
Then he and Cecily rode away, with no more said.

Bloody Feathers comforted Katie as best he could,
while Tully Roebuck and I dug Billy's grave on the
plain behind the China Pond. Since the earth that covered Des Montaignes was still loose, we decided to
economize, which meant uncovering him briefly so we
could tuck the small body of Long Dog Hawkins in with
him.

Billy, though, had his own private grave.

"Ever notice how all these famous gunmen are no
bigger than a pint?" Tully remarked as we worked. "Hill
Coe was small, too."

"I suppose presenting a small target helps one last, in
that profession," I said.

Katie cried and cried over Billy before she would let
us throw the dirt in.

"I didn't want nobody who didn't love him to kill

him," she said. "That's why I hurried. Billy was like me —he never had no place."

I thought, even allowing for her grief, that the remark was rather off. "Katie, this whole land is your place," I said.

She didn't answer. Her eyes were swollen. She cut one of the silver nuggets off her vest and laid it on Billy's breast.

"Heaven be your bed, *chapito*," she said. "*Soy el tuyo.*"

Then she got up and started back for Mexico, a woman with a sadly torn heart. Bloody Feathers rode with her out of town; when they left, La Tulipe left too, hobbling off with Bonaparte across the plain toward Colorado.

11.

Tully Roebuck rode back to Lincoln that afternoon, to his sheriffing and his blind daughter. I thought of going up to Winds' Hill and attempting to rid the earth of Cecily Snow, but of course I did no such thing. Instead, benumbed by life and death, I plodded over to the good hotel in Las Cruces and immediately penned the dime novel that I assumed would assure my glory and my income as well.

I called it *Billy the Kid; or, The Wandering Boy's Doom.* I expected high fame, but I suppose I was too quick off the mark, for the book sold poorly. The only thing that caught on was the nickname: now that Billy's risen in legend, the white star of the West, talk of Billy the Kid is all you hear—it's the one phrase I contributed to the language, of all the millions I wrote, though the book it introduced is forgotten, and was never believed.

The irony is that Tully Roebuck's silly memoir, written two years after my novel, caught the public fancy. It had been a terrible winter, Tully lost all his cattle and no doubt needed money, so he sat down with one of the Buntline secretaries and wrote *The True Authentic Adventures of the Notorious Billy the Kid.* It had the kind of lurid cover they used to put on my Orson Oxx tales, and it sold a million. Tully got so rich he began to buy racehorses, but he had only a year in which to enjoy his riches before Brushy Bob Wade ambushed him near the Bitter Lake and sent him where Billy is, and Hill Coe and all the rest.

Tully borrowed the nickname I had invented, but I bore him no grudge for that. What's puzzling to me still is how an earnest fellow such as Tully Roebuck could fool himself so easily and in the process confuse the story so completely.

It's true that Billy, as he was dying, asked Katie to let on that Tully had killed him—I suspect now that Billy didn't want it thought that he was killed by a woman, even one who loved him. But the puzzling thing is that Tully somehow convinced himself that he *did* kill Billy Bone. He claims in his booklet that he fired a second before Katie, which is nonsense—he was still inside the China Pond when Katie fired.

I was there and I know; and yet Tully is believed and I'm not. What makes it all the harder to fathom is that Tully was generally an honest man; still, he not only convinced himself of a wild lie, he convinced the public too.

Of course "eyewitnesses" kept popping up for years —cowboys who happened to be passing Greasy Corners at just the right moment and saw it all happen from behind one of the huts, unobserved by any of the people who were actually there that morning, though all of us had perfectly adequate vision and might have been primed to notice lurking strangers.

Because of the conflicting accounts of all these "eyewitnesses"—and also because newspapermen and historians, jealous of the fact that novelists get to make things up and they don't, encroach into fiction whenever they think they can get away with it—the brief, clear events of that morning in Greasy Corners have spawned at least a dozen theories already, and no doubt will spawn more. Every person in the town that morning has been championed by some "authority" as being the one who shot Billy down.

Some hold that Bloody Feathers shot him from atop the buffalo hides, and merely jumped down with the knife to take his scalp. Some hold that Isinglass shot him from behind the tent, or Cecily Snow through a slit in the tent, or Long Dog Hawkins from behind the hut. One man claims La Tulipe poisoned him; and the radical fellow from Roswell thinks I shot him because I was jealous of his advantage with Cecily. The fact that I had fifty opportunities to shoot him before we arrived in Greasy Corners has not occurred to the man.

But most of the "eyewitnesses" seem to favor Tully's account—you'd have to say it's the accepted account now—and maybe for the same reason that Billy himself favored making Tully his official killer: no one wants to admit that a Mexican girl killed the greatest outlaw of the era. The *Liebestod* business is hardly favored in our Old West.

They'd rather have it a man—it's that simple—though Katie, wild in her heartbreak, went on to a distinguished career in massacre, joining Villa and then Zapata, shooting down *federales* whenever they got in her way, and finally plunging all the way south to Nicaragua to foment revolution and blow up Yankee banana boats.

Of course, the books give her that: they allow her any number of *federales* and banana boats; they just don't want to give her the white star of the West, Billy the Kid.

No more was heard of La Tulipe, and little more of Bloody Feathers, the great Jicarilla; he never became one of the parade Indians so popular in Washington a little later, though he was mentioned as being at his

374

father's funeral, which occurred more than a dozen years after Billy's death.

Will Isinglass and Cecily Snow went back to Winds' Hill to resume their strenuous but I suppose not entirely unsweetened contest of wills. Cecily finished the drawings for her great book, but not before Isinglass got her with child a third time. This time, not to be thwarted, he found and took away the useful herbs recommended by the old Comanche woman; more than that, he nailed Cecily into her spacious third-floor rooms—for several months her food was sent up to her on a little elevator that Lord Snow had devised some twenty years before.

In the end, though, Cecily beat even Old Whiskey. She had had the forethought to hide the rope that Lord Snow had used in his great days as an alpinist. Just before the child was due she slid down the rope during a blizzard and escaped on her thoroughbred, making her way over a route cowboys call the Dim Trail into the Blue Mounds of Kansas. Of course, an expedition was raised at once; half the cowboys on the plains were sent after her, but only her sidesaddle was ever found. Most people now believe she died in the blizzard, but Tully —it was the last time I spoke to him, just before his own death—did claim that he had talked with a Whiskey Glass cowboy, a member of the posse, who claimed to have come across a coyote dragging a human afterbirth through the snow.

A few of the more radical fellows argue that Cecily Snow survived the blizzard and made it back to England —terribly disfigured and heavily veiled, some claim, though that sounds like Monk Lewis to me—and lived to direct the long legal battle mounted by Lord Snow's nephews, which eventually destroyed the Whiskey Glass ranch.

As to Cecily, I can't say—I've not bothered to tour the Cavendish or the Montstuart demesnes in search of her —but it's certain that Will Isinglass, the scourge of Kiowas and Comanches, suffered a long dismemberment at the torture stake of the law—until, in the end, the three million acres he once ruled had shrunk to fifty thousand. In his heyday fifty thousand acres would not have pastured his *remuda*.

I read of his death in a rooming house in Trenton, New Jersey, where I was conducting a pallid romance with a quarrelsome and affected parlormaid not half so appealing as Kate Molloy.

It seemed Will Isinglass, nearly one hundred at the time, had bought a motorcar—the first to be shipped to the eastern New Mexican plains—where he was living out his days with a scattering of cattle and a few pet buffalo he had acquired from Quanah Parker. The old man knew how to start the vehicle, but was vague about how to stop it; the car—they're the new buffalo, I guess; someday they'll cover the prairies in vast herds—ran away with him and sailed off into one of the canyons of the Canadian, crushing the great plainsman underneath it when it hit. They say he was emptying his pistol into the motor, in a vain effort to kill the thing, when the car went off the cutbank.

The ex-parlormaid only grew more quarrelsome as I sat in silence, holding the newspaper, with tears in my eyes—the story only ran six lines—and thinking about that great, violent old man.

12.

I went home, of course—rode Rosy to Denver and caught the train. Philadelphia was no different, nor was family life. Dora discovered me back in my study one morning, took a quick look, said, "You ought to trim that ugly beard," and went on with her life. The girls squealed "Papa!" a few times, and went on with theirs. Cook was the only person who asked where I had been; when I told her I'd been out West, she assumed I meant Cincinnati and talked for an hour about a sister of hers who had emigrated to Ohio. "Thank the Lord, she hasn't been scalped yet," Cook said, stirring her pudding.

Well, home life must have its little vexations everywhere. The worst I had to put up with was the insufferable Waddy Peacock, Dora's beau, who had been required to buy a mansion a block away so he would always be on hand when Dora needed an escort, which was often—she had not lost her taste for balls and socializing.

After some thought, I declined to trim my beard. Dora

took this refusal as an act of raw defiance and stopped speaking to me. She adopted Cook's view of my travels and let it out that I had contracted brain fever in Cincinnati and could no longer summon the coherence to fulfill my duties as a husband—at least that's what was reported by cronies at my club.

I soon gave up the club and the cronies, family life, parlormaids, and all the rest, to devote myself to art. It seemed to me I had real experience to draw on at last, and I set about to turn the rough scribblings I had done on the llano into books which I felt sure would far eclipse the popularity of Sandycraw, Orson Oxx, or even *The Butler's Sorrow*. How could material so colorful and so rich possibly miss? True, *Billy the Kid* had failed, but I dismissed that as a fluke.

So I all but nailed myself into my study and raced through a dozen books, confident that at last I had graduated from mere tales into literary works to be proud of. I wrote *Skunkwater Flats; or, The Desperate Battle*. I polished up *Mutes of the Mesa*, and *Sister of the Sangre* as well. I rewrote the ending of *Black Beans* to give it more human depth.

Then I applied myself to all of those vivid characters I had met on the plains. I wrote *The Missed Bottle; or, Hill Coe's Disgrace*. I wrote *Emperor of the Llano* about Will Isinglass; *The Ophelia of the Prairies* about Cecily, even generously excusing her behavior on grounds of madness.

The Girl Who Robbed the Governor; or, Jornado del Muerto was the first of my books about Katie; later I penned *The Flame of the Cantinas; or, The Pecos Beauty*. Mesty-Wooleh lived again in *The Negro of the Nile; or, Son of the Mahdi*; and I wept my way through *Joe Lovelady; or, The Cowboy's Lament*. To this day I only have to remember that kind, lonely man to feel decidedly weepy.

The brute fact is, all the books failed. I had once stood at the head of the Beadle and Adams list; I wrote *The*

Butler's Sorrow, the most popular dime novel of all time; but publishers are not long on sentiment, and after eight or nine failures it became clear they had ceased to look with enthusiasm on the parcels I mailed them so regularly.

Finally they sent one back—it was *The Trapper's Mistress; or, The Yellow Witch*—with a chilly note from some young editor I had never heard of. "Dear Mr. Sippy"—it read—"This Wild West stuff won't do. Our readers won't tolerate cowboys now; what we want are detectives, Pinkertons especially. If you care to send us a few Pinkerton yarns we'll give them prompt consideration. We all hope to see you return to the form you had when you wrote the great Sandycraw stories."

I don't think of myself as having a particularly frail spirit, but the fact is I never recovered from that letter: the sting was too sharp. No one wanted my new knowledge, my human depth—they only wanted my old, silly heroes—or, failing that, Pinkertons.

I never wrote again. As abruptly as it started, it stopped.

As it happened, Dora was looking particularly well just then: she seemed alight again after some rather shaded years—and a woman can flash as brilliantly as any firefly.

I decided—after all, I *was* married to her—to try my human depth on Dora, so I put out a hand, only to have it slapped away quite briskly; no more than the publishers did Dora want the new, the finer, me.

"If that's your attitude I wouldn't care if you moved back to Cincinnati," she said.

I did her one better, catching the train the very next day for New Mexico. Unwanted as a writer, or as a husband, there seemed little reason for me to make do with the small, smudged Pennsylvania skies and second-rate parlormaids, all of them a far cry from the glimmering ideal of the lost Kate Molloy.

In Las Cruces I built a fine house and did a good deal

379

of reading. I acquired a mule with a better disposition than Rosy's. Often I would ride to the top of the pass and look down on the ocean of plain, shimmering to the east. Now and again I would travel home, to marry a daughter and to marvel, only a little wistfully, at the lovely late light which Dora never again lost.

Though I never wrote another dimer or half-dimer—I never got over the fact that living had had such a disastrous effect on my powers of creation—the checks continued to flow in, from Sandycraw, from Orson Oxx, and from *The Butler's Sorrow*.

It seems, now I think about it, that I had embarked without knowing it on a kind of endless goodbye, starting that morning when J. M. Chittim dropped dead on the sidewalk. Goodbye to Chittim, and Cook, to Dora and my girls, to the winsome Kate Molloy—how I wish I'd kissed her.

From that time it had been goodbye to everyone: to the buffalo hunters and the buffalo; to Hill Coe and Happy Jack and all the sweethearts of Greasy Corners; to La Tulipe and Des Montaignes; to Viv Maldonado and Barbecue Campbell; to Sister Blandina; to Esteván and the mutes of the Mesa; to *los Guajolotes* and their flying leader, Katerina Garza; to Bertram and Mahmood and Mesty-Woolah; to Bloody Feathers and Isinglass and my lovely Cecily Snow, whose tongue was as exacting as her draftsmanship; to Joe Lovelady and our rough friend, Billy Bone.

Now I guess it's even goodbye to words, for I can't see to read them anymore, and don't care to write them. Of course I was never one of the great heroes of the language, such as Mr. Dickens or the poet Longfellow or W. D. Howells—*there's* a man who understood Yankees if anyone ever did—but, in my way, from the moment I picked up *Hurricane Nell, Queen of Saddle and Lasso*, I loved words and did my best by them.

I don't know what's to become of the old language now, thanks to a curious thing I myself had a small hand in popularizing. Once I was in Trenton—it was probably the time I heard of Isinglass's death—and happened to be drinking in a tavern with an acquaintance named Eddie Porter. I got to telling Eddie about my comical failures as a train robber, which caused him nearly to split his sides laughing. The more I elaborated on how hard it actually was to get a train to stop so one could rob it, the harder he laughed. And I suppose it *was* ludicrous, the thought of me robbing something; but then, cowboys and Indians used to chase those trains just for the sport, and that's all I was doing, really. I don't know what I would have done if one had stopped: bought a ticket home, most likely.

Eddie Porter worked as a camera mechanic for old man Edison. Next thing I knew he'd rented a train and a few horses and cowboy costumes—this was up in East Rutherford, New Jersey—and persuaded the company to do a moving picture of my adventures. They called it *The Great Train Robbery*. The thing caught on and probably earned more money than *The Butler's Sorrow*.

Eddie invited me to see it, and of course I did. The action moved so fast it made my eyes water a little, trying to watch, but I could tell it was my yarn that gave him the idea. Of course, his bandits got the train stopped, which is more than I ever did—the crowd whooped when they got caught as if it was all real.

I figured right then it was goodbye to the dime novel: for who wouldn't rather sit in a vaudeville house, munch a sandwich, and watch the whole story flow by like a pure dream, with perhaps a snatch of burlesque afterward, than squint at print in a book?

Not long after that, I happened to be in Denver, and who should I run into but the old Whiskey Glass cowboy Dewey Sharp—one of the ones who had had the forethought to leave Greasy Corners just a few hours before Billy Bone got killed.

But Dewey was as foolish as Tully Roebuck; he argued up and down that he *hadn't* left Greasy Corners at all; he had ducked out on Waco Charlie and the rest, got drunk in a wagon, and woke up just in time to see the shooting. I didn't argue too strenuously; by then half the old-timers in the West had convinced themselves they had been in Greasy Corners the day Billy Bone got killed.

The point about Dewey is that he was just finally getting around to his long-awaited trip to California. He had bumped into a motion-picture man—they were as common then as buffalo hunters had once been—and filled him full of Greasy Corners stories, all of them featuring that young Galahad, Billy the Kid. The man got all fired up and wanted Dewey to come right away to Hollywood, California, so they could make a picture about it.

"Come with me, Sippy—you know more about it all than I do," Dewey said. It was an unusually generous admission, I thought.

Having little else to occupy me, I did go with Dewey and saw the first palm trees I had seen since Dora and I did the Nile. The motion-picture man was a fan of my Sandycraw tales and promptly hired me to do the scenario for Dewey's stories. All Dewey got to do was wrangle the horses—it annoyed him bitterly. We called the picture *Sweethearts of Greasy Corners,* and it turned out to be the biggest hit of 1908.

I had better specs by then and could see fine. I don't know where they came up with the little actor who played Billy, but for my money he was not only good, he was too good. I cried all twenty-five times I saw the picture: it reminded me of all my hard goodbyes, and of my murdering friend, the wandering boy himself, Billy Bone, white star of the West, whose dust is now one with the billions and billions of particles that compose that ancient plain.

—Larry McMurtry